P9-AFZ-816

THE DARK DESCENT OF ELIZABETH FRANKENSTEIN

ALSO BY KIERSTEN WHITE

Paranormalcy

Supernaturally

Endlessly

Mind Games

Perfect Lies

The Chaos of Stars

Illusions of Fate

And I Darken

Now I Rise

Bright We Burn

Delacorte Press

NOTE: ALL CHAPTER TITLES ARE TAKEN FROM JOHN MILTON'S *PARADISE LOST*

 Published in the United States by Delacorte Press, an imprint of Random House Children's Books, a division of Penguin Random House LLC, New York.

Delacorte Press is a registered trademark and the colophon is a trademark of Penguin Random House LLC.

Visit us on the Web! GetUnderlined.com

Educators and librarians, for a variety of teaching tools, visit us at RHTeachersLibrarians.com

Library of Congress Cataloging-in-Publication Data
Name: White, Kiersten, author.
Title: The dark descent of Elizabeth Frankenstein / Kiersten White.
Description: First Edition. | New York : Delacorte Press, [2018] | Summary: The events of Mary Shelley's *Frankenstein* unfold from the perspective of Elizabeth Lavenza, who is adopted as a child by the Frankensteins as a companion for their volatile son Victor.
Identifiers: LCCN 2017037621 | ISBN 978-0-525-57794-2 (hc) | ISBN 978-0-525-57797-3 (glb) | ISBN 978-0-525-57795-9 (ebook)
Subjects: | CYAC: Characters in literature—Fiction. | Monsters—Fiction. | Scientists—Fiction. | Murder—Fiction. | Horror stories.
Classification: LCC PZ7.W583764 Dar 2018 | DDC [Fic]—dc23

The text of this book is set in 12-point Adobe Jenson Pro.
Jacket design by Regina Flath
Interior design by Ken Crossland

Printed in the United States of America
10 9 8 7 6 5 4 3 2 1
First Edition

Random House Children's Books supports the First Amendment and celebrates the right to read.

For Mary Wollstonecraft Shelley,
whose creation still electrifies
our imaginations two hundred years later

— *and* —

For everyone made to feel like
a side character in their own story

Did I request thee, Maker, from my clay

To mould me man? Did I solicit thee

From darkness to promote me?

—John Milton, *Paradise Lost*

PART ONE

HOW CAN I LIVE WITHOUT THEE?

ONE

TO BE WEAK IS MISERABLE

LIGHTNING CLAWED ACROSS THE sky, tracing veins through the clouds and marking the pulse of the universe itself.

I sighed happily as rain slashed the carriage windows and thunder rumbled so loudly we could not even hear the wheels bump when the dirt lane met the cobblestones at the edge of Ingolstadt.

Justine trembled beside me like a newborn rabbit, burying her face in my shoulder. Another bolt lit our carriage with bright white clarity before rendering us temporarily deaf with a clap of thunder so loud the windows threatened to loosen.

"How can you laugh?" Justine asked. I had not realized I was laughing until that moment.

I stroked her dark hair where strands dangled free from her hat. Justine hated loud noises of any type: Slamming doors. Storms. Shouting. Especially shouting. But I had made certain she had endured none of that in the past two years. It was so odd that our separate origins—similar in cruelty, though differing in duration—had had such opposite outcomes. Justine was the most open and loving and genuinely good person I had ever known.

And I was—

Well. Not like her.

"Did I ever tell you Victor and I used to climb out onto the roof of the house to watch lightning storms?"

She shook her head, not lifting it.

"The way the lightning would play off the mountains, throwing them into sharp relief, as though we were watching the creation of the world itself. Or over the lake, so it looked like it was in both the sky and the water. We would be soaked by the end; it is a wonder neither of us caught our death." I laughed again, remembering. My skin—fair like my hair—would turn the most violent shades of red from the cold. Victor, with his dark curls plastered to his sallow forehead, accentuating the shadows he always bore beneath his eyes, would look like death. What a pair we were!

"One night," I continued, sensing Justine was calming, "lightning struck a tree on the grounds not ten body lengths from where we sat."

"That must have been terrifying!"

"It was glorious." I smiled, placing my hand flat against the cold glass, feeling the temperature beneath my lacy white gloves. "To me, it was the great and terrible power of nature. It was like seeing God."

Justine clucked disapprovingly, peeling herself from my side to give me a stern look. "Do not blaspheme."

I stuck my tongue out at her until she relented into a smile.

"What did Victor think of it?"

"Oh, he was horribly depressed for months afterward. I believe his exact phrasing was that he *'languished in valleys of incomprehensible despair.'*"

Justine's smile grew, though with a puzzled edge. Her face was clearer than any of Victor's texts. His books always required further knowledge and intense study, while Justine was an illuminated manuscript—beautiful and treasured and instantly understandable.

I reluctantly pulled the curtains closed on the carriage window, sealing us away from the storm for her comfort. She had not left the house at the lake since our last disastrous trip into Geneva had ended with her insane, bereft mother attacking us. This journey into Bavaria was taxing for her. "While I saw the destruction of the tree as nature's beauty, Victor saw power—power to light up the night and banish darkness, power to end a centuries-old life in a single strike—that he cannot control or access. And nothing bothers Victor more than something he cannot control."

"I wish I had known him better before he left for university."

I patted her hand—her brown leather gloves a gift Henry had given me—before squeezing her fingers. Those gloves were far softer and warmer than my own. But Victor preferred me in white. And I loved giving nice things to Justine. She had joined the household two years earlier, when she was seventeen and I was fifteen, and had been there only a couple of months before Victor left us. She did not really know him.

No one did, except me. I liked it that way, but I wanted them to love each other as I loved them both.

"Soon you will know Victor. We shall all of us—Victor and you and me—" I paused, my tongue traitorously trying to add Henry. That was not going to happen. "We will be reunited most joyfully, and then my heart will be complete." My tone was cheery to mask the fear that underlay this entire endeavor.

I could not let Justine be worried. Her willingness to come as my chaperone was the only reason I had managed this trip. Judge Frankenstein had initially rejected my pleadings to check on Victor. I think he was relieved to have Victor gone, did not care when we had no word. Judge Frankenstein always said Victor would come home when he was ready, and I should not worry about it.

I did. Very much. Particularly after I found a list of expenses with my name at the top. He was auditing me—and soon, I had no doubt, he would determine that I was not worth holding on to. I had done too well, fixing Victor. He was out in the world, and I was obsolete to his father.

I would not let myself be cast out. Not after my years of hard work. Not after all I had done.

Fortunately, Judge Frankenstein had been called away on a mysterious journey of his own. I did not ask permission again so much as . . . leave. Justine did not know that. Her presence gave me the freedom I needed here to move about without inviting suspicion or censure. William and Ernest, Victor's younger brothers and her charges, would be fine in the care of the maid until we could return.

Another burst of thunder, this one rumbling through our chests so we felt it in our very hearts.

"Tell me the story of the first time you met Victor," she squeaked, clutching my hand so hard that the bones ached.

The woman who was not my mother pinched me and tugged my hair with brutally efficient meanness.

I wore a dress that was far too big. The sleeves hung down to my wrists, which was not the style for children. But the dress covered the bruises that covered my skin. The week previous I had been caught stealing an extra portion of food. Though I had often been bloodied by her angry fists, this time my caregiver had beaten me until everything went black. I spent the next three nights hiding in the woods at the lake, eating berries. I thought she would kill me when she found me; she had often threatened to do just that. Instead, she had discovered another use for me.

"Do not ruin this," she hissed. "Better for you to have died at your birth along with your mother than to be left here with me. Selfish in life, selfish in death. That's what you come from."

I lifted my chin high, let her finish brushing my hair so that it shone as bright as gold.

"Make them love you," she demanded as a gentle knock sounded at the door to the hovel I shared with my caregiver and her own four children. "If they do not take you, I will drown you in the rain barrel like the cat's last litter of runty kittens."

A woman stood outside, surrounded by a blinding halo of sunlight.

"Here she is," my caretaker said. "Elizabeth. The little angel herself. Born to nobility. Fate stole her mother, pride imprisoned her father, and Austria took her fortune. But nothing could touch her beauty and goodness."

I could not turn around lest I stomp on her foot or punch her for her false love.

"Would you like to meet my son?" the new woman asked. Her voice trembled as though she was the one who was scared.

I nodded solemnly. She took my hand and led me away. I did not look back.

"My son, Victor, is only a year or two older than you are. He is a special child. Bright and inquisitive. But he does not make friends easily. Other children are . . ." She paused, as though searching a candy dish for just the right piece to pop into her mouth. "They are intimidated *by him. He is solitary and lonely. But I think a friend like you would be just the gentling influence he needs. Could you do that, Elizabeth? Could you be Victor's special friend?"*

Our walk had brought us to their holiday villa. I stopped dead. I was amazed by the sight. Her momentum tugged me forward and I stumbled, stunned.

I had had a life, before. Before the hovel with mean and biting children. Before the woman who cared for me with fists and bruises. Before a life haunted by hunger and fear and cold, crammed into the dirty darkness with strange bodies.

I pushed one toe gingerly over the threshold of the villa the Frankensteins had taken for their time at Lake Como. I followed her through those beautiful rooms of green and gold, windows and light, pain left behind as I stepped through this dreamworld.

I had lived here before. And I lived here every night when I closed my eyes.

Though I had lost my home and my father more than two years before, and no child could remember with perfect clarity, I knew it. This had been my life. These rooms, blessed with beauty and space—so much space!—had graced my infancy. It was not this villa, specifically, so much as the general sense of it. There is a safety in cleanliness, a comfort in beauty.

Madame Frankenstein had brought me out of the darkness and back into the light.

I rubbed at my tender and bruised arms, as thin as sticks. Determination filled my child's body. I would be whatever her son needed if doing so gave me back this life. The day was bright, the lady's hand was softer than anything I had felt in years, and the rooms ahead of us seemed filled with hope for a new future.

Madame Frankenstein led me through the hallways and out to the garden.

Victor stood alone. His hands were clasped behind his back, and though he was not much more than two years older than me, he seemed almost like an adult. I felt the same shy wariness I would feel approaching a strange man.

"Victor," his mother said, and again I sensed fear and nervousness in her voice. "Victor, I have brought a friend."

He turned. How clean he was! It filled me with shame to be wearing a much-patched, too-big dress. Though my hair was washed—my caregiver said it was the best thing I had to recommend me—I knew my feet inside my slippers were dirty. I felt, as he looked at me, that he must surely know, too.

He tried on a smile like I tried on castoff clothing, shifting it around until it mostly fit his face. "Hello," he said.

"Hello," I said.

We both stood, motionless, as his mother watched.

I had to make him like me. But what did I have to offer a boy who had everything? "Do you want to find a bird's nest with me?" I asked, the words tumbling out in a rush. I was better at finding them than any of the other children. Victor did not look like a boy who had ever climbed a tree to spy on nests. It was the only thing I could think of. "It is spring, so their chicks are all nearly ready to hatch."

Victor frowned, his dark eyebrows drawing close together. And then he nodded, holding out his hand. I stepped forward and took it. His mother sighed with relief.

"Have fun! Do stay close to the villa, though," she entreated us.

I led Victor out of the garden and into the spring-green forest that surrounded the estate. The lake was not far. I could smell it, cold and dark, on the breeze. I took a wandering path, keeping my eyes trained on the branches above us. It felt vital to find the promised nest. As though it were a test, and if I passed, then I could stay in Victor's world.

And if I failed . . .

But there, like hope bundled into twigs and mud: a nest! I pointed to it, beaming.

Victor frowned. "It is high."

"I can get it!"

He considered me. "You are a girl. You should not climb trees."

I had been climbing trees since I could walk, but his pronouncement filled me with the same shame my dirty feet did. I was doing everything wrong.

"Maybe," I said, twisting my dress in my hands, "maybe I can climb this one, and it will be the last tree I climb? For you?"

He considered my proposal, and then he smiled. "Yes, all right."

"I will count the eggs and tell you how many there are!" I was already scrambling up the trunk, wishing my feet were bare but too aware of myself to take off my shoes.

"No, bring the nest down."

I paused, halfway to my goal. "But if we move the nest, the mother may not be able to find it."

"You said you would show me a nest. Did you lie?" He looked so angry at the idea that I had deceived him. Especially that first day, I would have done anything to make him smile.

"No!" I said, my breath catching in my chest. I reached the branch and scooted along it. Inside the nest were four tiny, perfect eggs of pale blue.

As carefully as I could, I worked the nest free from the branch. I would show Victor and then put it right back. It was difficult, climbing down while keeping the nest protected and intact, but I managed. I presented it to Victor triumphantly, beaming at him.

He peered inside. "When will they hatch?"

"Soon."

He held out his hands and took the nest. Then he found a large, flat rock and set the nest on top of it.

"Robins, I think." I stroked the smooth blue of the shells. I imagined they were pieces of the sky, and that if I could reach high enough, the sky would be smooth and warm like these eggs.

"Maybe," I said, giggling, "the sky laid these eggs. And when they hatch, a miniature sun will burst free and fly up into the air."

Victor looked at me. "That is absurd. You are very odd."

I closed my mouth, trying to smile at him to let him know his words had not hurt my feelings. He smiled back, tentative, and said, "There are four eggs and only one sun. Maybe the others will be clouds." I felt a warm rush of affection for him. He picked up the first egg, holding it to the light of the sun. "Look. You can see the bird."

He was right. The shell was translucent, and the silhouette of a curled-up chick was visible. I let out a laugh of delight. "It is like seeing the future," I said.

"Almost."

If either of us could have seen the future, we would have known that the next day his mother would pay my cruel caregiver and take me away forever, presenting me to Victor as his special gift.

Justine sighed happily. "I love that story."

She loved it because I told it just for her. It was not entirely the truth. But so little of what I told anyone ever was. I had ceased feeling guilty long ago. Words and stories were tools to elicit the desired reactions in others, and I was an expert craftswoman.

That particular story was almost correct. I embellished some, particularly about remembering the villa, because that was critical to lie about. And I always left off the ending. She would not understand, and I did not like to think about it.

"I can feel its heart," Victor whispered in my memory.

I peeked out the edge of the curtain as the city of Ingolstadt swallowed us, its dark stone homes closing around us like teeth. It had taken my Victor and devoured him. I had sent Henry to lure him home, and now I had lost them both.

I was here to get Victor back. I would not leave until I had.

I had not lied to Justine about my motivation. Henry's betrayal stung like a wound, fresh and raw. But I could survive that. What I could not survive was losing my Victor. I *needed* Victor. And that little girl who had done what was necessary to secure his heart would still do whatever it took to keep it.

I bared my teeth back at the city, daring it to try to stop me.

TWO

WHAT HATH NIGHT TO DO WITH SLEEP?

DARKNESS FROM THE STORM had already claimed the sky, rendering the sunset a moot point. But it could not have been much past nightfall when we reached the lodging I had hastily written ahead to arrange. I did not know whether Victor was allowed guests in his rooms here, or what state those rooms would be in. Though we had lived in the same house until he left, assuming I could stay with him here felt too risky. The Victor who had left two years earlier was surely not the same now. I had to see him again to figure out who he needed me to be. And Justine certainly would not approve of us staying in a young, single student's rooms.

Thus it was we found ourselves standing beneath umbrellas in the drearily persistent rain, knocking on the door of Frau Gottschalk's House for Ladies. The carriage waited behind us, the horses stamping their impatience on the cobblestones. I wanted to stamp alongside them. I was finally here, in the same city as Victor, but I would not have time to seek him out until the morning.

I pounded until my fist stung beneath my glove. The door cracked open at last. A woman, lit in yellow lamplight that made her look more wax than human, glared at us with startling ferocity.

"What do you want?" she asked in German.

I rearranged my face into a pleasant and hopeful smile. "Good evening. My name is Elizabeth Lavenza. I wrote about taking rooms for—"

"House rules! We lock the doors at sundown. If you are not inside, you are not getting inside."

Distant thunder echoed, and Justine trembled beside me. I twisted my full lips into a penitent shape, nodding in agreement. "Yes, of course. Only we just arrived, and had no way of knowing what the rules were. It *is* a sensible requirement, and I am so grateful that, traveling as two young women, we will be trusting our stay to a woman so well equipped to care for the safety and well-being of her lodgers!" I clasped my hands to my heart and beamed at her. "Indeed, I feared before we arrived that we might have made a hasty decision in seeking rooms here, but I see now you are as an angel sent before us for our protection!"

She blinked, wrinkling her nose as though she could smell my insincerity, but my face proved too adequate a shield. Her frown deepened as her beady eyes darted back and forth, examining us and the waiting carriage.

"Well, hurry and get out of the rain, then. And keep in mind this rule will never be broken again!"

"Oh, yes! Thank you so much! We are so fortunate, are we not, Justine?"

Justine's head was ducked, her eyes fixed on the steps beneath us. She spoke mainly French, and I was not certain how much of the landlady's German she understood. But the tone and demeanor needed no translation. Justine acted like a pup that had been struck for disobedience. I hated this woman already.

I directed the coachman to leave our trunk in the hallway. It was an awkward dance. The landlady would not allow him to have more than one of his feet inside at a time. I paid him generously for his service, hoping to retain him for the return trip—whenever that might be.

The landlady slammed the door behind him, locking two deadbolts. Finally, she drew a large iron key from her apron pocket and turned it in the knob.

"Is it a dangerous city, after dark? I had not heard that." The town revolved around the university. Surely a center of learning could not be that threatening. When had the pursuit of knowledge merited so many locks?

She grunted. "Doubt you hear much of Ingolstadt up there in your pretty mountains. Are you sisters?"

Justine flinched. I shifted so I was physically between her and the landlady. "No. Justine works for my benefactors. But I love her as a sister." The resemblance between us was not so strong that it was an easy assumption we were blood. I was fair-skinned, with blue eyes and golden hair I still cared for as though my life depended on it. I had finished growing sometime in the last year, petite and fine-boned. Sometimes I wondered, if I had been given more to eat as a young child, would I have been taller? Stronger? But my appearance worked in my favor. I looked fragile and sweet, incapable of harm or deceit.

Justine was taller than I by nearly a hand. Her shoulders were broad, her hands strong and capable. Her hair was a rich brown, shining with red and gold in the sunlight. Everything about her shone. She was a creature born for all days gentle and warm. But in her full lips and downturned eyes was the hint of sorrow and suffering that kept me tied to her, reminded me that she was not so strong as she looked.

If I could pick a sister, I would choose Justine. I *had* chosen Justine. But Justine had had other sisters, once. I wished this horrible woman had not dragged their ghosts into this dismal entryway along with the rest of our luggage. I reached down and took one handle of the trunk, gesturing for Justine to take the other.

She regarded our landlady with wide eyes and a stricken expression. I looked at the landlady again more closely. Though she bore no immediate resemblance to Justine's mother, that sharp and cutting tone of voice and the dismissive way she had answered my innocent inquiry were enough to upset poor Justine's nerves. I would have to do my best to keep Justine from interacting with her. Hopefully this would be the only night we required anything from this wax-faced harpy.

"I am so glad we found you!" I said again, beaming, as she harrumphed past us to a narrow flight of stairs. Then I turned and winked at Justine over my shoulder. She gave me a wan smile, her pretty face pinched with the effort of pretending.

"You can call me Frau Gottschalk. The house rules are as follows: No gentlemen past the front door, ever. Breakfast is at seven sharp and will not be served to anyone seated after that. You are to always be presentable when in the shared spaces of the house."

"Are there many other guests?" I maneuvered our large trunk past a poorly wallpapered corner.

"No, none. If I may continue, shared spaces are for quiet activities during the evening, such as needlework."

"Or reading?" Justine said hopefully, her tongue tripping over the German. She knew how much I loved to read. Of course she would think of me first.

"Reading? No. There is no library in the house." Frau Gottschalk glared as though we were the silliest creatures in existence for assuming a house for ladies would include books. "If you want books, you will have to visit one of the university libraries or booksellers. I would not know where they are. Washroom is here. I only empty bedroom chamber pots once a day, so have a care not to fill them too high. Here is your room." She pushed open a door, clumsily carved with an approximation of flowers that were as lovely as Frau Gottschalk's face was kind. The door creaked and cracked as though protesting its use.

"Dinner is your responsibility. You may not use the kitchens for any reason. And supper is served promptly at six, which is also when the door is locked for the night. Do not think my kindness tonight will happen again! Once that door is locked, no one can open it." She held out her heavy iron key. "You cannot open it, either. So no sneaking each other inside. Keep curfew."

She turned in a complaint of stiff skirts, then paused. I prepared my smiling gratitude for her wish of "Have a good night" or "Enjoy your stay," or, most hopefully, an invitation for a late supper.

Instead, Frau Gottschalk said, "Best to use the cotton on your bed-side tables for your ears. To muffle the . . . sounds."

And with that she disappeared down the unlit hallway, leaving us alone on the threshold of our room.

"Well." I dropped the trunk on the worn wood floor. "This is dark." I eased blindly through the room. After stubbing my toes against the foot of a bed, I felt my way over to a tightly shuttered window. I tugged on the shutters, but there was some latching mechanism that I could not see.

My hip bumped against a table, and I found a lamp. Fortunately, the wick was still lit, though barely. I turned up the gas. The room was slowly revealed.

"Perhaps it would be best to leave the lamp dimmed," I said, laughing. Justine was still by the door, wringing her hands.

I crossed to her, taking her hands in my own. "Do not let Frau Gottschalk bother you. She is just an unhappy soul, and we will not be here long. When we find Victor tomorrow, he can direct us to better lodgings."

She nodded, some of the tension leaving her face. "And Henry will know someone kind."

"Henry will know everyone kind by now!" I beamed in agreement;

it was a lie. She thought Henry was still in the city. Their easy friendship had been part of the lure to get her here. Believing Henry would be waiting for us comforted her.

Henry, of course, was not here. If he were, doubtless he would have made friends of the entire city. Victor, on the other hand, would have only Henry. I had broken that between them. And though I knew I should feel bad for Victor, I was too angry with him and with Henry. I had done what was necessary.

Henry had gotten what he wanted, at least in part. It was all well and good for them to be exploring, studying and working for the futures they had already secured by virtue of their births. Some of us had to find other means.

Some of us had to lie and deceive in order to travel to another country, chase those means down, and drag him back home.

I turned back to our sad room. "Would you like the cobweb bedspread, or the one that appears to be made of funeral shrouds?"

Justine crossed herself, scowling at my humor. But then she pulled off her gloves, nodding firmly. "I will get the room up to standards."

"*We* will. You are not my servant, Justine."

She smiled at me. "But I am forever in your debt. And I love opportunities to help you."

"Just so long as you do not forget that you work for the Frankensteins. Not for me." I took the other end of the quilt she was lifting and helped her fold it. The blankets beneath were in better shape, protected from dust by the quilt. "Let me open this window and then we can beat the devil out of this."

Justine dropped her end of the quilt, her stricken look making it obvious she was somewhere else entirely. I cursed my thoughtless choice of words.

* * *

Victor was low with one of his regular fevers, but in the recovery phase, during which he slept like the dead for two days before coming out of his fog. I had not been out of the house in a week for caring for him. Henry dragged me away with the promise of sun and fresh strawberries and finding a present for Victor.

After the boatman dropped us off at the nearest city gate, we strolled down the lane of the main market before following the sun on its narrow pathway through the charmingly crowded wood-and-stone buildings. I had not realized how much I needed this bright and clear day of freedom. Henry was so easy to be with, even though things had begun to shift between us. But that day we felt as if we were young children again, laughing without a care. I was drunk on the sunshine, on the feel of the breeze on my skin, on knowing that no one needed me at that precise moment.

Until someone did.

I did not realize I was running toward the screaming until I found its source. A woman built like a cudgel was standing over a girl around my own age. The girl had curled in on herself, arms over her head where her brown curls had come free from her cap. The woman was shouting, spittle carrying her words down to the girl.

"—beat the devil out of you, you worthless little whore!" She grabbed a broom from where it rested against the door and lifted it high over her head.

In that moment, I was no longer seeing the woman in front of me. I was seeing another hateful woman with a cruel tongue and crueler fists. With a blinding flash of anger, I leapt in front of her, taking the blow on my own shoulder.

The woman staggered back, shocked. I raised my chin defiantly. The anger drained from her face, replaced with fear. Though she lived in a decent part of town, she was obviously from a working class of people. And my fine skirts and jacket—not to mention the beautiful gold locket I wore around my neck—marked me as coming from much higher in the ranks of society.

"Pardon me," she said, fear combining with her angry exertions to make her voice breathless and tight. "I did not see you there, and—"

"And you attacked me. I am certain Judge Frankenstein will want to hear of this." It was false—both that he would want to hear, and that he was still an active judge—but the title was enough to make her even more frightened.

"No, no, I beg you! Let me make it right."

"You have injured my shoulder. I will need a maid to help me while I recover." I crouched down and gently pried the girl's hand away from protecting her own face, never taking my eyes off the hateful woman. "In exchange for not involving the law, you will give me your servant for my own."

The woman could barely contain her disgust as she looked at the girl, who was uncurling, her movements skittish, like those of an injured animal. "She is not my servant; she is my oldest daughter."

I tightened my fingers around the girl's to anchor myself, and to prevent myself from striking the woman. "Very well. I will have the contract of employment sent to you for a signature. She will live with me until I decide otherwise. Good day." Tugging on the girl's hand, I dragged her stumbling behind me. Henry was hurrying toward us, having been left behind in my rush. I ignored him, quickly crossing a street and darting into a side alley.

The rush of emotions I had worked so hard to contain came over me, and I sagged against a stone wall, breathing heavily. The girl did the same, and we rested there, my head level with her shoulder, our breaths and hearts racing like the rabbits we were on the inside: always watchful, always afraid of attack. I had not outgrown it after all.

I knew I should go back to find Henry, but I could not manage to yet. I trembled, feeling all my years of separation from my caregiver stripped away.

"Thank you," the girl whispered, wrapping her slender fingers around mine so that neither of our hands shook anymore.

"I am Elizabeth," I said.

"I am Justine."

I turned to look at her. Her cheek was bright red from being struck. It would blossom into an ugly bruise by the next day. Her eyes, large and wide-set, stared back at me with the same gratitude I remembered feeling when Victor accepted me and took me away from my own painful life. She looked about my age or, judging by her height, perhaps a year or two older.

"Is it always like that?" I whispered, brushing a soft curl away from her cheek and tucking it behind her ear.

She nodded silently, closing her eyes and leaning down to rest her forehead against mine. "She hates me. I have never known why. I am her daughter, her own child, same as the others. But she hates me, and—"

"Shhh." I drew her close so that her head nestled into the curve of my neck and shoulder. If it was luck that my own beauty had saved me from a life of cruelty and want, then I would extend that same grace and luck to Justine. Though we had only just met, I felt a soul-deep connection to her, and I knew we would be part of each other's lives forever.

"I do not actually need a maid," I said. She tensed, so I hurried on. "Can you read?"

"Yes, and write. My father taught me."

That was fortunate. An idea took root. "Have you ever considered being a governess?"

Justine, puzzled, stopped crying. She straightened to look at me, her delicate eyebrows raised. "I have been in charge of educating and caring for my youngest siblings. But I never thought of pursuing it outside of the home. My mother tells me I am too wicked and stupid—"

"Your mother is a fool. I want you to never again think of anything she told you about yourself. It was all lies. Do you understand?"

Justine held my gaze as though I were a rope pulling her in from drowning. She nodded.

"Good. Come. I am going to introduce the Frankensteins to their new governess."

"Are they your family?"

"Yes. And now you are, too."

Her innocent eyes shone with hope, and she impulsively kissed my cheek. The kiss felt like a cool hand on a fevered brow, and I gasped. Justine laughed, then embraced me again. "Thank you," she whispered in my ear. "You have saved me."

"Justine," I said, my voice as bright and cheerful as the boardinghouse was not, "will you help me open the window?"

She blinked as though waking up. If I remembered our first meeting with that much clarity, I could not imagine what my ill-chosen words had made her remember about the time before we found each other. Maybe it had been selfish of me to make her come along to Ingolstadt to find Victor. She had always felt so at home in the Frankensteins' isolated manor. The lake served as a buffer between Justine and her old life. She devoted herself entirely to her two young charges, and she was happy. While I had craved escape, I had not thought what disruption might mean for her.

I wish I had found her earlier. Seventeen years with that woman! Victor had saved me when I was but five.

Victor, why did you leave me?

"It is locked." She pointed to the top of the window, where the shutters were fastened to the frame.

I leaned close, peering up. "No; they have been nailed shut."

"This is a strange house." Justine gently placed the quilt on a rickety chair.

"Just one night." I sat on my bed, the ropes beneath the mattress straining. On the table between the two narrow beds was the only fresh thing in the whole room: the promised cotton for our ears.

What was it we were not supposed to hear?

* * *

After Justine's breathing went steady and slow with sleep, I eased out of bed, hungry and restless. I longed for the nights when, sleepless or plagued by nightmares, I could sneak down the hall and crawl into Victor's bed. He was nearly always awake. Reading or writing. His brain never stopped, sleep too much of a nuisance. Perhaps that was why he was plagued by his fevers—his body forced him to finally shut down.

Knowing that whenever I was awake he would be, too, made life less lonely. The last two endless years I would lie in bed, wondering if he was awake. Certain he was. Certain that, if I could just get to him, he would shift over and let me curl up next to him and his work. To this day, nothing comforted me more than the scent of paper and ink.

I wished horrible Frau Gottschalk had a library, if only so I could bring a book to bed with me.

Confident that all my years of nighttime creeping would keep me safe, I slowly turned the doorknob. I remembered that the door creaked and would need to be moved with utmost care.

But my memory mattered not. The door was locked. From the outside.

Suddenly the room, which before had merely been too small, was suffocating. I could almost smell the rank breath of other children, feel the press of scabbed knees and brutal elbows. I closed my eyes and breathed deeply to exorcise the demons of my past. I would not go back to that. Ever.

But still there was not enough air in the room. I went to the shutters and did my best to pry them open without waking Justine. As I worked, I went over my plan.

I would go to Victor's residence in the morning. I would not accuse or get angry. That never worked with Victor. I would smile and embrace him and remind him how much he loved me, how much better his days were with me in them. And if he brought up Henry, I would be perfectly innocent.

"What?" I whispered to myself in absolute surprise. "He asked you *what?*"

My finger got caught beneath one of the slats. I swore viciously beneath my breath, working it free. It was warm and wet. I stuck it in my mouth before the blood could stain my nightgown.

And if Victor did not seem to respond to my sweetness, I would simply cry. He never could stand it when I cried. It would hurt him. I smiled in anticipation, letting the meanness at my core stretch like ill-used muscles. He had left me *alone* in that house. I had Justine, yes, but Justine could not keep me safe.

I needed Victor back, and I would not let him abandon me again.

One of the slats finally slid free. Clutching it like a knife, I pressed my face against the opening to look down upon the empty street. The rain had stopped, clouds stroking the swollen moon like a tender lover.

Everything was still and quiet, shining wet and as clean as a city ever got. I saw nothing. I heard nothing.

I replaced the slat and then sat guard in front of our bedroom door, certain the only threat in Ingolstadt was the person we had paid to lock us in a dusty room.

Sometime before morning I startled awake, nearly falling from the chair. Dazed and half-asleep, I was drawn to the window as certainly as I had been drawn to Justine's animal cries of pain that day in Geneva.

The street was empty. Had I dreamed a cry that pierced so deep—that my very soul recognized? Plagued by memories I did not wish to possess, I resumed vigil until dawn and the long-awaited click of the key to freedom.

THREE

IN WANDERING MAZES LOST

Breakfast was a sour affair. Though I tried my best, Frau Gottschalk was impervious to my charms. Perhaps I overestimated them, or perhaps they were so well honed to the Frankensteins after all these years that they were worthless elsewhere.

It was not a comforting thought.

Frau Gottschalk refused to relinquish the key to our room—for our "protection," as though guarding the virtue of young women were part of her contract. Her bread was somehow burned and doughy at the same time, her milk as fresh as I felt after such a sleepless night, and her company unbearable.

We beat a hasty retreat from the house. As the door closed and locked behind us, I let out a deep sigh of relief. At least that would be the only night we would have to spend there. Once we found Victor, we could get resettled.

Everything would be resettled.

I pulled out Victor's last letter—from nearly eighteen months before, my fingers impulsively twitching into claws as I traced the date—

and looked at his address. Though I had memorized it, the letter felt like a talisman that would guide us to him.

"Should we find a carriage?" Justine eyed the sky dubiously. The clouds were heavy with the threat of more rain. But I did not want to waste time finding a man to hire, and I certainly would not go back inside to ask Frau Gottschalk for help.

"After so long in the carriage yesterday, a walk will be just the thing." Two years previous, when Victor was preparing to leave, I had copied a map of Ingolstadt. I took care to add all the flourishes and artistic details he seemed to admire when I did them. He used to laugh at how useless my art was, but he always showed it off proudly when the rare visitor came to the house.

I had the map I had used as the original. There were no flourishes because it was for me, and what was the point?

Tracing the lines of streets like a fortune-teller reading a future in a palm, I tapped my finger in time to my heartbeat. "Here," I said. "Here we will find Victor." Justine and I linked elbows and stepped carefully across the muddy borders of the cobblestone street, letting the currents of ink on my map draw us to our destination.

"Victor Frankenstein?" a man with a mustache as wiry and anemic as his frame asked, speaking French. "What do you want him for?"

"I am his cousin," I said. I was not, but it was the term we had been told to use for each other. His father and mother were always careful not to let us call each other brother or sister. Though they fed and clothed and educated me alongside him until he left for the city school and then university, they made me keep my own surname and never formally adopted me.

I lived with the Frankensteins. I was not one. And I never forgot it.

The man let out a wheezing sort of grunt, tugging on the ends of his mustache. "I have not seen him in more than a year. He said he needed more space. Arrogant bastard he was, too. Claimed I was spying on him, as if I would be interested in the lunatic scribblings of a student. I am a doctor, you know!"

"Oh?" Justine said, upset by his agitation and seeking to soothe him. "Of what?"

He rubbed the back of his neck, squinting up and to the side as though something had caught his eye. "Eastern languages. Poetry, specifically. Chinese and Japanese, but I know some Korean as well."

"I am certain that is ever so useful to you here, running a student boardinghouse." I offered my cutting words with a dagger of a smile. How *dare* he insult my Victor.

He narrowed his eyes. "Yes, I can see the family resemblance now."

Realizing I was playing this wrong, I shifted my face. Let my eyelids hang just a bit heavier, tilted my chin, smiled as if I had never had a secret. "Poetry is so beautiful! Your boarders truly are fortunate. Imagine how oppressive being aided through school by a mathematician would be! Everything cold numbers. Your rooms must be highly in demand. I can only assume Victor needed more space for some practical reason."

Now the man looked confused, thrown by my abrupt shift and already doubting the meanness he had seen. "Er. Well. Yes. He never said why he needed more working room."

"Do you have his new address?"

His eyebrows warred between wry and apologetic. "We have not kept in touch since he called me a fool with silk between my ears."

I put my fingers to my mouth in mock outrage, though really it was to cover my grin. How I had missed Victor! "The strains of his studies must have been great indeed for him to act in such a manner. He has probably remained a stranger since out of tremendous guilt for his ill-treatment of you." I pulled out one of the cards I had written up that morning. Frau Gottschalk had added the cost of the ink to our bill. "If you remember anything, or if he comes by to apologize, will you be so kind as to let me know? We are staying at Frau Gottschalk's House for Ladies for a short time." I held out the card and pressed it into his palm with slightly more contact than was necessary. This time his look was less confused and more dazzled.

I was *not* good with only the Frankensteins after all. Frau Gottschalk was simply terrible. Though we left Victor's old housing no closer to finding him, some of my confidence was restored.

Justine pointed out a café and we stopped to have tea. The decor left a bit to be desired, if one desired things like taste or elegance. But it was relatively clean, and the tea was hot. I wanted to rest my face over the steam, let my soul steep in the heat alongside the tea leaves.

"What should we do now?" Justine had her hands beneath the table, worrying at something. We were the only women there, the rest of the patrons easily identifiable as students by their ink-stained fingers and ghostly pallor. Every brow furrowed by intense concentration made me miss Victor even more. However, most of the brows unfurrowed and rose in interest as Justine and I spoke. I pretended not to notice. Justine did not have to pretend, as she always seemed genuinely unaware of the effect we had on men. I, however, was perfectly aware of my beauty. I considered it a skill, alongside speaking French, English, Italian, and German. It was a language of its own, in a way; one that translated well in different circumstances.

"Do you have any other letters?" Justine asked. "Contacts we can use?" I saw now she held a little lead soldier toy, rubbing it like a talisman. William's, most certainly. Of the three Frankenstein boys, I had no use for any but Victor. Justine loved the other two enough for both of us.

I stirred my tea, letting the dented silver spoon clink against the plain china. Ingolstadt was not a large city, but it was by no means small.

It had an impressive student population. There would be no shortage of housing for young men, *if* Victor had taken up a new residence in a house like his previous one.

"This is a mystery." I grinned conspiratorially at Justine. "Just like the ones I tell you."

Her attention was tugged back from where it doubtless hovered over William and Ernest back at Frankenstein Manor. "Will there be a jewel thief and a daring midnight ambush?"

I dropped two cubes of sugar into Justine's tea. She liked things as sweet as possible, though she would never take more sugar than anyone else at the table unless pushed. "Well, since we are hunting a scholar, I think jewels are out of the question. And our landlady would have us on the streets if we were caught out at midnight. But I promise at some point we will unmask a villain."

Justine laughed prettily, and now I *knew* every eye in the café was on us. I could feel them. It was like wearing an extra layer of clothing. Just a touch heavier, just a touch more constricting.

I resisted the urge to tug at my high lace collar. My eyes closed and I twitched once, imperceptibly, against the confines of my pristine and expensive clothing.

It was both a relief and an agony when Victor was deemed socialized enough to begin attending the local school instead of staying home for private tutoring. I had more hours to myself during the day during which I did not have to be anything to anyone, so long as I kept up my language lessons and my art. Yet I was bitterly jealous of Victor. Every morning he was rowed across the lake to other children and other minds, to learn and to grow, while I was left behind. I always stood at the dock until he disappeared, every muscle tense, wanting to be with him but also longing to run.

I used the time to wander. Though I had been half feral during my years before the Frankensteins, here my explorations had always been at Victor's side and therefore entailed a certain amount of wariness. I had to be accountable to him always, in my emotions, my reactions, my expressions.

Alone, I discovered the raw natural beauty of his home in a new way. The snowcapped mountains loomed along the skyline, watching all I did. I nicknamed them Judge and Madame Frankenstein. The lake, placid and beautiful and mysterious, I nicknamed Victor. But the trees—the trees were mine.

Most mornings I had to dutifully visit Madame Frankenstein and play with boring little Ernest. I did not care about him, but it made Madame Frankenstein happy. She had told me when she was still pregnant with him, her stomach distended and horrible in a way I could not understand, that it was because of me she had finally been able to bring another child into the house.

I would have been happy to never see the baby. But I did not let her suspect that as I cooed over him long enough until I could slip back outside.

As soon as I was out of sight of the house, I would take off my white dress and set it carefully in a cleaned-out tree hollow. Then, free to wander without fear of damaging my clothes and bringing home proof of my transgressions, I would prowl through the trees like a wild creature.

I discovered warrens, nests, burrows, all the hidden places of things that creep and crawl, leap and bound, fly and flee among the deep green and loamy brown. Though my heart was filled with joy among them, my journeys served a dual purpose: if I discovered where the animals I loved lived, I could deliberately avoid them when I was with Victor.

When I could not be outside, during the depths of winter or in the afternoons when Victor returned, I studied his schoolwork or looked at paintings and read poetry. It delighted the Frankensteins. They saw it as evidence of my good breeding that at such a young age I was so attuned to the arts. But really, it was a way of escaping back into the wilderness when I was trapped inside.

If I could have worn nothing but my slips, I would have. But clothes were part of the role I played. And I never stepped out of character where they could see me.

"Elizabeth?"

I stopped stirring my tea, which had gone cool as I stared out the fog-covered window. I smiled at Justine to cover my lapse in attention. She returned my smile to let me know she did not mind. Things were always so with Justine. I could never do anything to make her cross with me. It was a tremendous relief not to have to choose each word and expression with care. Sometimes, though, our relationship felt as false as the one with my benefactors. I wondered if she truly was *that* good, or if she merely acted that way to avoid being sent back to her monster of a mother.

No. I did not really wonder. If there was any pure good in the world, anything as clear and unsullied as freshly fallen snow, it was Justine's heart.

"What were you thinking of?" she asked.

"I was remembering the first time Victor left me to go to school. That was when he was thirteen, and it was just the local school in Geneva. He brought back all his books so I could study, too. And he brought back the most wickedly funny reports of his poor schoolmaster." I could scarcely believe that was only five and a half years ago. Now Victor was nineteen, and he had not brought back anything, not even himself.

"Oh!" I set down my spoon and abandoned my cold tea for good. "His schoolmaster! I have just thought of our next clue. In one of his earliest letters he describes two professors at length. He seemed particularly keen to work with one, though both had knowledge he hoped to gain. Surely they will be able to direct us to him!"

I pulled out the meager collection of letters I had from Victor. Four, total, and three of those from his first month away. After that, seven months passed until the next. And after that, nothing.

I had Henry's letter, too, from six months previous. But there was only one, and I did not care to read it ever again. The least he could have done was give me Victor's new address before abandoning us both. But my anger had cooled after steeping for so long, to be replaced with gnawing fear. Victor's extended silence could be attributed to any number of his less pliable traits. After all, I had been the one to gentle him. So long in my absence was not good for him. Or for us.

I stood, anxious for the day's work to be done. "Let us visit some professors."

FOUR

HALF LOST, I SEEK

Professor Krempe was not nearly so unpleasant to look at as Victor had written. But Victor was so precise, so meticulous in his pursuit of perfection in all things, that someone with features as lopsided and coloring as uneven as Professor Krempe's would be nearly unbearable for Victor to converse with.

If Victor could not fix it, he could not be around it. It was the fear of being unable to fix things that had driven him from Geneva. Had he found the answers he sought here?

Professor Krempe offered as little in the way of hope as he did in physical beauty. But his voice was kind and his expression apologetic. "He asked me for more chemistry books than a dozen students could need, and wrote me feverishly intense letters filled with the most astonishing and frequently absurd questions. But that all stopped more than a year ago. Indeed, until you young ladies knocked at my door, I assumed he had left his studies and moved on."

My throat tightened at the thought of it. Moved on? No. Surely he was still here. He would not have gone to another city entirely without telling me. Even Henry had had the decency to tell me, if nothing else. "Do you perhaps have the address he was at when last he wrote you?"

"I do, but I doubt it will help. There was another friend looking for him, now that I think about it. A young man, handsome, with a round, friendly face and startlingly blue eyes."

"Henry!" I said, too quickly and with far too much force. I blushed and smiled to cover my emotion, toying with my gloves. "Our friend Henry came to study here, as well. Do you know where else he went to look?"

Professor Krempe shook his head with genuine remorse. "I am sorry. I had an address for Victor that your Henry had already visited and found vacant. I do not know where he went next in his search. I see so many young men. I remember Henry only because he was so friendly, and I remember Victor for his remarkable intensity." The professor paused, scratching his pockmarked chin thoughtfully. "I think he did not like me. He seemed uncomfortable in my presence. I was keen to work with him, though."

"I am certain he liked you! You are one of only two professors he wrote of to me. He is simply . . . bright. He has an unusual mind, and it can be hard for him when talking to new people."

Professor Krempe nodded. "I hope he has done well, wherever he ended up. I have never seen questions such as his, and doubt I ever will again. He was on the path to either genius or lunacy." Realizing he had gone too far—I was unable to hide the panic his words brought to the surface—he held up his hands and laughed. "I jest. My odds are on him having taken up a different line of study and simply not needing me anymore. Somewhere he is plaguing a history professor with questions about the dental-care habits of ancient Mesopotamia."

I held out a card, writing a smile onto my face with as much elegant determination as I had written out my information. "If you do think of anything that might help us find him, or if he happens to contact you—"

"I will send word immediately. It was lovely to meet you, Miss Elizabeth. Miss Justine." He paused, and his next sentence was so studied and casual I suspected he hoped I would not notice how desperate it was. "If you find him, please let him know I would like to see what he has been working on." He smiled. "I am ever so curious about his studies."

"I will." I would not. This man had done nothing to help me.

As I turned, my eyes lingered on his walls. They were lined floor to ceiling with books. The room smelled of leather and paper and dust. I had always been jealous of Victor for leaving. Now I knew to be jealous of what he had left for.

What I would give for the freedom to declare myself a student, to spend years in dusty rooms, in dusty tomes, learning and puzzling and asking questions of the brightest minds to be found! And to study what I chose, when I chose, with whom I chose. To think that all those years ago, I had been forced to trick Victor into doing what I would have given anything to do.

When Madame Frankenstein had Ernest, it did not bring about the change I expected or feared. I worried she would no longer care to have me around. But the baby was another boy—her third, though the second died in infancy—and she seemed more desperate than ever that I be with Victor at all times.

We spent the next two years throwing ourselves into whatever Victor decided we should study. I learned poems to perform for his parents, and helped care for the baby some. But, to my relief, my main responsibility remained Victor. Better to be lying on a bed of moss being a corpse for examination than bouncing a drooling toddler on my hip!

I did too good a job of socializing Victor, though. He had taught me to read and write and learn, possessively proud of my sharp mind and keen memory. I taught him to react calmly, to smile in a believable way, to talk to others as a peer instead of an aloof critic. With me at his side, his sharp, cold edges blurred to acceptable degrees.

The changes in him did not go unnoticed. One morning when we tumbled into the breakfast room to eat before running outside, Judge Frankenstein stopped us.

"We are having guests today." He said it as though handing down a guilty verdict, and watched us closely for our reactions.

Madame Frankenstein's hands fluttered in front of her face as she searched for an appropriate facial expression. She finally settled on excitement, though her eyes were too bright and her mouth too tight across her white teeth. "A new family," she said. "One that does not know us from— One that does not know us."

Victor and I exchanged a look. I still had not asked what had happened to the other Frankenstein baby, the one who came after Victor and before Ernest. Whatever had transpired, it was awful enough that the Frankensteins had left Geneva and traveled—and therefore found me. So I did not care about that lost baby except as far as its role in my salvation.

But it was obvious in Madame Frankenstein's nerves that these guests had been chosen precisely because they had arrived in Geneva after the events that had driven the Frankensteins abroad. Victor's eyebrows had already begun drawing together, but there was something wild about his stillness that warned me this would not end well.

I grabbed his hand beneath the table, beaming at him. "Victor and I will perform a poem."

Whatever feral instinct had been surfacing in Victor's demeanor, it was settled by the ridiculousness of my offer. "You know I do not recite poetry," he said, shaking his head. "That is your job."

"Well, I will perform a poem and you can take all the credit, since I only know how to read and appreciate poetry because of your tutoring!"

This made him laugh, but I could tell by the flush of his cheeks that he was pleased. Interacting with new people would be easier for him if he could use me as a shield. I let him do that.

I would do anything for him.

"It is settled, then," Judge Frankenstein said. "Monsieur Clerval is a merchant. From common stock, but he has done uncommonly well and quickly climbed the ranks of society. He is quite wealthy now. And he has a son, Henry, who is your age."

I did not question that Judge Frankenstein was talking about Victor's age. He rarely addressed me directly. He rarely even looked at me.

Victor tensed. Unheeding, his father continued. "I have heard good reports of the new schoolmaster in town. If you can get along with Henry, perhaps you can join the school."

I squeezed Victor's hand urgently. I could see him panicking again, every line in his body taut. "May we be excused? We have a lot to prepare!" I stood before waiting for permission to leave, curtseyed to make up for it, then dragged Victor from the room.

"What are they thinking?" he shouted, pacing the length of the playroom we had yet to cede to the baby. "Inviting strangers here. As though I need them to find a friend for me. As though I care."

"Victor," I said. "Think of everything you could learn at a school! We can only learn so much here on our own. We are already running out of books to study. But if you have access to more, a good teacher . . ." I gestured expansively. "We could get further in a month than we can in a year on our own."

He lowered my hands back to my sides, pushing them down from where they had encompassed a broad and open imaginary future. "You know you cannot go to school."

"Of course I know that, silly." I tried to keep the sting of his words from showing. I had not actually thought of it. I was always *with Victor. I had pictured us going to school together. The realization that I would not—could*

not—go with him rushed over my head like the lake waters closing around me. I struggled to get to the surface so I could take a breath and control how I was feeling.

"So you want to be separated from me?" His dark eyes flashed like lightning, and I knew a tremendous thunder would follow.

We had been inseparable for years, such that I did not know where he ended and I began. "No! Never. But I cannot go to school, which means you will have to learn enough for both of us and bring your knowledge back to me here. You will be like my own explorer, going off into the wilds to discover treasures for me. Please, Victor." I was only eleven, but I wanted more. I had never thought of it before now, but the idea of having the freedom of a few hours each day had already sunk in deep, pulling at my lungs so I realized how suffocating my life had been.

I wanted to go with Victor. I could not. But if Victor left, no one would need me. At least for those few precious hours. And then he would return, and bring back more things I could learn.

All I had to do was make sure Henry and Victor got along. I beamed at Victor, already certain of my triumph.

Victor and I greeted Henry wearing all white, our hands clasped as a united front. Henry's smile was shy, but it hid nothing. His round face was open and utterly incapable of deception. Where Victor was cold and removed from the world, and I was as deceptive as a sour strawberry, Henry was exactly as he appeared to be: the most pleasant boy in existence. Even his blue eyes were as clear as the lake on a summer day.

Part of me scorned him for his inability to hide his desperation to be our friend. He would have crawled on the floor and barked like a dog if we had declared that the game we wanted to play. He watched Victor with a hunger that made my teeth ache, it was so sweet. If my love of Victor was entirely selfish, Henry's was the opposite.

And I, accustomed to viewing other people only in terms of what they meant to me, felt my heart crack open with the gap-toothed grin that split his face when he saw our discarded chest of play clothes. "Do you have any swords?" he asked, digging through them. "We can put on a play!"

His parents might have brought him here in hopes of securing further social advantage, and Victor's parents might have brought him here in hopes of securing further socialization for their own troubled son. But Henry?

Henry was here to have fun.

"I like him," I whispered to Victor. "He is silly. We should keep him."

Henry held up a length of tattered purple velvet and squinted as though imagining Victor wearing it as a cape. "Victor should be king. He has that regal quality about him. He is far handsomer than I, and looks smarter, too."

"And he likes you," I whispered, nudging Victor with my elbow. He had gone silent and still as soon as I said I liked Henry. "So he is at least a little bit intelligent."

Victor gave me a half smile, apparently mollified. I let Henry dress me as a queen, and Victor deigned to be king. That afternoon, we put on a short play for our delighted parents. I stood between the two boys, resplendent in fake finery, ebullient with real joy.

If I could not go to school, Victor's going was the next best thing.

Professor Waldman, our next stop, had a bland but perfectly symmetrical face and clothes with the precise tailoring of a man who cared about appearances. He had been far more highly regarded than Professor Krempke by Victor in his letter, but he had a similar report. After a flurry of demands on his time and his studies, he had not heard from Victor in more than a year. He did not remember whether another young man had come looking for Victor because he had neither the time nor the patience for such a thing—nor, clearly, did he have the time or the patience for two silly girls asking about a promising student who had so deeply disappointed him by disappearing.

"Perhaps you should check the gambling dens, the tavern back rooms, or the bottom of the river," Professor Waldman said meanly. "We seem to lose quite a lot of men to those." He shut the door without ceremony in our faces. An ugly and tarnished brass knocker sneered at me, mocking my failure.

I vowed that if we were not locked in that night, I would return and throw a rock through his window.

Justine trembled, lifting a hand to her forehead and ducking so her hat would hide some of her expression. "Elizabeth, I am so sorry. We tried. I know how you have worried, but I do not think we should stay here. We have no more information to go on. If Victor—when Victor—wants to be found, he will write. You said yourself he is unpredictable and can descend into moods that last for months."

I shook my head, clenching my jaw. I had worked too hard, too long, to give up now. I had spent my entire life being what Victor needed.

Now I needed him, and he *would* be found.

"We know Henry found him," Justine continued, gaining confidence as she steadily talked herself into leaving. "Perhaps they went abroad, or pursued studies elsewhere. Naturally, a gap in communication could be expected then. Letters get lost, or delayed. I am certain if we go home, something will be waiting." She finally tipped her head back up, beaming in anticipation. "Ernest will be so relieved to have us home. He will run up with the letter! And with little William on my lap, we will laugh and laugh at the poor timing that would have saved us this whole miserable trip!"

Justine's imaginative theory was plausible. But her scenario held no comfort for me. I refused to believe that Victor had gone on from this city. Not yet. Victor had promised that one day *we* would tour the continent together. Return to Lake Como. Trek through the ominous and wild Carpathians. Explore ruins in Greece. All the places we had read about.

And besides, with the last letter Henry sent me, I could not imagine any scenario in which they had reconciled.

I leaned forward and kissed her cheek. "I have one more place to look. Please?"

She sighed, already letting go of her true desires for my sake. She wanted nothing more than to be back at the Frankensteins' isolated manor, tucked away in the nursery with little William. And I was keeping her from it. "*What if he forgets me?*" she had asked on the way here, as though a five-year-old would forget the woman he knew better than his mother. The woman who had taken over entirely when his mother died. A few days in the care of the daft maid would not replace Justine.

"Where else can we look?" she asked.

"The place you always go when you need answers." I grinned, taking her hand and leading her back to the street. "The library."

FIVE

WITH PURPOSE TO EXPLORE OR TO DISTURB

Rich dark wood, polished by both time and careful hands, grew from the floor to the ceiling in perfect straight lines. In place of branches, shelves. In place of leaves, books.

Oh, the books.

I was light-headed from breathing in as deeply as possible, trying to absorb the knowledge here by sheer force of will. I trailed my hands along a row of spines, their worn leather bindings labeled with gold because of the treasure contained inside.

"Can I help you young ladies?" A man glared at us. His face was pinched around a pair of spectacles, having slowly grown to fit them rather than finding a pair that fit his face. His skin was as pale and stretched as the parchment he guarded.

I wanted more time with the books. I wanted to spend the day in a quiet corner, sitting against a window, lost in words and worlds I had never been given access to.

But there was no time. If I did not find Victor today, Justine would make us go home. And I could not return to that place. Not without what I came for. I could not go back to running the whole household for that silent, ungrateful man, worried every day that this would be the day he informed me I was no longer necessary. That my time as a temporary Frankenstein was at an end. That I was well and truly on my own forever.

This librarian could and would help me. I smiled benignly. "Yes, actually. I am looking for my cousin. He has recently moved, and we began our trip before his letter with his new address reached us."

Justine turned her head sharply at my falsehood, but I pushed on.

"I am afraid his landlord has been ill and was not able to rescue Victor's new information from an overzealous maid. So you can see our dilemma! We are quite desperate to find him. As he loves nothing more than books, and this is the finest library I have ever seen, I am certain we will find some trace of him here!"

The man sighed in exasperation but visibly softened. I was not here for his precious books. I was just a girl looking for a boy.

"A great many students use our books. I doubt I will be of any help. What is his name? Victor?"

"Yes. Victor Frankenstein."

"Oh." His eyebrows lifted in surprise and recognition, nearly dislodging his spectacles. "I *do* know that name. He used to haunt these rows, often here until we closed for the night. Several times I even found him waiting on the steps for us to open in the morning; I suspected he never went home. An odd, intense young man."

I beamed. "That is our Victor!"

"Well, I am sorry to say he has not been here in—"

"A year?" I said with a defeated sigh.

"More like seven or eight months. At that point, he had exhausted even this library's tremendous reserves."

My heart beat faster as my hopes expanded. That would have been after he left his original lodgings! "And do you have his address?"

"No."

My hopes were dashed. I tried to keep my expression from showing my true despair as I reached into my purse to withdraw one of the last cards I had written up. "If you think of—"

"You might try the bookseller."

I paused, my fingers still buried in silk. "Who?"

"There is a bookseller three streets over. A foreigner. Turn left out of the library, and then the next right. He specializes in difficult-to-obtain science and philosophy tomes that are both too expensive and too radical for us to stock here. I gave his name to your cousin, and that was when he stopped visiting us."

I could have kissed his papery cheek! Instead, I settled for the more appropriate gift of a blinding smile. His own lips, unused to that expression, twitched upward as though remembering what such happiness felt like.

"Thank you!" I took Justine's elbow and spun her, practically running out of the building.

"Slow down," she cautioned. She grabbed my arm to stop me before I stepped into the street just as a carriage clattered past.

I laughed, breathless with nerves. "You have saved me! See, we are finally even."

"Oh, Elizabeth." She tucked a strand of hair fallen free from my hat back into place, pulling a pin out of thin air to secure it. "Are you hungry? Should we find somewhere to eat before talking to the bookseller?"

I could see the exhaustion in her face. Normally it would be enough for me to acquiesce, but I could not. Not when I was so close.

Or so far.

Because if this bookseller did not know how to find Victor, I had no other ideas. And I could not stand the tension of delaying either reality: finding Victor, or having to go home without him as protection.

* * *

The Frankensteins took me from Lake Como and on their travels through the rest of the continent. I was too young to appreciate anything other than a full belly and no one hitting me. But not so young that I did not realize the precariousness of my situation. When we finally approached their secluded residence, located across a lake from Geneva and accessible only by boat, it was as though I was being rowed across the sky. It was a brilliantly clear day, the water around us a perfect reflection of cloudless blue.

The house appeared in the trees like something from a fairy tale. Lying in wait and ready to devour us. Sharply angled roofs cut like teeth against the sky. Everything was pointed—the windows, the doors, even the wrought-iron gates that slowly swung open to admit us.

I instinctively knew this house was a predator. But I was clever like a rabbit, fast and smart and tiny. I took Madame Frankenstein's hand and beamed up at her.

"Oh," she said, always surprised when she remembered me. She smiled, stroking my hair. "You will like it here. It will be good for Victor. Better. Better for us all."

I was taken to a room by one of the three servants they kept. The four posters of the bed echoed the lines of lead through the windowpanes, all of them like bars in a cage. But the mattress was soft and the blankets warm. Thus every small animal is lulled into security.

In the mornings when I awoke, I always spent a few precious seconds in bed with my eyes squeezed shut. I remembered the feeling of an empty stomach, the blows of angry fists, the fear and the cold, and always, always the hunger. I held on to that until I could open my eyes and smile.

I had been traded to the Frankensteins for a few coins, and lived in fear that they, too, would sell me. By their grace I lived, and so I did all in my power to keep their love. Perhaps they would have tolerated some disobedience, but I would not risk it. Not ever.

Victor liked me, but he was the child. Madame Frankenstein hardly seemed capable of getting out of bed most days. I could not depend on her kindness to sustain me. And Judge Frankenstein had never so much as addressed me, treating my presence in their company with the same indifferent indulgence he might have had his wife taken a notion to bring in a stray dog.

I needed to be something they would love. And so when I got out of bed, I left behind anything I wanted and slipped into sweetness as softly as I slipped into my warm socks.

Victor was odd. But I had only my caretaker's feral children to compare him to. Victor never bit me, never stole food from me, never held my head beneath the lake until I saw stars in the darkness coming to claim me. He did watch me carefully, as though testing my reactions. But I was more careful than he was, and never showed anything but the sweetest love and adoration.

It was after our first few quiet weeks in the house by the lake that I understood, finally, the fear I had seen ghosting across his mother's and father's faces sometimes when they looked at him.

I had been getting ready in my room and was pulling on my shoes when I heard the screaming.

My first instinct was to hide. There was a spot in my wardrobe that looked too small for a body, but I had fit myself neatly into it just to test it out. My window also opened, and I could scamper out, down the trellis, and be hidden in the trees in no time.

But that was not what people in beautiful houses did. And if I wanted to stay here, I could not fall back on my old ways.

I crept out of my room and down the hall, then padded silently down the stairs. By now I recognized Victor's voice, though it was twisted by rage in a way I had never heard. It was coming from the library, a room where I was not allowed.

I paused outside, then pushed the door open.

Victor stood with his back to me, in the middle of a whirlwind of destruction. Torn and shredded books encircled him. His chest heaved, his narrow shoulders shuddering as he screamed with a sound more animal than human. In his hand, he clutched a letter opener.

On the other side of the room, his parents stood, their backs to the wall, faces frozen in fear.

I could still choose to leave.

But Judge Frankenstein looked at me. He never *looked at me. That day, there was desperate pleading in his eyes. And the heavy weight of expectation, as well.*

Instinct took over. I had freed animals caught in traps. This felt the same, somehow. Humming low and deep in my throat, I approached Victor slowly. I reached up and gently stroked the back of his neck, the hum turning into a half-remembered lullaby. He froze, his frenzied breaths catching and then calming. I continued stroking the back of his neck, working my way around him until we were face to face. I looked up into his eyes, which were wide, the pupils dilated.

"Hello," I said. I smiled at him.

He regarded me with that furrowed brow. I moved my hand from the back of his neck to his forehead, smoothing away his tension. "Elizabeth," he said. He looked down at our feet rather than facing the destruction he had wrought.

I took the letter opener from his hand and set it down on a table. Then, holding his now-free hand, I said, "We should have a picnic."

He nodded, still breathing too hard. I turned him toward the door. As we left the room, I glanced over my shoulder to see the abject relief and gratitude on his parents' faces.

He had not hurt anything, not really, *but he had succeeded in cementing my place in their family. I might have been his, but he was mine. After that day we were truly inseparable.*

"He needs me, too," I said.

"What?" Justine asked, pausing in front of a house with a dreary gray door.

I shook my head. "Look, there!" Across the street was a bookshop. It squatted beneath an overhanging residence that left the windows in perpetual shadow.

This time I waited to be certain we would not be killed by a passing horse, but only for Justine's sake. Then I dragged her across the cobblestones as quickly as I could. Anxiety choked me as I pushed through the heavy door of the shop.

A bell chimed in muted resignation, signaling our entrance to the cramped stacks and dangerously leaning shelves. Where the library had been stately and impressive, this room was overwhelming and claustrophobic. How one could begin to find a sought-after treasure in here was beyond me.

"Just a moment," a surprisingly high and feminine voice called from an unseen location. The room could have gone on for leagues, as far as I could tell—any view of the expanse was blocked by the shelves. It was a labyrinth of knowledge, and I had no strings to mark my way. I would have to wait for this Minotaur to come to me instead.

Justine stood near the doorway, hands clasped primly in front of her. She gave me a tight, hopeful smile. I was too jumbled with nerves to return it. I was about to shout for the bookseller to please come and help us, when a woman not much older than we were appeared from behind a shelf. Her apron was covered in dust, and a charcoal pencil had been shoved into her pinned-up hair.

She was pretty in a way that seemed imminently practical. Her beauty was not a performance or a necessity; it was simply part of her. Her hair and skin were both darker than most in this region. There was something sharp and intelligent about her eyes that promised a lively mind, and I immediately wanted to know her. And I wanted to know, too, how a young woman had come to be working in a bookshop.

"Oh! You are not who I was expecting." She smiled, puzzled.

"Who were you expecting?" I felt my heart racing, wondering if Victor was due at any moment!

"The usual dour-faced and double-chinned professor to yell at me about our prices and inform me I am robbing him, *robbing him*, he says, and he will not have it! And then he pulls out his money anyhow, because he cannot get what he needs elsewhere." She clapped her hands together, rubbing them free of the dust I suspected never stopped clinging to her. "But you two are like flowers delivered by a sweetheart! I was about to close up for lunch. What books do you need?"

"No books. We are actually searching for my cousin."

"I am afraid I sold the last cousin yesterday and have no cousins stocked on my shelves. I can order one for you, but it will take *weeks* to arrive." Her eyes twinkled with amusement, but then she saw my desperation and her expression turned gentle. "This sounds like a complicated story. Will you join me for lunch and we can discuss it there? I get so little time with other women!"

I opened my mouth to decline, but Justine spoke first, relief bubbling from her. "Oh, yes! That would be lovely. We have had such troubles since we got here last night."

"I can tell from your accent that German is not your first language." The bookseller shifted to French with ease. "Is this better?"

Justine nodded, beaming with gratitude. I had no preference, but it was kind of her to take Justine's comfort into account.

"I am sorry for your reception. That is Ingolstadt. Not known for its warm welcomes during this season. In fact, it is preparing to again demonstrate how much it wishes we were not here." She pointed at the window, where the first warning drops of rain traced dirty lines down the glass. "We have to go outside and around the corner. Hurry!"

She pushed out the door and we followed her, huddling beneath our single umbrella. She walked ahead of us, unconcerned about the rain. I envied her dark skirts. Mine would show every trace of mud and filth the city had to offer. But I had to wear white, knowing I would see Victor. *Hoping* I would see Victor.

"Here we are!" She stopped in front of a plain door around the corner. Pulling out a key, she unlocked it.

"I thought we were going to a café?" I asked.

"They are all wretched and overpriced. I can feed you better." She turned and grinned at us, her teeth crooked like the shelves in her bookstore, crowding together in a pleasant sort of way. "I am Mary Delgado." She looked at Justine first.

"Justine Moritz. And this is Elizabeth Lavenza."

"Pleased to meet you both. Now, come out of the rain." We followed her into a cramped landing area, cluttered with so many books it might as well have been a shop, too. Books were piled on a table, pushed in stacks against the walls, and taking up nearly every step on the stairs ascending to the second story. A narrow path led straight up between the looming tomes.

"Mind the books," she said, climbing the stairs with practiced ease.

I leaned down to see some of the spines. There was no organization I could see. Poems beneath political tomes beneath religious texts beneath mathematical theory. I let my fingers linger on a book of philosophy, then drew them away. My white lace fingertips were still perfectly clean. These books were all regularly used, with no collected dust.

I *did* mind the books. I minded them very much, and I wanted to know more about all of them. Instead, we followed Mary up the stairs and into a cozy sitting room. This one, surprisingly, contained not a single book. A worn but clean sofa was paired with an overstuffed leather chair, both kept company by a cheerful fire.

"Sit," Mary called from another room, into which she had already disappeared. "Please, sit."

We did as instructed. Justine sighed happily, pulling off her gloves and unpinning her hat. I perched on the edge of the couch.

"You look like you are ready to flee," Justine observed.

I removed my gloves, too, but left my hat in place. I wanted to pace the room like a caged animal. Instead, I stared into the fire, willing the hypnotic flicker of flame to calm my mind.

Mary set down a tray of sliced bread, cold roast chicken, and a wedge of light, nutty cheese. "It is not much, but better than the overpriced swill they cheat the students with!" Before I could open my mouth to ask her about Victor, she disappeared again, reappearing with a tea service. When she had set that down, too, and seated herself, it was finally acceptably polite for me to begin speaking.

"Now, what type of cousin are you in the market for?" Mary's eyes sparkled. Adoration and annoyance warred within me. In other circumstances, I would want to be her friend. But right now, she was all that stood between my future and my perilous present.

"Victor Frankenstein."

She paused with her teacup halfway to her lips. "*Victor?*"

"You know him, then?"

She laughed. "Victor's voracious buying habits financed my uncle's book-hunting trip abroad. He left last month, as giddy as a child when he walked out the door. I think my uncle would adopt Victor if he could. He has suggested on several occasions that I should try to marry him."

I repented of my previous thoughts. I did not like Mary. Not at all. My teacup trembled in my hand, and I set it down lest I break it.

She must have sensed my reaction, because she laughed again. "You need not fear on my behalf. I have more than enough company with my books as it is. I would never survive having to make room for someone like Victor."

Victor did take up a tremendous amount of room in one's life. And when he left, all that vacant space buzzed, demanding to be filled.

I did not quite trust Mary still, but I needed her. "Do you know where Victor is, then?"

Mary opened her mouth to answer, then hesitated. "I have just realized that I do not know who you are or what you might want with Victor. And the last few months have taught us all to be cautious."

"What do you mean?" Justine asked. "Our landlady, too, seemed frightened and overly zealous about safety."

"It is all just rumor. A sailor missing. The corner drunk, there one day and vanished the next. People move, people leave without telling anyone, it happens. Especially among the lower classes, who have less to tie them to one place. But there is a certain undercurrent of . . . not fear, but concern, that has gripped the city recently."

"I assure you I have no intention of murdering Victor," I said, forcing a smile. Making him disappear from this city, perhaps. But if he was such a good client, she would not want anything to lure him away. "He is my cousin. He left us in Geneva two years ago—"

"After his mother died," Justine added.

"—yes, after his mother died, to study here. We have not heard from him in some months, and I am worried. He can get intensely obsessive and forget to care for himself as he should. We wanted to make certain he is well."

Mary raised an eyebrow. "But you do not know where he lives?"

Justine answered. "His friend Henry came several months ago to check on him, but—"

I coughed pointedly. Justine had been so silent with the men! But something about this Mary had her at ease. Justine was not controlling the conversation the way she should have been.

"Did your Henry not report back?" Mary watched me curiously, her expression shrewd. Why would the men swallow all my implausible explanations, but this girl catch every snag?

"He did," I said. "Though he has always been less than meticulous and neglected to give us an actual address for Victor."

"And Henry cannot help you now?"

I had avoided answering Justine's questions about where Henry was, allowing her to assume he was here, too, and could help us. She trusted him. It had made her more comfortable coming. But if I wanted answers from Mary, I would have to provide some as well. "Henry left for England not long after he found Victor," I said, setting down my teacup and leaning forward so I could not see Justine. "You can imagine what an exasperating trip this has been!"

Justine whipped her head around. "England? You knew? But you said he was here!"

"He was. Until about six months ago."

I finally looked over and her expression made me feel as fragile as my teacup. I braced for anger, but found only hurt and gentle reproach. "Why did you not tell me?"

"I knew you would worry, coming to an unknown city without someone you trusted here. But Victor is here, and I trust him. I am sorry I did not tell you about Henry. I needed you to come. I cannot do this alone."

Justine kept her gaze on her food, but one of her hands disappeared into her purse, where I was certain she clutched the little lead soldier. "You should have told me."

"I should have." I searched her face to see whether she was more upset with me or with Henry. I had never been able to tell whether Justine held any feelings more than friendship for him. I had never encouraged them, exactly, wishing to hold on to all my options. But now those options were gone for both of us. I reached out and squeezed her arm, drawing her close to me. She came, though reluctantly. "I am sorry. It was selfish of me to keep that from you. But I am so worried about Victor, I could not think straight."

Justine nodded, silent. I knew she would forgive me. And I did not regret what I had done. We were here now. We would find him. And our success would wash away all my manipulations to get here.

Mary leaned back, picking up a piece of chicken with her fingers and popping it into her mouth. She had watched the whole exchange with silent interest. "So Victor came to study and stopped writing. And then Henry came to check on him, and immediately left without giving you Victor's address?"

"That is the sum of it," I said flatly. "You know how inconsiderate men can be of our feelings. They get so busy with their lives that they forget we are left at home with nothing to do but fret over them."

"That is my experience, as well. Since my uncle left I have had not one letter from him. It is vexing." She wiped her fingers on her apron. "I do not know this Henry. If he came by the bookshop, he must have spoken with my uncle. But your description of Victor is true, and your concern seems genuine. He is an odd and obsessive young man. Quite rude a lot of the time, frankly. But I did not mind, since I got the impression he was rude to everyone and not just me because of my sex and heritage. He has not been in the shop for a few months now."

I wilted. Lying to Justine, deceiving her, and, worse, potentially giving Judge Frankenstein a firm excuse to throw me out—all for nothing!

"But," Mary said, leaning forward and putting a finger under my chin to lift my face. She smiled at my devastated expression. "I *do* have a delivery request from his last order that should have an address. It may no longer be current, but I know my uncle was stopping to see him on his way to the continent, so—"

"Please, give it to me!" I was too obviously desperate. She could press any advantage from me, ask anything, and I would give it.

Instead, she stood and left the room. Justine ate, not looking at me. I should have apologized more, but I could not manage anything with my nerves in their current state.

Finally, Mary returned with a slip of paper. "Here it is." She passed it to me. It was not the old address I had already checked. And the date was from only six months before!

Mary had also brought a cloak and an umbrella.

"You must need to return to the shop," I said, standing. Justine sighed over the remaining food but did the same. "Thank you so much for your kindness and help!"

"With my uncle gone, I seldom have customers. The shop will keep for a few hours while I take you to Victor's residence. It is not in a friendly part of town."

Justine laughed, and I was grateful for the sound, even though it was sad. "No parts of this town have been friendly."

Mary smiled tightly. "Perhaps I phrased that too gently. It is in a part of town that no woman should visit alone, and even two women should not venture if they are unaware of their surroundings." She fastened her cloak and took a hat from a hook by the door, settling it on top of her hair and covering the pencil. "Also, I am wildly curious. I have seen the types of books Victor pursued. I would like to know what he has been doing with all his studies. And to know what could have possessed him, that he would shamefully neglect two such lovely and concerned friends."

"We all would," I muttered darkly, following her back out into the weeping city.

SIX

ROUND HE THROWS HIS BALEFUL EYES

At another time, I might have seen the charm of Ingolstadt. The steep roofs in warm oranges, the cheerily painted rows of homes along wide, open streets. There were several green park areas, and a cathedral soared over the city, keeping watch. I felt it on the back of my neck, tracking my movement. Its spires were sentinels, visible nearly everywhere we went. Was God watching? If so, what did he see? Did he care for the obstinate machinations of one small woman with only seventeen years to her credit?

If he was watching, that meant he had *always* been watching. And if he had always been watching, what a spiteful, mean old man he was to watch and do nothing. For me. For Justine.

No. Justine would insist that God had answered her prayers by sending me. And she would probably say that God had answered my prayers by sending Victor.

But that was not possible. I had not prayed as a child, and I certainly did not now. Surely God, so stingy with his miracles, would not answer an unoffered prayer. I did not repent of my distance from God. If I wanted help, I would find it for myself.

We passed an old building overlooking a city square. All colors were muted by the clouds and the rain, blending together like a palette of paint being rinsed clean. I knew from my study of the map that Mary was leading us toward the Danube River and the outskirts of the city. I had embraced confidence both for Justine's sake and my own, but it was a relief to have someone else leading us. Since I joined the Frankensteins and we settled at the lake house, I had not been anywhere except Geneva. This city, pleasant though it might have been, was a stranger. And strangers were not to be trusted.

We passed through the commercial center, then into more residential streets. The medieval wall around the city was maintained in good repair and still marked the boundaries of Ingolstadt. We walked along it until we came to a passage through an unused gatehouse that would lead us out. The noise of the rain against our umbrellas hushed for one long breath as we walked beneath the wall.

In that moment I thought I heard again the noise of my dreams. The haunting cry of a soul so alone, even being in hell in the company of the other damned would be a comfort.

I whipped my head to the side, peering into the dark recesses of the gatehouse. There were doors there, barred, but one looked as though it had recently been forced open and clumsily drawn shut again. "Did you—"

Mary waved dismissively. "It is an old city. Even the stones mourn the passing of time. It is not much farther, though we must cross the bridge."

Justine, however, looked as unnerved as I felt. "We cannot be gone much longer," she said. "Mind the hour. Frau Gottschalk will lock us out."

"Charming," Mary said, her voice the only bright thing out that dreary afternoon. "Hurry, then."

We left the ancient borders of the city. This section of the Danube was crowded with boats for loading or unloading goods, though most sat idle, waiting out the rain. We nearly made it over the bridge without incident, until a passing carriage splashed murky puddle water on our skirts. The thought of showing up to see Victor in a dress anything other than pristinely white filled me with terror. All the insecurities of our first meeting engulfed me, and I felt I was once again the little girl with dirty feet.

What could I offer him now? I had seen no trees for climbing, no nests filled with eggs. I had no tiny, fragile hearts to give him as an offering, only my own. I lifted my chin, determined not to be weak. I would be his Elizabeth, the one so carefully shaped with his help. And he would remember, and love me again, and I would be safe.

Henry, who had abandoned and betrayed me, would never again get a single beat of my heart. I should never have let him so far in. He had threatened everything from the start.

Those fleeting childhood years, when Henry guided our play and Victor was satisfied with his school studies, were suffused with light and the closest I had ever felt to ease. There was something remarkable in having Victor and Henry—the one so prone to fits of anger and cold aloofness, the other so bright and joyful and open to the wonders of the world without questioning how they existed—revolve around me.

I saw in the hungry way Henry sought Victor's attention and favor that Victor's love was rare, and rare things are always the most valuable. In turn, I became even more what Victor wanted me to be. Lovely. Sweet. Brilliant and quick-minded but never as smart as him. I laughed at Henry's jokes and plays, but I saved my best smiles for Victor, knowing he collected them and secreted them away.

I had become this girl in order to survive, but the longer I lived in her body, the easier it was to simply be her. I was twelve, on the cusp of leaving childhood behind forever. But we still played like children. I was Guinevere to their Arthur and Lancelot, acting out the dramas Henry lovingly cobbled together out of pieces he stole from great playwrights of eras past. The trees were our Camelot. All our foes were imaginary and therefore easily defeated.

One day we were playing a variation of kings and queens. I lay in a magical sleep upon my forest bed. Henry and Victor, after much travail, had found me. "She is the most beautiful girl in the world! A sleep like death has claimed her. Only love can awaken her again!" Henry declared, raising his sword to the sky. Then he leaned over and kissed me.

I opened my eyes to find Henry looking at me in shock, as though he could not believe what he had done. I dared not look at Victor. I squeezed my eyes shut again, not reacting to Henry's kiss.

"I thought perhaps it would— I thought it would wake her," Henry said, stumbling over the words. He sounded frightened.

"She is not sleeping." Victor's voice was as brittle as morning-frosted grass. "Here, see? No life in her veins." He lifted my wrist, which I kept limp. "She is dead. But we can trace the pathways her heartbeat would have used in life." Victor drew a finger along the blue veins in my pale arm, up and up to where my sleeve started. My arm twitched at the contact.

"Be still!" Victor whispered, catching my open eye. "Here, I have my own blade, sharper and subtler than your sword. We will see if she bleeds now that she is dead."

"Victor!" There was no laughter in Henry's voice. My wrist was tugged away, and I was pulled out of my corpse character and into Henry's arms.

"You cannot do that!" he said.

"Just a small cut, to see what is under the skin. Do you not wonder?" Victor's anger this time was not a storm raging out of control. It was darker and deeper, like the bottom of the lake—cold and unknowable. It was a new type of anger, and I did not know how to soothe it.

"Elizabeth does not mind." Victor's knife winked in the sun as though it wanted to play, too. "She is always concerned with the beauty and poetry of

the world, but I want to know what lies beneath every surface. Give me your hand, Elizabeth."

Henry, on the verge of tears, tugged me farther away. "You cannot go around cutting people open, Victor. It is simply not done!"

I did not know where to look or how to respond. But I knew staying with Henry—on his side—would offer me no benefit in the long run. And I could not risk Victor's anger. I had never been the target of it! Henry had put me there, and I resented him for it.

I extricated myself from Henry's arms and placed a dainty kiss on Victor's cheek. Then I put my arm through his and held his elbow as I had seen Madame Frankenstein hold Judge Frankenstein's. "He was only playing. You are the one who ruined the pretend by kissing me without asking first."

Victor radiated coldness, but his surface was as smooth and clear as glass. "I am done with your games for today, Henry. They are boring."

Henry looked from one of us to the other, hurt and bewilderment on his kind face as he tried to understand how he had been the one in the wrong.

"Henry does not understand how to play corpse; that is all," I said. "It is our special game. We are getting too old for it, anyhow." I looked to Victor for confirmation—desperate for it. I needed to mend this. I could not lose Henry. He was such a bright spot in my life.

Victor nodded, one eyebrow raised dispassionately. "I suppose we are. I will be fourteen next month. We are going to the baths to celebrate. Did Mother tell you?"

I could not let him leave Henry angry. Who was to say if our friend would ever return? Victor did not let go of grudges lightly. The year before, the cook had served a meal that made him ill. Victor refused to eat food prepared by him for an entire week, forcing his parents to dismiss the cook and find another. I did not want Henry dismissed, even if he had complicated everything.

Laughing with gaiety, I squeezed Victor's hand and beamed up at him. "Do invite Henry and his parents. Otherwise, I am afraid you and your father will go off hunting together and I will be left alone with little Ernest."

"But you told Mother you love Ernest."

"All he does is cry and wet himself. I will be miserable trapped with him! And miserable without you. If Henry is there, you will have a reason to tell your father no. And he can take Monsieur Clerval instead."

The tight remnants of anger around Victor's eyes finally disappeared. "Of course Henry should come."

I turned my smile on Henry, and he nodded, relieved but still confused. "Go and tell your parents, Victor," I said, "so they know to plan for the Clervals. I will see Henry to the boat."

His anger shed like a coat, Victor calmly walked away.

I kept a distance between Henry and myself, though, as we walked back to the dock. We were nearly there when he grabbed my arm and forced me to stop.

"Elizabeth, I am sorry. I am not sure what I did wrong."

I gave him a light, careless smile. I used smiles like currency. They were the only currency I ever had. My dresses, my shoes, my ribbons—they all belonged to the Frankensteins. I was a guest in them, just as I was a guest in that house. "You punctured Victor's make-believe. You know how sensitive he can be."

"I am sorry I kissed you."

"I am sorry for that, too." I lifted my fingers to my lips to find my easy smile had abandoned me. "You cannot do it again."

His face was a portrait of disappointment. "Will you answer something for me? Truthfully?"

I nodded. But I knew I would not, regardless of what the question was. The truth was not a luxury I could indulge in.

"Are you happy here?"

Henry's simple question landed like blows on my shoulders, and I flinched away from it as I would have from my old caretaker's fists. "Why would you ask me that?"

"Sometimes the things you say sound more like the lines I write than like what you are actually feeling."

"What if I am not happy?" I whispered, smiling, though it was a physical pain to do so. "What would you do? What would anyone do? This is my home, Henry. The only one I have. Without the Frankensteins I have nothing. Do you understand?"

"Yes, of course I—"

I lifted a hand to cut him off. He could not understand. If he could, he would never have asked me such a stupid question. "But I am *happy. What would I choose but this life? You are such a strange boy. We are together nearly every day! You know I am happy here. And you are happy here, too, or else you would stop coming."*

He nodded, worry clouding the open expanse of his face. I could not bear to look at it, so I drew him close in a hug. "I am happier when you are here," I said. "Never leave us. Promise."

"I promise."

With his promise—because Henry was as truthful as I was not—I took him to the boats and waved him cheerfully away. I would have to be more careful with my two boys, with the balance there. I did not want to think what would happen if I lost Victor's love. Losing Henry's would simply hurt.

But I had had enough of hurting for an entire lifetime. I resolved to keep Henry near me always. I would use both of them as my protection.

Henry had asked if I was happy.

I was safe, and that was better than happy.

"So, what is your relation to our Victor?" Mary asked Justine. I chafed at her use of the possessive.

Justine startled, drawn out of the silence into which she had retreated. I walked as close to her as I could, but I still felt a distance between us I would need to work to heal.

She smiled reflexively. "I am employed by the Frankensteins. I started just before Victor left, so I do not know him well. But I take care of his brothers. Ernest, the elder, is eleven. He is such a good boy! So clever, and though he could do without a governess now, he still minds me. He is thinking of entering the military. It makes me scared just thinking of it, but he will be a fine and steadfast soldier someday. William, the baby, is such a dear! He has dimples sweeter than candy, and the softest curls. I worry about how he is sleeping without me. I sing him to sleep every night."

"William is hardly a baby," I said. "He is nearly five. You spoil him."

"It is not possible to spoil a child so wonderful!" Justine gave me the harshest look her gentle countenance was capable of. "And you will appreciate my generosity of love when you have your own babies for me to be nursemaid and governess to."

Her declaration startled me so much I laughed out loud, a welcome relief to the pressure that was beginning to build unbearably inside my chest. "If I ever have babies, you will already be a mother, and we will raise them as beloved cousins."

Justine made a funny noise in the back of her throat. I thought, with a pang of guilt, about Henry's absence and what that might mean for Justine's private hopes. I had been selfish. I would make it up to her. I linked my arm through hers and drew her closer. "Justine is the best governess in the entire world, and the young Frankenstein boys worship her. The nicest thing I ever did for them was find her."

Justine blushed, ducking her head. "It is I who have benefited most."

"Nonsense. Any life is instantly improved by the addition of you."

Mary laughed. "I concur! You have already rescued me from a dusty, lonely afternoon. And brought me to such an excitingly aromatic destination . . ."

She pointed to a cluster of brick buildings skulking along the riverbanks. We could already smell them as we turned off the bridge, the scents exacerbated by the moisture. There was a tannery somewhere in the distance, shit and piss competing to be the most overwhelming assault to the senses. We hurried along the row. The tannery stench faded but was replaced by the sharp metallic reek of old blood. Perhaps a butchery.

"All the things a city needs to survive but would rather not look at—or smell," Mary said, stepping gingerly around a mysteriously discolored puddle. Outside one of the buildings on the corner were a couple of viciously hungry-looking men. Between them stood a middle-aged woman wearing a suggestively low-cut blouse. She was less alluring than depressing, but the purpose of the establishment was immediately clear.

"Why would Victor live out here?" asked Justine, sounding afraid as she drew closer to my side. In spite of the dreadful circumstance, relief buoyed me. We would be fine. Justine had probably already forgiven me.

Mary stepped around the prone body of a man who was almost definitely sleeping off too much drink and *probably* not dead, though none of us moved to check. "People come out here for any number of reasons. The city is cramped, and you can find much larger spaces here. The rent is cheaper because of the smells and the distance to the city center and university." She shrugged. "They also come out here if they want to avoid being noticed or found."

"Victor is not *hiding* from us," I snapped. "He is a genius, and with that comes a level of carelessness about the regular maintenance of life and relationships that most people do not understand."

"He is fortunate to have you, then. Since you understand."

"I do." My raised eyebrow was met with an infuriating smile.

"You might like Henry," Justine said thoughtfully. "He is nothing like Victor. He loves stories and languages and poetry."

I squeezed Justine's arm. "I am certain Mary would like Henry, as everyone likes Henry." As everyone *liked* Henry. With his last letter, I was certain Victor no longer did. And I did not, either. He had failed us all.

"Here we are." Mary stopped, and Justine and I turned to look.

The building, sitting on the edge of the river, was so ugly and misshapen I could not believe Victor had agreed to live here. The mere existence of such a thing—more like a brick-and-stone growth than an actual architectural piece—would upset him. There were no windows on the ground floor, or even on the second floor, that I could see. A narrow line of them marched drunkenly parallel to the roof. On the roof itself, I thought I could see a window that had been cranked open like shutters to the sky. Which was a bad decision, as it was raining. There was also an odd sort of chute from the roof to just past the riverbank.

"Should we knock?" Justine asked dubiously.

"Shouldn' go 'n there." We all three jumped, shocked, at the slurred and sloppy voice behind us. The man from the gutter—definitely not dead, then, though he smelled as if he had spent many long hours dancing with death—was leaning precariously behind us. I had not known the human body could be at that angle unsupported and remain upright.

"Excuse me?" I asked.

"Bad place."

I did not have the patience for a drunkard. Not when Victor was quite possibly beyond a single door. "As far as I can tell, this whole quarter is a bad place. I do not see why this building should be any different."

"Tell you a secret." The man shuffled closer. His breath was as putrid as an unwashed chamber pot. I could not back away, boxed in by Justine on one side and the door on the other. I stepped closer to the man, shielding Justine with my body. He beckoned me even closer.

One of his eyes was filmy white. His beard was patched and unkempt, the skin beneath splotched red and purple. He ran his tongue along his few remaining teeth, eyes darting back and forth as though he was fearful of being overheard.

"Well?" I said.

He moved even closer. *"Monsters!"*

I jumped in alarm and shock, and he cackled with laughter at his trick. He took a step back, and I saw immediately what would happen—a raised pile of discarded bricks was behind him, and then a steep drop into the river.

I did not warn him.

He stumbled into the bricks and lost his balance, his arms spinning like a windmill. The splash with which he entered the river was deeply satisfying.

"How awful!" Justine covered her mouth in horror. "What if he cannot swim?"

"He fell quite close to the side." I turned my back on his desperate splashing. "I am certain there will be something to grab on to. Besides, listen to his cursing. That is far too energetic for a man struggling for air. He is fine. And a good soak might improve his smell."

Angry, exhausted, and ready to be finished, I reached for the iron doorknob. I withdrew my hand with a cry of pain and surprise. A shock had stung my fingers through the holes in my lace glove. Shaking my hand to dislodge the lingering pins and needles, I stepped aside and let Mary try her luck with her far more practical leather gloves.

The doorknob turned.

The door opened.

"Oh, no," I whispered.

SEVEN

I SUNG OF CHAOS AND ETERNAL NIGHT

I THREW MY ARM out, blocking Justine and Mary from entering Victor's building. "It could be dangerous. Stay here."

The scent of old blood was strong here, too. There was something else, though. Something rotten. I gagged, putting my hand over my nose and mouth.

The entry—if it could be called such—was filled with scattered and torn pages of books. Mary's eyes lingered there. Mine were fixed on the door ahead of us. A ladder traversed the wall to a trapdoor that led to the upper story. A door to our side listed open to reveal a dirty washroom. The only illumination was the rain-dampened daylight lingering at the door with us, as unwilling to enter as we were.

"If it might be dangerous, we should stick together." Mary leaned down to look at the pages on the floor.

I crouched low and picked up the exterior of the book that had been so violently destroyed. I knew this book. It was the alchemical philosophy Victor had lost himself in during our holiday at the baths. And I knew Victor. I was not worried for Mary and Justine's safety.

I was worried for *his*.

"What is that?" I pointed outside. "Has the man climbed out of the river already? He needs help!" Justine and Mary rushed out the door.

I slammed and locked it.

"Stay here," I told Henry. He was not suited to whatever would need to be done. Because I knew that scream—it had been little Ernest. Whom we had left downstairs alone with Victor while the nursemaid was asleep and the adults traveled to town. We were trapped by rain and boredom in this holiday cottage. I had gone upstairs with Henry out of perverse curiosity. Out of a desire for something exciting to happen.

Selfish, stupid.

Henry's hands tightened in their embrace. "But—"

I shoved Henry away, ran out the door, and locked it from the outside. I practically threw myself down the stairs, burst into the sitting room, and took in the scene in one wide-eyed glance.

Ernest, howling in animal shock, holding his arm. It had been cut almost to the bone and was dripping blood onto the floor. A puddle had already formed.

Victor, sitting on his chair, staring white-faced and wide-eyed at his brother.

The knife, on the floor between them.

Victor looked up at me, his jaw clenched and his fists trembling.

I knew only two things for certain:

One, I had to help Ernest so he did not bleed to death.

And two, I had to find some way that this would not be blamed on Victor.

Because if it was blamed on Victor, maybe he would be sent away. Certainly I would be. What use would the Frankensteins have for me if I could not control Victor?

I would protect all three of us.

I grabbed my shawl and wrapped it around Ernest's arm as tightly as I could. The knife was a problem. I picked it up and forced the nearest window open, pushing the knife out into the rain and mud, where all traces of its crime would be quickly erased.

I needed a culprit. No one would believe Victor was innocent no matter what he said. They were all prejudiced against him. If only I had been down here, where I should have been! I could have been a witness. Henry, too.

Ernest had stopped howling, but his breath was quick and fast like an injured animal's. His nursemaid had not even woken from her laudanum-aided sleep.

His nursemaid.

I darted from the study and into the back of the house, behind the kitchen, where her quarters were. The room was dim and too warm, and she snored lightly from her bed.

I picked up her bag of sewing supplies and retreated.

Back in the study, neither of the Frankenstein boys had moved. I pulled out the nursemaid's sharp scissors. I dipped the blades into the pool of blood on the floor, then dropped them nearby. Victor watched in silence.

My shawl was growing heavy and dark with blood around Ernest's arm. "The wound needs to be closed," Victor said, finally breaking out of his stupor.

"Cleaned first. Get the kettle." I reached into the nursemaid's sewing bag and found a tiny needle and the thinnest thread I could.

Ernest looked up at me. I was so angry with him for being stupid enough to threaten everything. "I will fix this," I said, pushing his hair back from his sweat-soaked forehead. "No more crying."

He nodded, silent.

"You should not have cut yourself." I stroked his cheek and pulled him close. "That was naughty to play with the scissors and cut yourself."

He whimpered, nuzzling his head against my shoulder.

Victor returned with the kettle. I held out Ernest's arm, careful not to pour the water where it would wash the scissors clean. He cried out again, but he was exhausted from fear and shock and quickly quieted. The only sound was Henry's pounding on the locked door above us.

"Hold the skin together." I frowned in concentration, mirroring Victor's standard expression. It was just sewing, after all, and I had done plenty of that at Madame Frankenstein's side. Victor aided, watching closely. I sewed the wound shut as neatly as I could manage. My work was as good as any surgeon's. I never had much artistic flair for needlework, but apparently I was good with skin.

Closed, the cut only seeped blood, making me hope that Ernest would suffer no long-term ill effects. I rushed back upstairs to the hall linen closet, ignoring Henry's shouts, and pulled out a clean towel. I ripped it into strips—wishing I could use those stupid scissors—brought them downstairs, and bound Ernest's arm tightly.

Then I curled up in the armchair with him snuggled into my lap.

Victor stood in the center of the room, watching us. "I should learn to sew," he said. "When we get home, you can teach me."

"Get Henry out of his room and tell him that Ernest got into the nursemaid's sewing bag and cut himself. Tell him I was so busy helping that I forgot to let him out."

"Why did you lock him in, in the first place?" Victor asked, puzzled.

"Because I did not know what was happening." I gave him a look heavy with meaning. "And I needed to protect you."

Victor looked impassively at the floor, where the blood was congealing around the scissors. "I can tell you what happened. I—"

"We know what happened. It was the nursemaid's fault for leaving out her sewing supplies. She is stupid and lazy and still sleeping. She will be punished and relieved of her duties. Ernest will be fine." I paused to be sure Victor understood that this was our story, no matter what. "And we are fortunate that she is stupid and lazy and convenient, and nothing like this will happen again. Will it?"

Victor looked more thoughtful than sheepish. He nodded curtly, then turned to go get Henry. By the time the Frankensteins and Henry's parents returned, Ernest was sleeping warm and silent in my arms. Victor was reading the same volume that had obsessed him the entire trip, and Henry was fretting and pacing.

"Little Ernest got into the nursemaid's sewing supplies and cut his arm horribly!" Henry was filled with melodrama as he threw himself at his mother for a comforting embrace. "Elizabeth and Victor stopped the bleeding by sewing his wound shut!"

Madame Frankenstein rushed into the room, ripping the boy from my arms and waking him. He immediately began crying and fussing again—she was always disturbing him like that, with no sense of how to handle him—and she called for the coachman to take them to a doctor.

Judge Frankenstein quietly surveyed the room: The blackened puddle of blood. The scissors so artfully placed. The nursemaid still absent. And Victor reading.

There was a narrowing of the eyes, a cloud of suspicion in his terrible judge's face. I kept my head lifted, my face clear of any guilt. But he did not look at me. He looked only at Victor. "Is this true?"

Victor did not glance up from his book. "Elizabeth did a marvelous job with the stitches. If she were not a girl, she would have a bright future as a surgeon, I think."

His father ripped the book out of Victor's hands with an explosively violent gesture. "This is garbage," he said, sneering at the book and tossing it on the floor. "Surely you can do better things with your mind. And surely you can afford to give this current crisis more of your attention."

Victor looked up at his father looming over him, something going vacant behind his eyes. I rushed to his side. "Come, Victor," I said. "I have blood on my hands. Help me wash them while your father sorts out the situation with the nursemaid."

"Thank you for your quick thinking and action," Judge Frankenstein said. "You saved my son."

I could not tell which son he spoke of, and I suspected I was not intended to. Victor stood, picking his book up off the floor, and followed me upstairs. I made him read aloud to me to calm himself as I washed the afternoon from my skin.

That night, when I snuck into his room, unable to sleep, I found him still reading. "I like this book very much," he said. "The ideas are fascinating. Did you know you can turn lead into gold? And that there are elixirs that can extend and even restore life?"

I hmmed *as I crawled into bed next to him.*

"Elizabeth," he said. "You never asked me what actually happened this afternoon."

"It is fixed now. It does not matter and I do not care. Read me some more of your book," I said, closing my eyes and falling asleep.

Justine and Mary pounded on the door just as Henry had those years ago on holiday.

I would demand that Victor take me on holiday after this.

Bracing myself, I shuffled through the dark entry of Victor's residence and pushed the inner door open. The smell here was not so bad. Stale and sour, but not noxious. Windows along the back of the building were filmed over so that I could barely see. Above me, water dripped incessantly against the ceiling—probably on the upper-story floor from the two windows on the roof left open.

Once my eyes adjusted to the dimness, I made out a long room. A table with two chairs was pushed against a wall, stacked with papers and dirty dishes. A sink had been artlessly installed; a bucket beneath caught excess water. There was a stove next to me, but it was unlit, the room frigid with undertones of creeping river-damp.

In the opposite corner, a cot was piled high with a jumble of blankets, and—

A hand, trailing off the side.

I closed my eyes.

I counted ten steady breaths as I removed my gloves and tucked them into my purse. And then I walked across the floor, knelt by the bed, and took the wrist between my fingers.

"Thank you," I whispered fervently. I had been wrong: I did have it in me to pray after all. The wrist was warm—burning, in fact. I pulled back the mess of quilts to reveal Victor sprawled on his stomach, his dark curls wild, his forehead hot and dry. He was probably dehydrated. I had no way of knowing how long he had been in this fevered state. At his worst, one of his fevers had lasted more than a fortnight. And with no one here to care for him!

I cursed Henry with more fervor than I had prayed with. He had abandoned both of us—me to long-term peril, and Victor to immediate risk. He knew how Victor was! He knew that Victor was not to be left alone. How selfish of him to leave because his feelings were hurt. How privileged of him to be able to value his own feelings over the safety of others because he himself had never known what it was to be afraid.

"Victor," I said, but he did not even stir. I stroked his cheek. And then I pinched his arm. Hard. Harder.

No response.

Satisfied that Mary and Justine would find nothing too alarming, I ran back to the door and unlocked it. Justine was crying, and Mary was livid.

"What do you mean, locking us out?" she demanded.

I inclined my head meaningfully toward Justine. "I could not bear to expose you two to anything horrific. Neither of you has the responsibility to Victor that I do."

Justine looked up at me, her face as pale as death. "Is he—"

"He is dangerously sick with a fever. We will need a doctor. And we should move him to a more healthful location. I am certain this building contributed to his state."

"I can go and fetch a doctor. I know one." Mary regarded me with no small amount of distrust. "Should I take Justine with me?"

"She can stay and help if she wants."

Justine's eyes widened as she looked in at the dark hallway leading to the darker room.

Mary and I traded a look of understanding, and I spoke again. "Actually, yes. I think it would be best if Justine went with you. She can inform the doctor of Victor's history of fevers."

Justine nodded, the relief washing across her face. "Yes. Yes, I will do that. And I can hire a carriage, too. We cannot ask Mary to pay for anything."

"Very smart! What would I do without you?" I beamed at her to let her know she was handling this all quite well. I dug a few banknotes out of my purse, my last remaining address cards falling onto the wet steps beneath us. I did not bother to pick them up; the ink would run and stain the silk lining of my bag.

"We will hurry," Mary said.

I waved at them until they turned toward the bridge. Then I shut the door and locked it once more, not wanting unexpected visitors. I checked on Victor again; he had not moved. His breathing was shallow but steady and unlabored. I drew down the blankets farther. He was wearing breeches and a shirt, as though he had collapsed in the midst of working. He even had shoes on, scuffed and unshined.

I sat next to his head, looking down at him. He was thinner, paler. Judging by the length of his sleeves, he had grown, too. And not purchased new clothes for his changed frame. I wet a cloth that did not smell moldy, then put it over his forehead and sighed. "Look what happens when you are alone. Look how much you need me."

He stirred, eyes fluttering open but wild and unseeing. "Do not—" he croaked.

"Do not what?" I leaned close to his face.

"Henry. Oh, Henry. Do not tell Elizabeth."

He was delirious, then. He thought I was Henry, and he did not want Henry to tell me something. He had shifted on the bed, revealing a metal object beneath himself. I eased it free. It was a key, perhaps to the front door. I slipped it into my purse.

"Of course," I said. "It will be our secret. What should I not tell her, though?"

"It worked." He closed his eyes, shoulders shaking. I could not say for certain, but I thought he was weeping. I had never seen him cry. Not even when his mother died. Not even when he thought I was going to die. Victor did not cry; he raged. Or, worse, he did not react at all. What could make him cry? "It worked. And it was terrible."

He settled back into unconsciousness. The only noise was the insistent tap of water dripping on the ceiling, like the knocking of a stranger demanding to be let in.

I looked up. What had worked?

Leaving Victor, I went back to the entry and pondered the ladder. I put out a hand to touch the rough wood. My fingers trembled, then curled in on themselves, away from the rung. I had always considered myself brave. There were not many things that made me squeamish or that I was afraid to face. But my flesh recoiled at the thought of climbing up that ladder. It knew why before my mind fully processed it.

Then I realized:

The smell.

There was nothing down here to account for that lingering scent of old blood and rotting meat. Which meant it could only be coming from whatever was above this ladder.

And I had to discover it before anyone else did.

EIGHT

HORROR AND DOUBT DISTRACT HIS TROUBLED THOUGHTS

EACH RUNG LASTED AN eternity. I lingered longer than I should have. I knew I had to see what was beyond the trapdoor, but part of me desperately hoped it would be locked.

I reached it and pushed tentatively.

It was not locked.

I shoved it open and rushed up the last few rungs, pulling myself into a space that was dim but still brighter than the windowless entry.

The sound of rain hitting an ever-deepening puddle competed with the wild pounding of my heart to make music of discord and chaos. In place of a symphony to accompany me, there was a stench.

A stench of things rotten.

A stench of things dead.

And above and around it all, burning fumes that made me cough and gag.

I pulled out a handkerchief and covered my nose and mouth, wishing I could cover my stinging eyes, as well. But I needed them.

The dripping noises were different up here, though. Now that I was in the room, they had a faint metallic quality, hitting something other than the warped and blackened wood floors. In the center of the room, illuminated by the cloud-choked day, a pool of water rippled and shifted, gathering in the center of a table before dripping off the sides to meet with the water on the floor. The table was situated directly beneath the open roof panels.

I stepped closer. Broken glass crunched beneath my boots. The table had held my attention, but now that I looked down, I saw that the entire room was littered with shattered glass containers. Someone had gone to a tremendous amount of trouble to break everything in here.

Most of the larger glass pieces were sticky and wet with whatever had been held inside. It smelled to me like some death-tainted form of vinegar. Chemicals that preserve yet corrupt in equal measure.

Some of the glass remains bore . . . other substances. Gelatinous mounds on the floor. Poor, sad pieces of—

I pulled my gaze away. Something about the nearest spill made my eyes refuse to focus on it. It had no recognizable form, and yet I knew—*I knew*—I did not want to look at it.

My boots crunched and scraped as shards of glass embedded in their soles. I crept toward the table. Whether because it was the center of the room or because it was the best-illuminated feature, I was drawn toward it, pulled on a current.

The table itself was metal, as large as a family dining table. Around it were various apparatuses I did not know the meaning or use of. They looked complicated, all gears and wires and delicate tubing. And every one, like the glass containers, had been smashed beyond repair.

A pole, also metal, wrapped in some sort of copper wiring, extended from the head of the table to the windows in the roof. But it, too, had been warped. It was bent, the wires dislodged and hanging from it like hair ripped from a doll's head.

The water pooling on the table was thicker and darker along the edges, as if rust had been pushed outward. It smelled sharp and metallic, but with something organic beneath it all. Something like—

I pulled my finger back from where I was about to touch the near-black stains.

It smelled *almost* like blood. But whether the water dilution or the chemicals in the room had affected it, I did not know. Because I knew the scent of blood. And this was so close, and yet different in a way that repulsed me more than anything else here.

"What were you doing, Victor?" I whispered.

A clattering noise surprised me, and I whipped around. My bare hand brushed the side of the table, giving me another shock like the door handle had. I cried out, stepping away. My arm was numb. Though I could command it to move, I could not feel the movements.

Terrified, I searched for the source of the sound. Again! This time, of sharp things scratching at a surface. A flurry of movement, black darker than the shadowy corners of the room. I lifted my arms to defend myself from—

A bird. Some misshapen carrion thing, scratching and pecking at a massive trunk that took up nearly the length of the wall on the side closest to the riverfront. The bird must have gotten in through the roof opening.

Cross with it for scaring me—and with myself for being so easily frightened—I reached down for the nearest thing on the floor to throw.

My fingers closed around a long knife unlike any I had seen. It was shaped like a surgeon's scalpel, though no surgeon would need a scalpel this large. Other points of metal among the glass on the floor winked invitations for exploration. A saw, too small for wood. Clamps. The wickedly sharp and absurdly long metal tips of needles, glass vials attached to them broken and jagged.

The bird cawed darkly, a sound like laughter.

What was in the trunk?

* * *

It was the fall before the first winter I would spend cocooned inside with the Frankensteins. The leaves were so scarlet that even the light had a crimson tinge. Birds circled overhead: those that were leaving and those that were hardy enough to survive the long dark of the mountain winter.

Victor and I were walking the paths we had made in the undergrowth when we heard a desperate thrashing.

We crept toward the noise, both of us silent without agreeing to be so. Victor and I often functioned that way—I could respond to his needs without being told. Some sense, some careful attunement, always guided me.

I gasped when we found the source of the commotion. A deer, far bigger than either of us, lay on its side. Its visible eye rolled wildly, chest heaving as it panted. One of its legs was twisted at an unnatural angle. The deer struggled once to rise. I held my breath, hoping, but it crashed back to the forest floor and lay still save its desperate breaths and an odd keening sound. Was it some instinctive, unconscious noise? Or was the deer actually crying?

"What could have happened?" I asked.

Victor shook his head. His hand, which had grasped mine, slowly released. I could not take my eyes away from the deer until Victor spoke. The trembling determination in his tone pulled all my attention.

"We cannot let this chance pass," he said.

"What chance?" I saw only the wounded thing in front of us. "Do you want to help it?"

"There is no helping it. It will die."

I did not want it to be true, but he was right. Even I knew that if prey animals could not run, they could not survive. And this deer could not so much as stand. It would slowly starve to death lying on the cold forest floor, covered by the falling leaves.

"What should we do?" I whispered. I looked around for a large rock. As much as I hated to even consider it, I knew that the kindest thing we could

do was end its suffering. It never occurred to me to run to the house for help. The deer was ours, our responsibility.

"We should study it." Victor leaned closer, laying his hand on the deer's flank.

I did not want to do that again. Not ever. But I mournfully supposed that once the deer was dead, it would not much care what was done with its body. And as always, Victor's happiness was my first priority.

I nodded, misery siphoning away the afternoon's happiness like the winter cold slowly sucking the color from the trees. "I will find a rock we can use to kill it."

Victor shook his head. He reached into his pocket and pulled out a knife. Where he had gotten it, I had no idea. We were not allowed knives, and yet Victor nearly always had one. "It will be better to study while it is still alive. How else can we learn anything?"

His hands shook as he lowered the knife; he looked sad, but more than that, he looked angry. He almost vibrated with intensity, and all my instincts were to soothe him. To distract him from this. But I did not know how to calm him, whether I should calm him at all.

Then the knife went in. It was as though that thing I saw sometimes beneath Victor's surface, struggling to get out, had been released with the first cut. He sighed, and his hands steadied. He no longer looked afraid, or angry, or sad. He looked focused.

He did not stop. I did not stop him.

Red leaves. Red knife. Red hands.

But white dresses, always.

The deer stopped keening. It did not die as Victor tugged the knife through the skin over its stomach. I had imagined it parting like the crust of a loaf of bread, but it was tough, resistant. The sound of tearing made me sick. I turned away as Victor strained to make progress with blood coating his hands and making the knife slippery.

"It will be harder," he said, breathing heavily with exertion, "to get

through the ribs before the heart stops beating. Run to the house and get a bigger knife. Hurry!"

I ran. I did not beat the failure of the heart. Frustration and disappointment twisted Victor's face as I held out the long, serrated knife the cook would be blamed for losing.

He accepted the knife and got to work on the now-still rib cage. I turned away again, keeping my eyes on the scarlet leaves trembling above us. A single leaf fell, and I marked its lazy path down until it landed in the darker crimson pooled at my feet.

I saw nothing. I heard everything. Knife ripping skin. Blade against bone. All the delicate viscera that support life spilling like slop onto the forest floor.

Victor learned about the paths blood takes in a living creature, and I learned the best ways for cleaning that blood from hands and clothes so that his parents would never know the course of our new studies.

When I crept into Victor's room that night, I found him drawing the deer still alive, but flayed so that all the parts he had seen inside were showing. He shifted to let me into the bed. I could not get the deer's noise out of my head. Victor actually fell asleep before I did for once, his face at peace.

That winter was long and cold. Banks of snow as high as the first-story windows sealed us in, away from the world. And while his parents did whatever it was they did when they were not with us—we were utterly uncurious about them—we played games only a child like Victor could design. He had been inspired by the deer. And so we played.

I would lie silent and still, like a corpse, as he studied me. His careful, delicate hands explored all the bones and tendons, the muscles and tracings of veins that make up a person. "But where is Elizabeth?" he would ask, his ear against my heart. "Which part makes you?"

I had no answer, and neither did he.

* * *

The metal scalpel in my hand was a sort of comfort. Though nothing in this room threatened me, I could not fight the instinct telling me I was in danger. Telling me to flee.

"Shoo!" I stomped toward the bird. It fixed one baleful yellow eye on me, clacking its murderously sharp beak.

"Get out!" I ran the rest of the way, startling it. In a flurry of feathers, it flew past me and into a black hole in the wall I had not noticed. I followed it, finding the beginning of the chute that ran from the building to the river. It was large enough that I could have comfortably crawled through. Doubtless it had been added to dispose of refuse. But it was so large! What had been the purpose of this building before Victor?

Chest heaving, I looked down at the trunk that had so fascinated and occupied the wretched bird. The trunk was made of wood, painted with thick black tar to seal it. An inelegant but effective form of waterproofing.

I tried to lift the lid, but it was locked. Crouching, I found a heavy padlock securing it. With trembling fingers, I pulled out the key I had found beneath Victor.

It fit.

I wished desperately it had not.

With a well-oiled click, the padlock sprang open. I unhooked it, opened the latch, and then heaved the long lid upward.

The force of the smell was a physical blow. I fell back onto the ground, cutting my hand on a shard of glass. The scalpel skidded away along the filthy floor. I turned my head and vomited, my stomach seizing my whole body in spasms to propel me from this.

Coughing, I found my handkerchief and held it to my face instead of binding my hand. I stood, my legs shaking, and looked down.

There were . . . parts.

Bits and pieces, like sewing materials discarded but saved for the day when perhaps they might be useful. They could not have been too old, because the decay was minimal. Bones and muscles, a femur so long I could not guess what animal it had come from. A hoof. A set of delicate bones like a puzzle waiting to be pieced together. Some of the parts had been roughly sewn together.

A sheet of parchment, tacked to the lid of the box, shifted in the breeze from the open roof. It bore lists: Types of bones, types of muscles, missing parts. The name of a butcher shop. A charnel house. A graveyard.

This was a supply box.

"Oh, Victor," I sobbed. I yanked the list free and shoved it into my purse. Lowering my head, I saw in the far corner something square and inorganic wrapped in an oiled sheet. I reached in as carefully as I could, gagging again as my hand brushed something cold and soft. I pushed past it and grabbed the item I wanted. I pulled it out and slammed the lid of the trunk closed.

It was a book. For some reason, though, it frightened me more than anything else in the room. Moving away from the horrible supplies, I opened the well-worn leather covers of Victor's journal.

His handwriting, tiny and cramped, as though he feared not having enough space to get his thoughts down, was as familiar to me as my own. There were dates, notes, anatomical drawings. At first they were of animals and humans. And then they were of something . . . not quite either. I skimmed the words through my tears, his handwriting growing more frantic with each passing page.

The final page was a drawing of a man. More than a man. The proportions were wrong, the scale monstrous. And beneath it, written with so much force it was carved into the paper, the words *I WILL DEFEAT DEATH.*

I closed the journal and dropped it on the floor. Numb, I went back to the trapdoor and climbed down, closing it over my head. One hand still had not recovered from the shock of touching the metal table, and the other was cut. I slipped, falling down the last few rungs. I stood just as an insistent fist pounded on the door.

I opened it. "Sorry!" I said breathlessly. Justine, Mary, and an older gentleman stood waiting. "This quarter frightens me. I did not want anyone else to get in."

"Elizabeth!" Justine took in my bloodied hand and doubtless wild expression.

I forced a smile. "I slipped trying to tidy up. Come, we must get Victor away from here."

I led them into the room, hoping they would not be curious. Fortunately, Victor's state was so obviously dire that they did not bother exploring anywhere else. Though Mary peered around the room with narrowed eyes, she helped leverage Victor out of bed. "What is that smell?" she asked.

"We have to get him into the carriage. Hurry!" I rushed them through the entryway, praying they would not look up and want to check the room there. When they were all safely outside, I closed the door firmly.

"At least it is over now," Justine said with a relieved sigh. I still had work to do, but I smiled in companionable relief as though I, too, were leaving that horrible place behind forever.

Justine took my elbow, wrapping my hand in her clean handkerchief. My dress was covered in dirt and grime. Bright spots of my own blood stood out as if it had been spilled on filthy snow.

"You were right to come," Justine said. "He needed you."

He always had. And he did now more than ever. I had to help Victor get well, and I had to protect him. I could not let anyone discover the truth:

Victor had gone mad.

NINE

THIS HORROR WILL GROW MILD, THIS DARKNESS LIGHT

The doctor, a stately gentleman whose clothes told a story of a satisfied and wealthy clientele, had a room in his offices for cases like Victor, where the patient needed both seclusion and extra care.

I saw Victor safely settled, taking care to inform the doctor of his history of intense, prolonged fevers.

"He grows quite delirious," I said, smoothing Victor's curls away from his forehead and placing a damp cloth there. A matronly nurse hovered nearby, waiting for me to get out of her way. "He may say things that make no sense or sound horrible, but when he wakes he will have no memory of them because they are nothing more than fever dreams."

The doctor nodded impatiently. "Yes, I am quite familiar with fevers. There is no need to expose yourself to further strain, Fräulein Lavenza. He will be well taken care of. You may visit him in the mornings, but we reserve the rest of the day for quiet repose. It is good you found him when you did. Another day or two and he might have perished from burning away all his body's fluid."

"Yes," I murmured, kissing Victor's cheek and then moving away from his bed. "That is a bad thing to burn."

Some things, however, still needed burning.

In the sitting room, Mary and Justine waited. Justine was fidgeting nervously, looking at the ever-decreasing light out the window. She shot up like a spark from a flame when she saw me. "Elizabeth! How is Victor?"

"They have settled him in. I am certain he will be well. Thank you, Mary, for securing such a capable doctor so quickly. We were lucky to find you, for a number of reasons."

Mary nodded, pulling on her gloves and adjusting her hat. "I am glad I came with you. My uncle would be happy I helped Victor. I wonder now if he was the last person to see Victor well. Though, obviously, Victor must have been in good health at that point. Otherwise, my uncle would never have left him there."

"Unlike Henry," I said, my thoughts dark and already clogged with ash and char.

Justine edged closer to the door. "Henry left so many months ago, though. He would have stayed, as well. Do we have anything else to do here? It will be nightfall soon, and we will be locked out!"

Mary looked quizzical.

"Our landlady leaves much to be desired," I explained. "She locks the door at sunset and has informed us that if we are not inside by that time, we will not get inside at all." I realized then that I had a problem. I could not be locked in all night, but I needed some reason to impose more on Mary's hospitality.

"Actually . . ." I paused thoughtfully, as though it were only just occurring to me. "I would hate for some crisis in Victor's health to happen in the night and be unable to receive word of it or rush to his side. Mary, you have already done so much for us, but could I beg one further favor?"

"Of course. You need not even ask. You are welcome in my home this night and any others you might need. Though I have only one spare bed."

"I can sleep on the floor," Justine offered.

"Nonsense. We have a perfectly good room we have already paid for." I paused again, exaggerating my thought process for their benefit. "I need to pick up some new clothes for Victor so he has clean items for the morning. I will buy them—I have no desire to go back to his residence! Mary, could you see Justine back to the boardinghouse and safely stowed inside? And then I will meet you back at your house to be available should Victor need me. It should only be for this one night, after all. Tomorrow we will have a much better sense of how quickly he will recover."

Both women accepted my perfectly sensible plan, though Mary seemed alert to how often I had sent her and Justine away together. But it worked. And it was a plan that situated me closer to the river, in an unlocked room, with no dear friend highly attuned to me to startle awake upon my leaving.

I left Mary's address with the doctor and waved Mary and Justine away in the carriage, then turned resolutely to face my unwelcome tasks.

There was a graveyard connected to the city cathedral, but that was too public and did not match the name of the one on Victor's list. I once again slipped outside the walls protecting the good people of Ingolstadt—this time avoiding the gatehouse that had troubled me so the first time.

It was nearing sundown when I reached my destination. The trees were hunched over, weeping with accumulated rain. A one-room house on the edge of the meandering green expanse had a light in the window, and I knocked determinedly. At the last moment I drew my cloak closed to cover my dirty, bloodstained dress.

A man as hunched as the trees opened the door. "Can I help you?"

"I am here on behalf of my father, who is the caretaker of the cemeteries in Geneva. He has had a recent string of grave robberies and is at pains to gather information. As I am here to visit my sister and her family, he has asked me to inquire whether you have experienced anything similar."

The man frowned, looking out past me. "You alone?"

"Yes." I lifted my chin and smiled as though the fact were neither unusual nor troublesome. "My sister has recently given birth and cannot leave the house. I only just remembered my promise to my father and slipped out to fulfill it before she needs me again."

He sighed, rubbing at the white stubble on his jaw. "They been taking jewelry?"

"Yes."

"Well, nothing like my troubles, then."

I frowned. "What do you mean?"

He raised a bushy eyebrow at me. "I live next to a university. When people steal from my cemetery, they do not take jewelry off the bodies. They take the bodies themselves." He shook his head. "Dirty, damnable business it is, too. I have been offered money for the bodies, but I have never taken a bribe. Not a single one. I patrol most nights, but I am an old man. I have to sleep sometimes."

I nodded, my sympathetic horror unfeigned.

"Tell your father to consider himself lucky it is just the jewelry that goes missing. Much easier to hide than a gaping hole where someone's brother was laid to rest."

"I—I will. Thank you, sir."

He waved sadly and closed the door. I turned toward the cemetery. As evening quietly claimed the day, everything turned from green to gray to black, soft and silent. I imagined creeping in with a shovel, looking for the most freshly turned soil. Digging until my hands blistered.

Then pulling a body free, tugging its limp weight, tripping over roots and low headstones, the body falling to the ground that was supposed to have claimed it, kept it safe . . .

It was all so much *work*. I could imagine Victor doing it once, twice even. But surely he had found a better way.

The other address listed was a charnel house, a sort of repository for bodies of the poor. Deceased who had no relatives or benefactors with money to pay for proper preparations ended up there to be buried in paupers' graves.

Where the cemetery had been damp and serene, the charnel house was dank and repulsive. I knocked on the door and was greeted by a person with more of weasel about him than man. His tiny eyes were narrowed in suspicion, his few remaining teeth blackened and sharp.

"What do you want?" he growled.

I raised an eyebrow imperiously. "I am here on behalf of an interested buyer."

The man coughed so long and hard that I feared he would lose a lung. Finally, he spat a blob of mucus onto the floor at his feet, some of it landing on one of his boots. I suspected that was the only polish they ever got. "Let me guess: Henry Clerval?"

I gasped in shock. Henry had bought bodies for Victor? I could not imagine it. It made no sense.

And then I realized—Victor must have used Henry's name so that his would not be known by so low a creature as this man. It was clever, really. And it made my job easier: I would not have to try to bribe this man into silence about Victor's activities.

"Yes," I said. "Henry sent me."

"So mister high-and-mighty needs more supplies, does he? Why would he send you?"

"He has been ill. But he is finally able to resume his . . . studies."

The man sneered, his mouth puckering with greed as he tried to sound casual. "Lots of other buyers these days. Buyers who pay in advance. Always a demand with the university. He thinks he can just come back and claim the best goods again?"

"What do you mean?"

"The tallest! The strongest! The strangest! Has a taste for the unusual, your Henry. Treats me like a market where he can haggle over the price of apples! I have not missed him, no, not one bit. But I have missed the payments he owes me."

His eyes kept darting to my purse, and I resisted the urge to clamp my hand over it. I was holding my cloak to hide my dress, and any movement might reveal my true state.

"I see," I said coldly. "I will have to consult with him as to whether he wishes to continue to give you his patronage."

The man's face twitched as he attempted to smile. "I can give you a deal. I just received two bodies—foreigners, no family to claim them. No one to complain if the bodies never find the cemetery grounds. But you pay now *and* pay what he owes me."

I stepped back, failing to hide the revulsion on my face. How could Victor have stooped so low? How could he have associated with such a repulsive man and such soul-curdling activities?

"Where are you going?" He lunged forward and grabbed my wrist, his hand cold. I shuddered at his grasp, imagining what else those hands had touched that day.

"I am leaving, sir. Let me go."

He yanked me closer. My cloak flapped open, and he noted my appearance, growing rougher. "Not until I get what Henry owes me! You think I am dirty because of what I do? That he can stay away and be clean and fancy?" He turned toward the open door, pulling me along with him. "I will show you what filth your Henry trades in. I will show you what he thinks he can forget debts on."

I should have screamed. I knew that I should be screaming. But I could not manage it. I had been too well trained in silence. But I could not go into that building. I had seen horrors this trip; I did not wish to see any more. And I did not want to know what he would do with me behind closed doors.

My heart racing, my tongue frozen, I reached up to my hat with my free hand and pulled one of the long, sharp pins used to keep it in place. And then I stabbed that pin down into the man's wrist as hard as I could, taking care to aim for the space between the two bones of the forearm so it would go all the way through.

He screamed in surprise and pain, releasing me. I turned and ran.

His angry shouts followed me, but thankfully, footsteps did not. When I was safely back within the city walls, I leaned against a brick building and struggled to catch my breath. My heart continued pounding as though I were still being pursued.

I wished I could not imagine Victor doing business with him, but I could. Victor had left, possessed by the need to defeat death, and without me here to temper his obsessions, he had descended to hellish depths.

I had driven Victor to this madness. I would repair it in any way necessary.

Secluded as we were across the river, our only regular company Henry and occasionally his parents, we managed to avoid most illnesses that took toxic root and spread like mold in Geneva during the long winter months.

When I was nearly fifteen, however, illness found me and staked its claim with ferocity to make up for lost time. I fell into darkness and pain. Doctors must have been called, but I was sensible of none of it, lost to the violence of a body destroying itself. My world burned. It ached.

And then it felt like nothing at all.

The border between life and death had fascinated Victor for so long. I had crossed that border coming into this world—changing places with my mother, who died as I was born. I felt certain that once again I was on the edge of it. On one side: Victor. Justine. Henry. The life I had built with such vicious determination. On the other: the unknown. But the unknown beckoned, promising rest from pain. Rest from sickness. Rest from the endless striving and manipulating and working, working, working just to keep my place in the world.

But a cool hand on my brow broke through. Whispered pleadings, an endless stream of them, led me from those dark, unknown lands like a trail of crumbs glowing white in the moonlight to lead me home. After a time, days or weeks, I finally opened my eyes to find my determined savior.

Madame Frankenstein.

I had expected Victor or Justine, the two in the house who loved me. But I had underestimated how much Madame Frankenstein depended on me. How terrified she was of what would happen if I were to leave them.

Her eyes shone with mania, and she pressed my hand to her hot, dry lips. "There you are, Elizabeth. You can never leave. I told you that. You have to stay here, with Victor."

I had not the strength to nod. My throat, parched and cracked, could not force out the words. But I held her gaze with my own, and we were in agreement.

Then Madame Frankenstein crawled onto the bed next to me and fell asleep.

Within a day I had regained enough strength to sit up and take some nourishment. But my gain was Madame Frankenstein's loss. She had disobeyed the doctor's orders, exposing herself to my illness in order to nurse me. The fever had abandoned me and claimed another prize.

When the doctor came to move her to her own room—which, it was clear, she would never leave again in this life—her fingers curled around my wrist like a manacle. "This is your family," she said, her voice rasping as though she had swallowed a live coal. The same coal burned with imagined red light in the intensity of her gaze. I realized she was not, finally, declaring me a true part of the family. She was assigning them to me as a burden lifted from her shoulders and deposited onto my own. "Victor . . . is . . . your . . . responsibility."

The doctor and Judge Frankenstein carried her from my bed. Her head lolled to the side so her eyes could watch me the entire time as they bore her away. I pushed out of the bed and away from the ghost of Madame Frankenstein already taking residence there, though she yet lived.

Sliding against the hallway walls for support, I stumbled to Victor's room. I found him, there, barricaded in amidst a fortress of books. His candle was burned low; his clothes, usually so meticulous, were dirty and in a state of disarray. His bed, unslept in, now functioned as a desk and bookshelf in one.

"Victor," I whispered, my voice not yet healed from long disuse.

He looked up, eyes unnaturally bright in contrast to the dark and hollow space around them. "I had to save you," he said, blinking as though seeing me and not seeing me at once.

"I am better."

"But you will not always be. Someday death will claim you. And I will not allow it." His eyes narrowed, and his voice trembled with fury and determination. "You are mine, *Elizabeth Lavenza, and nothing will take you from me. Not even death."*

"You forgot Victor's new clothes," Mary said, her lips pursed and her clever eyes examining my disheveled and breathless state. It was well past dark now.

I laughed, putting a hand to my head where my hat was askew due to the missing pin. "I could not find a shop in time. They were all closed, and then I got lost in an unfamiliar part of town. I have been wandering ever since! I am simply exhausted."

Nodding, but showing little sympathy, Mary showed me to my room.

I waited several sleepless hours, until I judged it was time for the second half of this night's unsavory activities. I longed for sleep. Longed to close my eyes and forget all I had seen and done. But I could not. Victor still needed me.

The clock in Mary's sitting room showed just past one in the morning when I slipped out, carrying the supply of oil I had stolen from her closet.

The city had an entirely different character at night. Streetlamps were few and far between, and the buildings seemed great hulking beasts at night, watching with black eyes that reflected myself back at me. It would be so easy to disappear here. To wander into the dark and never be seen again.

I hurried, my cloak drawn around me with the hood up. I felt pursued at every step, constantly checking over my shoulder. But I was alone. I paused at the gatehouse, shrinking further into my cloak and eyeing the doors warily. No sounds greeted me. The entire world was silent, as though holding its breath to see what I would do.

The journey over the river, which during the rainy day had been unremarkable, felt like crossing a bridge to another world. A few of the boats had torches burning, so that it looked like portions of the jet-black river were on fire. Like the river Styx, a passageway directly to hell.

Shivering, I moved faster. I needed this night to be over, this last task accomplished. Once it was, I would be safe. At last I came to Victor's residence. I would not call it a home. It was nothing of the sort. I lifted my hand to turn the knob—

The door was slightly ajar. I was certain I had closed it all the way when we left. Had I? I had been so eager to get Mary out and away from further exploration. . . . And Justine had been talking to me. . . . Maybe

I had not waited for it to latch. I nudged it open with my foot, not daring to light my lamp. But there was no other light inside. The trapdoor above my head was firmly shut. I peered into Victor's living quarters. The stove was still cold. I used one of my matches to light it, closing the flue and leaving the oven door open. Then I turned and—

A man loomed out of the darkness.

A shriek of terror left my mouth. Lashing out, I swung my container of oil into him. He toppled with a wooden clatter. The hat that had been atop the hatstand rolled away from me.

"Damn you, Victor," I whispered. I had not noticed the hatstand during my earlier trip, being quite preoccupied. I picked up the hat and was hit with a shock of recognition even in the dark. I knew this hat.

It was Henry's. I had purchased it for him, just before he left for Ingolstadt. I ran my fingers around the brim, feeling the velvet softness in contrast to the stiff shape of it. So Henry *had* found Victor when Victor was already living here. He had to have seen the madness taking hold. And still he had left.

Angry tears burned. He had left Victor, and he had left me. I did not know which betrayal hurt worse. Part of me, too, hated him for being able to decide to just leave. Some of us did not have that option, and never would.

I dropped the hat and poured some of the oil on it. I made a trail around the borders of the room until every last drop was emptied. Then I pushed Victor's table into its path, as well as his wooden bed. I found more oil next to his stove and added that, soaking the bedsheets while I waited for the stove to heat up.

Finally, I went into the hall and draped the bedsheets on the ladder.

Back in the living quarters, I lit a match and dropped it onto Henry's unfaithful hat. It burst into flames, which moved with liquid grace along the lines of oil on the floor. The heat was sudden and intense. I had done my job well. I backed out of the room, letting my eyes linger on Victor's time here being erased.

No one would ever know what he had studied, how far down the path of his madness he had been allowed to stumble alone.

I lit the bedsheets and watched the fire climb the ladder to the trapdoor. Then I shut the front door behind me. No one would see the fire until it had overtaken the second floor. By then it would be too late to salvage anything. I backed up to the edge of the stone wall lining the steep riverbank and waited. I wanted to see the fire claim the horrors of his laboratory. I had to be sure.

It did not take long. Soon there was a glow, and then a brilliant, explosive burst that blew out the windows. I ducked as glass rained down around me. Whatever chemicals had soaked into the floor up there, they did not mix well with fire.

I laughed, lifting my face to the dry heat radiating from the building. No. They mixed perfectly with fire. But there was no smoke rising from the windows in the roof. They had been left open. How—

A scrambling, bumping tumult rumbled down the chute above my head. The one that led from the building to the river. Before I could turn to see what it was, something enormous splashed into the water.

I covered my mouth in horror. Had someone been inside?

I leaned over the edge, peering at the placid black surface of the water. I saw only the reflected flames behind me. Nothing disturbed the surface.

Perhaps something had been lodged inside the chute and been forced out by the change in air pressure. But the front door had been opened when I'd arrived. Who would have been there? Obviously no one was in the habit of visiting Victor. Maybe the drunkard from earlier in the day? But I had heard his splash. It was far smaller than this one.

Perhaps a jealous rival. Professor Krempe had seemed a little too keen to know what Victor had been up to since they lost contact. Had Victor secluded himself because he was being watched? But who would care about the lunatic theories of a man playing with stolen corpses and desecrated animals?

A more dangerous possibility seized me. The charnel house man, reminded of Victor's debt by my visit, might have come to collect. I trembled, expecting him to arise with a roar and pull me into the water. But I could not turn away, could not expose my back to whatever awaited me.

I watched the water until my lungs burned from the smoke and I knew it was not safe or wise to stay at the scene of the crime. Nothing surfaced from the black depths of the river. It kept its secrets.

I would keep mine. And Victor's, too.

TEN

TO LOSE THEE WERE TO LOSE MYSELF

I HAD PLANNED TO slip out of Mary's house at dawn so I could check in on Justine and then spend the morning with Victor. But my nighttime activities caught up to my body, and I slept past the sun's rising.

Hoping Mary was a late sleeper or had already gone to open her bookshop, I pinned my hat, its stability precarious. I missed my lost pin but knew Justine would have extras. Then I rushed out of my room to grab my cloak.

Mary was sitting, holding it.

"Good morning," she said brightly.

"Good morning." I tried to imitate her tone to hide my annoyance that I would have to talk to her. I had things to do.

"I am not certain you will be able to wash the stench of smoke from this cloak." Her tone was conversational as she held it up. "Your dress from yesterday was already quite ruined by blood and filth, but this is a nice cloak. For arson, you should have worn an old one, or borrowed one of my uncle's."

I blinked, smiling blankly. "Forgive me, but I do not understand what you mean."

"There was a terrible fire on the other side of the bridge early this morning. The fire brigade was able to put it out, but not before it destroyed a whole building. Imagine! An entire building, and everything inside, burned beyond salvaging. It is assumed the stove chimney had not been properly cleaned."

"That is a shame." I sat opposite her, reaching for the cup of tea she had prepared for me. "I hope no one was hurt."

"No, the building was as empty as we left it yesterday. And I am quite certain the stove was cold and unlit then." She dropped my cloak and any pretense at delicacy as she leaned forward intently. "What did you find? Why did you burn it?"

"I do not know what you are talking about."

"Oh, please do not pretend. You may look like an angel, but I am not a fool. You locked us out. You were afraid of discovering something you wanted no one else to see. And then you had time there, alone, to explore. What was so awful that you had to go back and burn down the building?"

I smiled, knowing full well my smile was sweeter than summer strawberries, my blue eyes as clear and dazzling as the sky. "Maybe I just like fires."

To my surprise, Mary burst out with a wild laugh. It was the least feminine laugh I had ever heard. Nothing about it was prim or guarded. I wondered how she could even manage to breathe deeply enough in a corset to produce the sound. "Oh, I like you, Elizabeth Lavenza. I like you very much. I am a little bit afraid of you, but I think that makes me like you more. Well. I am going to throw your cloak out with the trash—in someone else's neighborhood, of course—and then we are going to fetch Justine and check on your Victor."

"You really do not need to come. You have already done so much."

"Not nearly as much as you." She grinned wickedly. "I have been stuck in the business of books for so long, I forgot how much fun being a part of a story can be." She stood, popping a biscuit into her mouth and swallowing it almost whole. "I do not expect you to tell me the truth. I am happy to puzzle over this mystery on my own. As long as you promise not to burn down my house." She looked at me, her expression shifting from playful to serious with a single movement of her finely shaped black eyebrows. "Please do not burn down my house."

I matched her sincerity, grateful that she would be complicit in silence. "I promise I have no intention of burning anything ever again. And I appreciate your discretion. I can assure you my intent was only to protect Victor. He was— His work there was the product of an unwell mind. If others were to discover it, it could ruin his chances for future success. I will not let that happen."

She nodded, pulling another cloak off a hook on the wall and handing it to me. It was worn, older than mine, but soft, and it smelled of ink and dust and leather, my favorite aromas. I felt instantly comforted wrapping myself in it.

"Will you answer something for me?" she asked as we sat in the back of a carriage on the way to the boardinghouse.

"Probably not with honesty," I said, surprising myself by telling the truth.

"I am going to ask anyway. What is Victor to you that you searched so hard for him and went to such lengths to protect him? Surely he must be more than a cousin. Are you in love with him?"

I looked out the window as we passed the city center, now sunny and bright, as though its nighttime version were a dream best forgotten. Oddly, Mary's having discovered my secrets freed up my willingness to talk. Normally I kept the truth behind closed doors and heavy locks, letting only careful shadows of it out into the world.

"He is my entire life," I said. "And my only hope of a future."

* * *

Victor left before the dirt had settled over his mother's grave.

"I will be back when I have solved it," he promised, pressing his lips to my forehead like a seal in wax.

And then I was the mistress of a house that had never been mine and still was not. I ran the household, overseeing basic management. Judge Frankenstein never gave me funds, always in charge of the budget himself. Madame Frankenstein's personal maid was immediately dismissed. I was to assume Madame Frankenstein's role but inherit none of her privileges. I was allowed only the cook, one maid, and Justine.

My relief at my unexpected foresight in getting Justine hired was immense. I had relatively little to do with Ernest, now attending school in town, and young William. Sweet though they were, children remained to me a foreign language that I could speak and understand but never felt comfortable with.

Justine flourished. She would have done the work of five household servants, but I did not let Judge Frankenstein realize that. She was not of low birth, after all.

In fact, I secretly suspected she was of higher birth than I.

Though I had kept my fears to myself all these years, with Victor gone and Madame Frankenstein dead, they bubbled to the surface whenever I ate a meal alone with Judge Frankenstein. With every delicate bite I took, every impeccably mannered sip of a drink, I wondered whether it would show. Whether he would know. Whether he already suspected.

They had bought me based on a lie.

It had to be the case. Looking back, it was laughable, really. Madame Frankenstein had told me the story they were given. It made no sense. How would a violent mite of a woman living in poverty in the woods come into possession of an imprisoned Italian nobleman's daughter? Her story, woven of political woes and Austrian-seized fortunes, was as juvenile as something I would tell to get William to quiet and go to sleep. "The beautiful wife died bringing an even more beautiful daughter into the world! And though she was an angel, her father, bereft and angry, could not give up his righteous fight against those who had wronged him! Taken far away to a dark dungeon, the father left his daughter to be raised in meanness and the lowliest estate, until the day a kind and generous family found her and instantly knew she had been born to more than that."

I would burn a book that defiled my mind with such trite nonsense. Instead, the more likely story: The woman had inherited me from a sister or a cousin. She resented another mouth to feed. When the Frankensteins took up residence at Lake Como and she saw their young son, she seized her opportunity. Took the pretty child and sold her, complete with newly brushed hair and a shining story to wrap her up in.

So it was that my mind was already gnawing anxious circles around my origin when Judge Frankenstein, gaunter and obviously in poorer health since the death of his wife, actually addressed me at dinner six months after Victor had left.

"Tell me, what do you remember of your father?"

My spoon paused halfway to my lips. I set it down so he would not see it tremble. He had indulged his wife for years, but she was gone now. Victor was fixed. The judge had no reason to keep me. What was I, after all, but a worthless stray whose usefulness was past?

I smiled. "I was so young when they took him away. I remember crying as the doors to our villa closed behind me and they loaded him, shackled, into a black carriage." I remembered nothing of the sort.

"Do you know what your mother's name was? Anything about her family?"

"Oh." I batted my eyes as though the dim light were difficult to see in. "Let me think. . . . I know I was named after her." I did know that much, at least. "Pretty little Elizabeth, as pretty and useless as the Elizabeth you came from. I spit on her grave for burdening me with you," *my caretaker still hissed in my memory. "But I do not know what her family name was. I wish I did. Then I would have something of hers to hold on to."*

"Hmm." His brows, wiry and gray with age, drew low over his dark eyes. Where Victor's eyes were lively and intense, the judge's were the heavy, forbidding brown of an aged gallows.

"Why do you ask?" I said as innocently as I could, keeping all trace of fear out of my voice.

"No particular reason." His voice slammed the conversation shut.

I would have avoided him after that, but it was not necessary. Most days he spent shut up in the library. When I would sneak in at night to find a book, I would find his desk littered with papers and half-finished letters. He looked increasingly troubled, and his trouble affected me most deeply when I found a list on his desk titled "Drains on the Frankenstein Estate."

There were no items listed, but it was not difficult to imagine my name at the top.

Without Victor, I had no reason to be here. And while the Frankensteins had been generous to take me in, they had also rendered me useless. If they had taken me on as a maid or even a governess, I would at least have employable skills, like Justine. Instead, I was treated as a cousin: pampered, and educated in disciplines that in no way translated into the ability to care for myself.

They had saved me from poverty and, in the same stroke, doomed me to utter dependence. If Judge Frankenstein kicked me out, I would have absolutely no claim or legal recourse to take anything with me. At any moment he could force me to leave, and I would once again be simply Elizabeth Lavenza, with no family, no home, and no money.

I would not let him do that.

I wrote Victor once a week without fail, desperate to remind him of how much he adored me. He had never mentioned when he might return. And then his letters stopped. Judge Frankenstein inquired about his son on occasion—making it clear that Victor had never bothered to write to his own father—and I resorted to making up responses, filling the ever-expanding months with stories about Victor's studies, the exasperating and admirable qualities of his fellow students, and always, always, how much he missed me.

Justine could sense my growing unease and increased her kindness toward me. It was no use. As much as I loved having her there, she could do nothing to protect me.

I needed Victor back.

Or at least, I thought I did, until Henry Clerval surprised me with a different possibility.

"Come into town with me," Henry said, nearly a year after Victor's departure. He was working for his father now, and we rarely had time together. "When was the last time you were there?"

I went, sometimes, with Judge Frankenstein. But it was always in his boat and then his carriage, all our destinations predetermined and run by his pocket watch and adherence to his schedule. The idea of going to town and simply wandering struck me as delightful.

"We will find a gift for Victor," I said, just like the last time we had gone alone. What gift could remind Victor to set a damned pen to a damned piece of paper and write me a damned letter?

Justine stayed behind with William, who demanded a game of hide-and-seek. Justine was always happy to do whatever he wished. We were silent across the lake. Henry manned the boat himself, since the servant who used to do it had been dismissed after Madame Frankenstein's death. In all our years as friends, we had been so rarely alone that even being together in a boat on the open lake felt surprisingly intimate.

I kept my eyes on the water, a delicate parasol protecting my face. Though it never got unbearably hot this close to the mountains, the sun could redden any complexion within a few minutes.

Henry did not mind. He tipped his head up, closing his eyes against the brightness as he pulled us across the lake with measured, confident strokes.

"You should marry me," he said, his voice as light and breezy as the afternoon.

The rippling brilliance of the sun reflecting off our wake dazzled my eyes, nearly blinding me. Had it affected my ears, as well? "What?"

"I said, you should marry me."

I laughed. He did not. He fixed his piercing blue gaze on me and gave me his purest, most sincere smile. I knew he had meant it.

And I was livid.

How could someone so effortlessly happy ever understand me? Would I have to pretend to be a new Elizabeth to keep him happy as a wife in some imaginary future? What Elizabeth would I be at his side? I had worked so hard to be Victor's Elizabeth, and I had failed.

The parasol felt heavy in my hands, my shoulders drawn downward with sudden exhaustion. I suspected I was more myself with Victor than I could be with Henry, though who I truly was remained a mystery even to me.

"Henry. I am only sixteen. I am not marrying anyone yet."

"But not never." He raised his eyebrows hopefully.

I could feel a blush that was not entirely deliberate. I ducked my head, smiling. And letting him see a glimpse of the smile. "No, I did not say never."

"That is good enough for now." Henry docked the boat, an extra spring in his step as he disembarked. "Tell me about where you came from before you joined the Frankensteins," he said as we took a leisurely stroll through the clean and well-kept streets of Geneva.

My annoyance flared back up. What would I have to tell him, to keep him loving me? I had only wanted his friendship, the relief from managing Victor all on my own. Would I now have to figure out how to be his friend and be what he wanted in a spouse? I did not want to marry Henry. It would be cruel of me; I would be miserable forever, knowing he deserved better love than I could offer.

But . . . I did not want to be without options. Victor had abandoned me. And the risk of becoming useless to Judge Frankenstein loomed ever larger as a threat. I sighed. I did not think Henry would mind if I was not actually of noble birth, but I knew he loved the romance of the story. "Imagine the shore of a lake. The water crystal clear. The bottom perfectly visible. But as soon as you reach in, or stomp through, the sediment is churned up, the water muddied, all the treasures inside the once-placid water hidden from view. Perhaps something could be found by digging, but why bother, when everything is fine as it is? That is all you need to know of my origins."

He reached for my arm, stopping me. Then he turned me so we were facing each other. "I am sorry," he said. "For all you have been through. I cannot imagine."

I laughed prettily, rising on my toes to kiss his cheek. It was the fastest way to end the conversation, as his cheeks burst into shades of pink and his ability to speak left him for several minutes.

After that, I made certain to fill our time with idle chatter, drawing him out about his idea for a new play. Though he had outgrown asking us to act them out, he still wrote them. He wrote poetry, too, and yearned to study more languages. He had so little time for it now, though, working with his father.

"I have heard that Arabic has the most beautiful poetry known to man," he said as we browsed a haberdashery. He idly stroked the ribbons streaming from a lady's hat. This was the one topic that could make him sad. Though my situation was obviously worse, Henry was also a prisoner to other people's expectations. His life had been mapped out for him from the day he was born: he would follow his father into business, expanding their family holdings.

I hated to see him sad. It felt like a too-tight collar, tugging at me. If I could fix Victor's rages, I could fix Henry's sadness.

And maybe I could fix my own situation, as well. "Henry. You must go to study with Victor."

"I could never. My father sees no purpose in it."

I pulled a hat off a shelf. It was stiff and well made, but the material covering it was velvety soft to the touch. I placed it on his head, stepping back to admire it. "You look like a poet." I smiled. He reached up and tentatively stroked the hat. I forged ahead, with my quickly hardening idea. "You will convince your father that the Eastern languages are useful. Think of how much is left unbought, unsold, because we cannot adequately communicate with the merchants there! Why, a man with the connections of your father and the skills to speak clearly with the merchants of Arabia and China could build an empire!"

Henry took the hat, turning it in his hands. "I have never thought of it that way. I could learn the languages because I love them—"

"And the poetry!" I added.

He beamed. "And the poetry!"

"To better understand their cultures and relate to them . . ." I smiled slyly. "It would be important and would aid you in gaining foreigners' trust."

He laughed. "You know, Elizabeth, I think you could convince Winter to leave early and give all his territory to Spring if only you could talk to him."

"That might be too big a task for even me. But we will convince your father yet of the practical uses of Arabic poetry. Then you will join Victor at university. And you will write me how he is. I worry about him." I paused. Henry offered two new futures. Good, sweet, dear Henry. "And if you meant it, about marrying me, you will need to talk to Victor. I know his mother always treasured the thought of Victor and me marrying, but he and I have never spoken of it. I do not know how he feels on the subject, and I could never enter into a betrothal without his blessing. We cannot hurt him."

"I would sooner die than hurt him!" Henry said. But his face was alight with earnest excitement. "I think your idea will work, Elizabeth. I will go to university. And then . . . then we will both have a future to think about." He smiled bashfully.

"Yes. A future." I smiled, feigning demureness. My mind whirled as I bought him the hat with the meager pocket money I had managed to save. Victor would return, afraid of losing me, or give Henry his blessing. Either way, I would be saved from the constant threat of destitution.

I hoped, for Henry's sake, that Victor would return. I suspected marrying me would be the great tragedy of Henry's life. He deserved someone who could accept a proposal with a joyful heart, not a calculating and conniving mind.

Besides, I already knew how to be Victor's. I did not want to learn how to be anyone else's.

Justine was waiting outside for Mary and me when we arrived. How long she had been on the walk in front of the boardinghouse she did not say, though I suspected it was from the moment Frau Gottschalk unlocked the door.

The doctor would allow only one of us in to see Victor, so Mary took Justine to the bookshop while I sat at Victor's side. He was already much improved, the color in his cheeks less alarming and his body able to sweat once again. The nurse showed me how to painstakingly get liquid into his mouth—enough that he would be hydrated, but not so much that he would choke in his insensible state.

After a couple of hours, I thought he was waking. He began muttering, his eyebrows drawing together in that expression that was as familiar to me as my own face.

"Too big," he muttered. "Too big. Too willful. I made thee out of clay."

I bathed his forehead and used this opportunity to get some water down his throat. He coughed, sputtering.

"No! Eve from a rib. The rib is smaller."

I stroked his cheek and his hand shot up and wrapped around my wrist. His eyes opened, red and furious. He pulled me close, his urgency palpable. "Eve," he said. "The rib."

"I understand," I murmured. "That is an excellent point."

Letting out a relieved sigh, he relaxed back into slumber. I realized the nurse had entered the room, and was grateful that Victor had not said anything suspicious.

"Good boy. Knows his Bible."

"Yes." I stood, straightening my skirts. In fact, that was one of the few books Victor had never found any use for.

With the doctor confident that Victor would be lucid within a day and that there was no danger of him worsening in the meantime, I spent the night in the boardinghouse with Justine. I had no secret errands to run, and I did not want any time alone with Mary, lest she think of more questions I would not answer.

Frau Gottschalk was predictably unpleasant. My dreams were worse. I once again awoke in the middle of the night, breathless with the feeling that I had been in the middle of a bleak conversation, pleading for my life. I went to the window with hopes I could work it open for a stirring of fresh air. The loose slat was easily removed, but I could not get through to the glass behind it. I pressed my face to it and looked longingly at the night.

And discovered the night was looking back.

On the street immediately beneath me, wrapped in the black shadows, a figure stood staring up at me.

No, not *at* me. No one could have known I was behind these shutters.

But the figure did not move. I watched, terrified that moving would reveal my presence. I had been able to put the chute and whatever or whoever splashed from it out of my mind, but now it rose like a specter. What if someone *had* been at Victor's laboratory? What if I had nearly killed someone, and the person had followed me here to exact revenge?

But I had not come back here after the fire. I had gone to Mary's house. So who would have known I was staying here?

Anyone I left the cards with. I squinted, as though narrowing my eyes would increase their ability to pierce the darkness. But I could not make out any features. I could not tell whether it might be Professor Krempe. The figure seemed far too tall for it to be the charnel house man. But it could have been Judge Frankenstein himself and I would have been none the wiser.

There was some strange trick of the darkness, though, a shifting and magnifying of perspective or perception that made the figure loom larger than life. It looked . . . wrong. The torso too long, the legs bending at not quite the right place. A bulk of chest that spoke not of excess weight, but rather of unnatural power.

Justine stirred, cooing in her sleep. I glanced over to see if she had awakened. When I looked back, the figure was gone.

Its unnaturalness did not leave my mind. It settled over me like a spider's web, invisible and impossible to brush off.

ELEVEN

WHEN FROM SLEEP I FIRST AWAKED

To MY SURPRISE—AND VAIN dismay—when I walked into Victor's convalescence room the next morning, he looked better than I did. Whatever damage my sleepless nights had done to my face, his time here had erased all traces of his feverish delirium.

He was propped up by a pillow and was surprised to see me when I walked in.

"Elizabeth! What are you doing here?"

I bit back my impulse to berate him, to inform him I was there to save his foolish life. Instead, I pressed my hands to my mouth and rushed to his side. "Oh, Victor! When I found you, you were in such a low state. I feared I was too late."

His eyes twitched. "You were the one to find me? I do not remember anything of the last few days. Weeks, perhaps." He rubbed his forehead, eyes searching the air in front of him for some hint of what he had missed. "Did you . . . What state were my rooms in?"

I smiled gently, taking his hand from his forehead and resting my cheek against his much cooler fingers. "You certainly could have used a maid. I did not have much time to look around. We rushed you right here. I am so sorry to report that the same night we found you, the stove caught fire and burned down the building. All your things were lost. And to think—if I had not found you, you would have been inside the inferno!" I let tears pool in my eyes.

He dropped his head back against the pillow, but I knew every expression of his face. He was the text I had devoted my life to studying. It was relief, not despair, that caused him to lose his strength.

"My time here has been for naught anyhow. I sought to puncture heaven and instead discovered hell." He closed his eyes. His eyelids were nearly translucent, traced with tiny blue and purple veins. I was reminded of the time when he mapped my own veins with his fingers, plotting the course of my heart with meticulous study.

"Victor," I said, needing to speak to him before he fell back into sleep. If he wanted to remain silent on what his mad studies had cost him, I was more than happy to let him keep those secrets. We would never talk of them again. I had erased the evidence from the world, and perhaps Victor's fever had erased them from his mind, too. But there was one mystery I could not set fire to and turn my back on. "Why did you never write? I was so worried about you that I sent Henry here just to find you. And then he left, too."

"Henry?" he echoed. But his eyelids twitched, tightening from their relaxed state.

"Surely you remember. He came six months ago. And he wrote that he had found you. But then I never heard from him—or you—again. That is why we came. I was so worried about you without anyone to look after you."

"I was working every day for us. For you. I never wrote because I had nothing to report. Surely you did not doubt that what I was doing was important."

I wanted to pinch him, to pull on his hair until he cried out in pain. I also wanted to press my mouth against his and devour him. Consume him. Instead, I smoothed his hair back from his forehead, playing with the silky curls. "I know. And I knew you would have been lost in your studies and forgotten how desperately I would want to hear from you. But Henry left you all alone. And that is not like him. Your condition when I arrived proved I was right to be worried. Henry should not have gone."

Victor opened his eyes and studied me shrewdly. "We did not part on good terms. You know why."

I feigned innocence. "I assure you, I do not."

"Do you know why Henry came here?"

"To learn Eastern languages so he and his father could open up trade with merchants from the Far East. I thought it was an excellent idea. He was unhappy, working as his father did, and this allowed him the freedom to pursue something he loved while remaining loyal to his father."

Victor's dark lashes swooped low as he narrowed his eyes. "It turns out that loyalty is not something Henry values highly."

"What do you mean?"

"Henry tracked me down when he arrived. I am not certain how he found me. Or how you did." He paused, curious.

"Mary Delgado."

"Who?" Victor's genuine confusion was a balm to my competitive spirit. She might have remembered him, but he had no use for her. All my initial regard for her settled back into place now that I had nothing to fear from her as far as Victor's affections.

"The bookseller's niece. She had a receipt from her uncle at the bookshop."

"Oh. Carlos." Victor tilted his head, a memory I was not privy to passing like a cloud over his face. "I wonder if that is how Henry did it, too. Clever of you. I would imagine he found some simpler route. He arrived at my door all smiles and energy. I was relieved to see him. I needed a break from the intensity of my studies. But I quickly discovered he was much altered from when I left him. Prone to long silences, and distracted. After a week I could bear it no longer and demanded that he tell me what the problem was. He confessed he had come here to ask for my blessing in pursuing a betrothal. With you."

"With me?" I frowned in feigned surprise. "But why would he ask that? I had always planned on him and Justine marrying. I had set my heart on it."

"Henry set his heart much higher. You can doubtless imagine my response." His eyes burned into mine. I could see his anger at just the memory of it. I could, in fact, imagine his response.

I took his hand in mine, lowering my eyes shyly. "Actually, Victor . . . I cannot imagine your response. It has been almost two years. Eighteen months without a letter. I feared—I feared perhaps by leaving me you realized I had no place in your life anymore. And we have never discussed our future. Not in any plain terms. I do not wish to engage you where you wish to be free, but my heart is as it ever was—"

"Elizabeth," he said, his tone firm and chiding. He lifted my chin and fixed my eyes with his. "You are mine. You have been since the first day we met. You will be mine forever. My absence should not have caused you to doubt the firmness and steadfastness of my attachment to you. It will never fade."

I nodded, this time the tears in my eyes bearing liquid truth as relief washed over me. I was still safe, then. I would have a place at Victor's side, no matter his father's wishes. No matter how much of a waste of resources I was.

He dropped his fingers from my chin, rubbed his eyes, and pinched the bridge of his nose. "I was neither kind nor gentle with Henry. His application for possession of you rewrote our entire history together, and I can no longer view any of his actions as friendship. They are revealed instead to be a long and subtle campaign against me." He paused. "When he asked, I demanded to know whether you reciprocated his feelings. If you had, I would have set my own feelings aside, of course." The twitch of his jaw told me he was lying, but I appreciated his efforts. "He told me you two had not spoken of it."

That, at least, Henry had gotten right. If he had told Victor the truth, this conversation would feel quite different. The last letter I had received from Henry was the only proof of my involvement. I would burn it when I got back to Geneva.

"I asked him to swear he would never try to capture your heart. He said he could make no such promises, as your heart was your own to give where you would and he would not reject it were it ever to be offered. I knew that our friendship was truly dead. I told him as much, and demanded he leave my presence and never darken my doorway with his traitorous lies again. He said he was going to study in England to clear his mind of both of us. And that is the last I have seen or heard from him."

"I am so sorry. I knew he had traveled on to England, but had I known what he came here for—" Had I known, I would not have done anything different. Not now that I had Victor back. Henry was a friend and comfort of my youth. But I would have been deeply unhappy trying to convince him I was happy. He saw too much. It would have been a constant burden, being married to him.

Victor shifted, and I adjusted the pillow for him. He closed his eyes again, the skin around them tight. "It is not your fault, of course. Men will ever strive for that which is out of reach. For that which is higher than themselves. For that which is divine."

I laughed, resting my head on his chest. "I have missed you so."

Victor unpinned my hat, letting my hair fall free, the way he preferred it. "And I have been lost without you. Tell me, how have you managed?"

"Poorly. I would have lost my mind without Justine. She has been a great comfort to me in your absence. She helped mend the wound of missing you, in some measure. I am so glad we brought her to the house."

"Hmm." He toyed with a strand of my hair. "I never guessed she would be a good companion for you. She always seemed simple to me."

"You never could see her worth."

"And yet you did, immediately. You do not take to many people like that."

"Justine is special. Just as I told you." I breathed deeply, closing my eyes. "And you let me save her, just as you saved me."

Justine, newly rescued from her mother, had been secreted away to my room. I instructed her to wait until I was ready. On the boat ride back from town, I had realized the flaw in my plan to save her.

The children already had a governess.

In my panic and agitation, I had sought only to take Justine away. I had not quite sorted through what I was taking her to. And I did not have the authority in the Frankenstein house to declare a change of employees. I did not have any authority there at all.

But I was never letting Justine go back to her mother's house. I would simply have to make sure that a vacancy arose . . . immediately.

And for that, I needed a coconspirator.

"Victor?" I said, sliding onto the bed next to him and brushing his dark hair from his forehead. It was cool, his color healthy. His fever had finally lifted while I was away. He blinked his eyes open, and I was relieved to see that they were clear and focused. Sometimes during his fevers, he would be seized by fits during which he knew neither me nor his family. He would ramble about things that made no sense, as though he were living an entirely different life.

"Elizabeth." He pushed himself up to sitting, then stretched, peering

through the dim curtained room to look at the clock against the wall. "How long has it been?"

"A few days. I am so glad you are well."

"What day is it? Did you miss me?" He asked as though searching for facts to fill in the blank spaces in his memory.

"Thursday, and yes, of course I did. I was in here most of the time."

He nodded. Then he looked at me closer. "You need something."

An unexpected prickling stung my eyes. As much as I thought my interior life was hidden from Victor, he saw me better than anyone. I leaned my head against his shoulder, hiding my face so it would not reveal anything I did not want it to.

"Do you remember where your family found me?"

He reached up and undid my hair where it was pinned beneath my hat. It tumbled down, and he played with the curls. "Of course I do."

"But you never met the woman who took care of me at Lake Como."

"No. Why? Do you miss her?"

"I hope she is dead. And I hope she suffered tremendously on her way out of this life."

Victor let out a quiet, surprised laugh, lifting my chin so he could look into my eyes. "Then I hope so, too. Why do you bring this up?"

"You saved me. And now I want to save someone else." I told him of Justine, the scene I had witnessed, my rash intervention. "So you see, I cannot let her go home. I want her to be here, with me." I realized my mistake and hastily corrected it. "With us. For the boys." I took his hands, holding them in my own. "I want to save her, just like you saved me."

Victor shook his head, clearly not understanding. "But you are special."

"I think she *is special."*

Something shifted in his face, as though a curtain had been drawn closed behind his eyes, shutting him off from me. He leaned back. I pushed ahead desperately.

"She is not lowborn. Her family lives in town. She is educated and sweet—already better off than I ever was!"

"But your father was a noble."

Years of suspicion crashed down around me, but I skirted what I feared was the truth of my heritage. "Perhaps. Or perhaps I was the daughter of a whore, and my caretaker lied." I smiled to pass it off as jest but watched for Victor's reaction.

Saying it aloud felt like setting down a burden so long carried the weight was forgotten until released. I took a deep breath, my lungs finally filling. My head was light with all the air.

Victor could not tell whether I was joking. "But you said the house we had at Lake Como seemed familiar," he said.

"Familiar like a dream, not like a memory. Of course I would have dreamed of light and comfort and happiness in the midst of a life in hell."

Victor's silence was interminable. Finally, he nodded. "It does not matter. I do not care who your parents were. I never did. Perhaps it matters to my parents, but they are stupid. I did not know or care where you came from that day in the garden when you became mine. And I do not care now." He leaned closer, focused on my face, all worry gone from his own. "You began existing the day we met. You are my Elizabeth, and that is all that matters." He leaned forward and pressed his lips to mine. It was the first time we had kissed.

His lips were soft and dry. If Justine's lips had felt like a butterfly on my cheek—a moment of surprising grace—Victor's were like a contract between us. A promise that I was his, and he would keep me safe.

I kissed him back, throwing my arms around his neck and pulling him closer to sign my own name to the contract between us. When he released me he sighed, his brows drawing down again.

"Very well. We will save this Justine. Though how giving her the care of Ernest and William is a kindness, I do not know."

I laughed, burrowing into him with my head against his chest and holding him as tightly as I could.

But it was one thing to have a partner, another to have a plan. Victor excused himself to get something to eat. I paced in his room, trying to figure out how to make the Frankensteins dismiss their governess, Gerta, without convincing them she had done something worthy of prosecution or imprisonment. I bore no ill will toward her. She was simply in my way.

I settled on forging a letter from her family—who lived several days away—that her uncle was sick and needed her to return home immediately. Like mine, her parents were dead. I did not know how close she was with her relatives, but I hoped it was close enough that she would be enticed to leave. The moment she left, I would put forward Justine as her temporary replacement, and then send a letter to Gerta that she was no longer required. A forged letter from Gerta would be sent to the Frankensteins, telling them that she had found new employment and would not be returning.

The plan could fall apart at any stage, but I was confident it was the least damaging option. I would also include in Gerta's dismissal letter a glowing recommendation to help her find employment with another family.

I had just sat down at Victor's desk with a quill and a pot of ink when he returned. "I did it," he said.

"What?"

"Gerta is gone. My mother will be desperate for a new governess."

I stood, shocked. When he had left the room, I thought he was going to eat. He had been gone only an hour. What could he possibly have done in an hour to get rid of Gerta so easily?

"Where did she go?"

"Home," he said simply.

"She would not just leave. How did you manage it?"

He paused, holding up one of my long curls, still loose from when he had unpinned them. "Sublime," he murmured, twisting my hair to catch the light streaming in from the window. "Why is it, I wonder, that I can find beauty in this? What is it about your hair—a natural phenomenon, one that holds no inherent value or purpose—that triggers happiness in me?"

"You are so strange." I took his hand and turned it to kiss his palm. "Now. Tell me. How did you get rid of Gerta?"

He shrugged, his eyes fixing on some point above my head. I noticed that his shirt and vest were slightly rumpled and askew. It was not like him to be anything other than immaculate when he was well. A remnant of the fever must be lingering. "I asked her to leave. She did. Tomorrow will be a good time to suggest to my mother that you know a suitable replacement."

He took my place at his desk, pulled out one of his books, and resumed the studies that had been paused by his illness.

Whatever Victor had done had worked. We never heard from—or spoke of—Gerta again. The next morning, I told a harried and upset Madame Frankenstein that I knew a perfect replacement governess. Justine was produced and immediately hired, and had only me to thank for her new life.

It was a struggle initially, finding a balance. I had to be careful not to make Victor jealous of my affection for Justine. Having so few people he loved in his own life, Victor was not inclined to share me. But when he was at school, I was free to spend time with her.

I would often join her in the nursery as she instructed Ernest while playing with and cooing over William. I interacted with the boys as required and pretended to be delighted with them, but Justine's adoration of them was sincere. When she praised Ernest's progress, she meant it. When she laughed and clapped at William's newest trick, her eyes shone with pride.

I had meant to do Justine a favor—and thus myself—but I could see that she was what I should have been to this family: an angel.

She was an angel to me, as well. She was the one person in the house who did not, to some extent, hold my fate hostage. Because she was an employee and I was a ward, she could do nothing to threaten me. But because I was not a Frankenstein, she was free to treat me as a dear friend and not an employer.

Perhaps I stared at her with as much joy and adulation as the young Frankensteins did.

I loved Justine.

Just as I loved Henry.

But I loved no one as I loved Victor, because I owed it all to him.

When the afternoon light grew warm and long, the doctor shooed me out.

"Inform your landlady you will be leaving in the morning," Victor said as I pinned my hat back in place. I still needed another pin to replace the one I had left in the charnel house man's wrist.

"Where will we stay? Do you have a recommendation?"

"You must return home."

I crossed my arms, obstinate. "Not without you." Then I paused, repenting of my forcefulness. It was never the way to win Victor's agreement. "Or will you stay on and continue your studies? I want to remain at least until you are fully well."

"It would be a waste of your time. And no, I am not going to stay, either. My failure here was complete. I need a fresh start. I will return home as soon as I have settled a few personal business matters. You must go ahead of me so I remember the goodness I have awaiting my return. It will make my time here pass far more bearably. I will not be more than a month behind you."

"A month!" I cried.

Victor laughed at my unhappiness. "What is a month to us, who have shared a lifetime? I am quite serious, though. Ingolstadt is no place for you."

I sighed. I both agreed and disagreed. I had not had a particularly good time here—but there had been something invigorating about being on my own, chasing down my own future. Answering to no one.

Still, I would do as Victor wished. I could go back knowing that he would follow, bringing my security with him. "Justine is quite unhappy here. She is desperate to be back home."

Victor's eyes narrowed with a twitch. "You mean back to work?"

I waved dismissively. "She does not consider it work. She adores William, and has been so good for Ernest."

"And she has been your dearest companion."

I looked toward the outer rooms, where Justine was waiting. She had been so good to accompany me. Without her, I never would have been able to make this trip. I had deceived her and pulled her away from the things she loved. As much as I wanted to remain and make certain Victor came back, I could not ask her to do the same. If Victor wanted me to go and Justine wanted to go, I could not justify staying. And I would have no one to help me do so. "If you think it best, I will return home for Justine's comfort. But you must promise to write me at least once, and send word ahead when you are on your way."

His eyes were heavy and dark with some meaning I found—to my great dismay—I could no longer read. It filled me with panic. What was he thinking? Was he upset? Was he just tired? Suddenly he was a language I did not know.

"I will most certainly send word ahead." He smiled then, and some of the tightness in my chest released. "You will know when I am coming. I promise."

"I will hold you to that." I leaned over the bed to kiss his forehead. I was entirely unprepared when Victor tilted his head up and met my lips with his own. A charge passed between us, and I gasped, pulling away. It reminded me too much of the one I had received in his horrible laboratory.

Victor looked amused. "Why, Elizabeth. Have you forgotten how to kiss me?"

I lifted my chin in the air, looking down at him imperiously, but with a hint of a smile. "You had better hurry home so you can remind me."

His laughter followed me out of the room, my steps lighter for it.

Justine stood, putting William's mending in her bag. How she had managed to pack it, I did not know. "How is Victor?" she asked. Justine had not gone back to see him. I offered to let her, but she blushed at the mere thought of seeing her employer's oldest son in a state of repose. What would she think if she knew how often I had shared his bed, however innocently!

"He is restored to himself. And he insists we go home immediately."

Justine closed her eyes and bowed her head, smiling in silent prayer. "I am so glad."

"That he is restored, or that we get to go home?"

"Both! And that we will have only one more night in that horrible boardinghouse."

I pursed my lips thoughtfully. I had already bidden farewell to Victor. Everything was settled between us. He loved me. I had secured my prize *and* protected Victor's reputation through a few careful acts of destruction. My future was once again free from the threat of poverty and destitution.

Judge Frankenstein could take himself straight to hell.

Smiling, I tucked Justine's hand into the crook of my arm. "We should leave tonight. As soon as we have secured our things. I do not want to spend another moment in this town, either."

Justine kissed my forehead, then pulled an extra pin from her hat and carefully pinned my hat more firmly in place. As we walked out the door, I glanced over my shoulder and thought I saw Victor passing back into his room. Had he come to say goodbye? Why had he not called out to us?

Perhaps he, too, was shy in front of Justine, wearing only sickbed clothes. He did not like talking to people in general, much less when he was ill. Or perhaps it had been the doctor, not Victor. It nagged at my mind as we hurried back to the boardinghouse. I would have been much more settled if he were returning with us.

But I had to trust that he would come home as he had said. Victor did not lie to me.

Back in our room at Frau Gottschalk's, I closed our trunk with emphatic flair.

"Oh!" Justine exclaimed with dismay. "What about Mary? She was so good to us. It would be rude to leave without saying goodbye."

I agreed. It would be rude. And also the most prudent thing to do, given what she knew of my activities while I was here. "Write to her and give her our regrets. Tell her I am grateful for everything. Particularly the cloak she lent me." I ran my fingers along its edge, surprised to find I already missed Mary.

Justine, ever dutiful, sat down at the scratched and peeling desk and proceeded to write a letter more sincere and elegant than I could have managed. Under other circumstances, I might have been friends with Mary. Circumstances under which I could afford such indulgences as friends, that was. She had her uncle and her shop. She had no need of me. And I had no need of her sharp and perceptive eyes. Besides, I had Justine and Victor. I had lost Henry, but that only showed how one truly *could* have too many friends.

Just before nightfall—saving us from the enthusiastic locks of Frau Gottschalk, who watched us leave with suspicious eyes after demanding extra coin for more ink usage—Justine and I settled in our carriage.

"Home!" I cried, pointing forward. The carriage bumped over the roads and out of Ingolstadt, back to the house on the lake that no longer threatened to spit me back out. We would ride all night for Justine's sake.

In the early hours of the morning, when the sun had yet to make any claim on the sky, I startled awake to a bright flash of lightning. Silhouetted against a hill parallel to our path, I thought I saw the figure from the street. The figure from my nightmares. It ran with inhuman speed, its gait close to a man's but horrifyingly off in some unnamable way. I closed my eyes in terror. Another flash of lightning forced them open.

Nothing was following us.

I sank back against the seat, closing my eyes and thinking only of home. The home that was, once again, mine.

PART TWO

WHAT IS DARK WITHIN ME, ILLUMINE

TWELVE

AT ONCE INDEBTED AND DISCHARGED

As Justine and I were rowed with patient and even strokes across the lake, I remembered my first time here. How frightened I had been. How the house had felt like a predator, waiting to devour me. Now, as I looked at it, it seemed infinitely lessened. Did the spires not stand up so much like teeth as grave monuments? Did the gates swing not so much to catch us as to wave us wearily inside?

I had pictured my return as triumphant. But I sat passively watching the house grow closer as someone else took me there. I realized then: for all my striving, all my hoping and fearing and traveling, I had worked this hard to stay in the same place.

The sun was almost setting, the day nearly done. I did not anticipate home and my bed the way I had expected. Justine sighed happily, taking my hand and squeezing it. "Look! William is on the dock, waiting for us!" She waved so vigorously at her little charge that the boat rocked.

I smiled, too, with a wave. Mine did not so much as add a ripple to the lake.

Everything was not the same, though. Judge Frankenstein, thankfully, had not yet returned from the mysterious trip that had allowed ours, making it less likely that he would speak with Justine and discover my illicit travels. Not that he ever spoke with Justine—in her more than two years at the house, I could not recall a single conversation between them—but it was still a relief. Being caught in my lie about Henry was more than enough. I did not want Justine knowing I had tricked her into chaperoning me without express permission.

With the judge gone, and with the freedom of knowing I would not be thrown out, I prowled the house with a possessive aggression. Perhaps some in my position, having finally obtained a measure of stability after so many months of worry, would collapse into bed, or spend their time reading or painting or simply relaxing. But art had long been a performance for me, a way to convince the Frankensteins of my value. There was no one to convince now. Art brought me no joy, and my canvases were left blank.

I moved from room to room, pulled by an invisible, nagging thread. Things familiar—my four-poster bed, the leaded windowpanes, even my own paintings—had a layer of uncanny discomfort. I walked as if in a dream through a simulated version of life in which I was certain that if I just turned around quickly enough, I would find the truth of the dream: A wall melted to reveal the bones of the house, groaning and fracturing under the weight of us all. The ghosts of Madame Frankenstein and her long-lost second child, watching how well I kept her charge, even beyond the grave. The desiccated corpses of my own parents, too unknown to be anything to me but lifeless husks.

Yet no matter how many rooms I prowled, no matter how many times I spun, certain someone was watching me, there was never anything worth noticing.

The house was the same.

The people in it were the same.

Victor was coming home, and we would be the same.

What, then, had changed?

The estate felt lessened and cheap under my newly critical eye. Now that I did not have to fear losing this sitting room, I saw that the velvet sofa was all wrong, the dimensions of it too big for the space. It was furniture designed for a grander room. Rather than improving the space with its fineness, it emphasized how claustrophobic the room was, how low the ceiling, how bulky the fireplace.

Everywhere I looked was the same. Soulless paintings too big for the walls they hung on. A dining table set for twenty that only ever fed four. It was all boastful artifice hiding the truth:

The house was dying.

I saw it all now: The dusty corners. The cracked and fading paint. The doors that did not hang quite right, either never closing all the way or closing so tightly I feared being locked inside a room, unable to open them again. Half of the fireplaces were boarded up. The other half either heated the rooms to stifling oppression or did little to cut the ever-present draft. Any room that might ostensibly have visitors was stuffed with overtly ornate furniture, scrolling wood and gilt and velvet. And any room that would not was either empty or a graveyard of broken, useless items.

The only room with any real life was the nursery. I spent more and more time there with Justine, Ernest, and William. And even though I had done my best to avoid the boys all these years—preferring to be responsible for only Victor rather than taking on even more Frankensteins—they were . . . rather delightful. It was probably Justine's effusive love of them infecting me, but Ernest was at an age where he tried to speak like an adult, and William was at an age where he tried to copy Ernest, and they were both so absurd and simple and easy to please.

"Actually," William said, watching Ernest pack his things for school one morning, "I am going to school soon, too."

"That is an incorrect use of the word *actually*," I said. "You were not correcting him or disputing any information, merely stating a fact."

Justine frowned at me. "You hush! If you dare correct another thing he says, I will banish you! And, William, you are not going to school soon. I have you all to myself for a few years yet."

William gave her a sloppy, wet kiss. I wanted to wipe my own cheek just seeing it. Ernest and I shared a knowing look of disgust, then laughed.

Victor had never been this way, even as a child. They were nothing like him. Maybe it was because they had Justine instead of me. Had I truly helped Victor, or had I made him even more unusual? The madness I had seen of his work in Ingolstadt made me wonder.

But he had gone mad without me. Not *with* me.

Shaking off the worry, I volunteered to see Ernest off at the dock for school. I was tempted to row into town with him and check to see if there had been any letters, but that promised anxiety. It had not been that long. I would wait.

Victor would write.

"Should I bring you back a flower?" Ernest called as the boat pulled away.

"No! Bring me back an equation. The most beautiful equation you can find!"

He giggled, and I smiled. It was unfeigned. These boys were too easy to make happy. They reminded me of Henry, which made me sad. So I went back inside, intending to stop at the kitchen to find some little treat for William. Soon I would spoil them as much as Justine did. I was doing it to make myself feel better, but it was working.

I paused in the grand entry, staring at the huge double doors that led to the dining room. There, carved into the wood more than a century before, was the Frankenstein family crest. How many times had I traced those lines, willing myself a place on that shield? How often had I imagined myself crouching behind that shield, claiming the protection of the Frankenstein name—a name that had never been given to me?

Someone pounded on the front door, and I jumped, startled. We were not expecting anyone. Indeed, we rarely had guests at all. Perhaps it was a letter!

The maid was in another wing of the house. I swished through the entry to the door, half expecting to find Judge Frankenstein there, glowering over being locked out of his own house. Instead, I opened it to find Fredric Clerval, Henry's father.

"Monsieur Clerval?" I gave him a puzzled smile. "To what do we owe the honor?"

He looked past me, searching for someone else. Henry had far more of his mother in his face. His father's features were flat and hard, eyes squinted from perpetual glaring. He looked like a man counting ledgers and never quite satisfied with the results.

"Where is Judge Frankenstein?"

"He is away, I am afraid. Would you care for some tea?"

"I would not!" He took a deep breath, steadying himself. But then his baleful eyes found me, and his glare deepened. "Have you heard from my son?"

The letter hidden in the back of my vanity drawer seemed to pulse in my mind. I still needed to burn it! "Not for some six months, I am afraid. The last he wrote me, he said he was going to England to further his studies."

Monsieur Clerval let out a derisive blast of air between his lips. "His studies! He has gone chasing poets! If ever there were a more useless waste of his time and mind, I cannot think of it." He leaned close. "Do not think I hold you blameless. I have no doubt some of this was planted in his mind by your influence. I curse the day I introduced him to your company. You and Victor have done nothing but corrupt him, make him miserable with the life he was given."

I wanted to stagger back. I wanted to agree, to apologize. Instead, I lifted my chin and raised my eyebrows in wounded surprise. "I am sorry, Monsieur Clerval. I am afraid I do not know what you are talking about. We have ever loved Henry as our dear friend, and want only the best for him."

"No one in this family wants the best for anyone but themselves." He threw a stack of parchment on the floor between us. "See that Judge Frankenstein gets these. And let him know I will no longer defer collection on his debts. He has ruined my son. I will ruin his fortunes."

He turned to stomp away—and found Judge Frankenstein standing in the doorway. I should have acted as hostess and ushered them to a sitting room. Judge Frankenstein looked at me, then at the papers Henry's father had thrown down. A mixture of fury and fear mingled, ugly and purple, on his face.

I dipped a respectful curtsy and then hurried to the nursery, my skirts swishing with my urgency. "Come!" I said, bursting through the door. "Let us go for a walk!"

Justine agreed, sensing my need. William, always one for time outside, raced ahead of us. We stayed close to the house. My neck prickled with the sensation of being watched. I whipped around, but the windows greeted me with blank reflections of nature. If someone watched us, it was not from there.

The wind whistled mournfully through the trees, shaking them. Somewhere to our right, in the morning shadows of the house, a twig snapped. I rushed to catch up to William, clasping his tiny hot hand as an anchor, trying to absorb some of his brightness as he pointed out interesting rocks and trees he wanted to climb.

"Elizabeth used to be an expert at climbing trees," Justine said, smiling.

I nodded, distracted and far away. My thoughts were still in the entry with Monsieur Clerval's accusations.

Had we ruined Henry?

* * *

Henry had been gone only two weeks when I received his letter.

To say I had been waiting patiently would be to perjure myself most horribly. I had been haunting the windows, looking out across the lake as though I could will his report to me.

My entire life hinged on Henry's activities in Ingolstadt. I hated him, and Victor, and the whole world for it. How was it that my future was entirely dependent on one boy who could not be bothered to put pen to paper, and another boy who wanted to spend the rest of his life with me, unaware of who I truly was?

I supposed that in some tawdry novel I would not be permitted to read but would steal from Madame Frankenstein's hidden store anyhow, I would have been torn between my two lovers and wasting away because of it.

In reality, I wanted to tear both of them apart.

It was not fair to them. But nothing in my *life was fair, and so I could not find pity for Victor, having to decide whether he wished to marry me or release me to someone else, or for Henry, being used as a whip to prompt Victor into some sort of action.*

I held the letter in my hands, staring down at it. Victor, or Henry. It had already been decided in my absence.

Though I had imagined tearing it open on the spot as soon as it arrived, I walked out behind the house into the deep woods there. Ahead of me loomed the mountains. I had spent many happy days at their feet, and even one perfect day on the glacial plains. Their silent strength brought me no peace now. I turned to the thickest portion of the forest, pushing through the brambles and bushes until I found a hollowed tree trunk.

And then, as though returning to my feral roots, I curled into it. I peered out, wondering: Could I live here? Could I make a nest, a home? Sleep deeply during the winter? Prowl the undergrowth at night for prey?

It was the type of fantasy that had sustained me before the Frankensteins. I knew better now. I would starve, or freeze. There was no home for me here in the wild, the place I loved best. I would have to settle for what I could capture on my own.

I opened the letter.

Henry's hand, usually sprawling with confident loops and self-indulgent flourishes, was shaky. The edges of the paper were splotchy, some of the ink smeared as though he had not waited for it to dry before folding it.

"Dear Elizabeth," I read, and I had my answer. No "Dearest Elizabeth," no "Better Half of my Soul," no "Dream of My Future Happiness." Henry was incapable of writing so plainly unless his heart was truly broken.

"I have spoken with Victor and expressed my desire to enter into an engagement with you. I am afraid I have broken our friendship irreparably. Where I saw in you two companionable friendship or the love between two people raised so closely, I failed to see the depth of his connection to you. It was a betrayal most unforgivable to assume I could ever come between you two. It is an attempted theft he will not overlook. Nor should he.

"In pondering my attachment to you, I suspect it stemmed from jealousy. I have always envied Victor. I wanted to be *him. And in place of being him, I wanted what was his. That included you. Please forgive my arrogance."*

The next several words were splotched beyond recognition. But the last paragraph continued, "to England to settle my mind and my spirits. I do not expect to contact you again. It is best for everyone if I leave behind my false friendship forever and attempt to become someone new.

"Forgive me,

"Henry Clerval."

Even Henry's signature lacked any flourish. It barely looked like his, though I knew it to be. It was as though someone else had possessed him and written this letter. But perhaps that was precisely what had happened.

The Henry I knew had always admired Victor and watched him with an almost jealous hunger. Had it all been an act, then? Was Henry a far better actor than even I was, convincing me, the ultimate liar, of his infallible sincerity?

That did not feel quite right. I wondered if perhaps Henry had genuinely believed his own attachment to me, and, when confronted by Victor, had finally realized the true motivation behind his actions.

Sometimes we were strangers even to ourselves.

So it was settled. Henry would leave, and Victor still wanted me. But where, then, was my letter from Victor? Did Victor want me, or did he simply not want Henry to claim me?

I curled deeper into my temporary burrow, hollower than the tree and less capable of providing shelter. I would wait for Victor's letter.

I had no other choice.

Justine caught me staring out a window at the evening landscape. I had been watching it since Monsieur Clerval left and we had finally dared to come back inside. Whether I was waiting for something, or fearful that if I looked away, I would miss some vital threat, I could not say.

"Where are you?" she asked, putting a gentle hand on my shoulder.

I sighed. "In the past."

She led me to the sofa and sat us down, so close that our legs touched. "I thought you would be happy. You did what you set out to do!"

I offered her the best smile I could manage. Soon I would have to go dine with Judge Frankenstein. I needed to get back to pretending. "You are right. I am afraid the trip was more exhausting than I had realized. I am not quite recovered yet."

"Thank goodness we will never have to do that again! All those decisions. I was frightened the whole time."

"Me too," I lied. "I suppose, returning home, I miss Victor all the more. And Henry, too. I am sorry he left for England without the blessing of his father." Justine had not seen Monsieur Clerval, and I did not mention his visit, or the papers he had left for Judge Frankenstein, though those things contributed to my lack of ease. No wonder Judge Frankenstein had wanted to excise me from their expenses. He had debts, apparently. What if I had secured Victor, only for him to be rendered a pauper?

I did not think that would happen. Wealth like his family's had a way of replenishing itself. And Victor was a genius. He would take care of me.

Justine clucked her tongue in sympathy. "Men are always doing things without thinking of how they will affect others. It is a woman's heart that is big enough to hold another's feelings. We will miss Henry, but we will be fine."

"I always imagined him as some part of our lives forever. Our friend. Even your husband." Or my own. I had not anticipated him leaving us behind entirely. If I had, would I have acted differently?

Justine laughed. "Oh, I could never marry Henry!"

I turned to look at her. "Then you are not upset? I had wondered if maybe you would feel it a lost opportunity."

"Goodness, no. I never want to marry. I want to stay here and raise dear William and Ernest. And I want to take care of your children."

My children. What a horrible thought. "But then you would never have children of your own!"

Justine nodded, her face clouding with sadness. "I do not want them."

"Surely no one has ever been more capable of being a loving mother."

"My mother was loving."

I frowned. "We are not thinking of the same woman."

Justine's eyes were pulled to the floor with the weight of her memories. "She was. Loving and gentle and kind. To my three younger siblings. What I did to so anger her that she could treat me with nothing but hatred and spite, I have never known. Maybe something was wrong inside her. Or maybe she saw something wrong inside me that I have not yet discovered."

I grabbed her arms and turned her toward me, my voice fierce. "There is nothing wrong with you, Justine. There never has been." I knew what it was to be rotten in the core—to hide sharp teeth behind a serene smile. Justine was not hiding anything.

"But do you see? How do I know I will not share my mother's madness? How do I know I will not make life a hell for a child of my own?" She patted my hands, removing them from her arms and settling back against the sofa. "I am so happy here with you. I want nothing more than what I have and can reasonably hope for in the future, now that Victor will return. I am glad it is all settled."

I was happy to hear it, for her sake. But something in me recoiled at her words, and I realized what the ghost haunting my return truly was.

I was haunted by the diverging future I had given up. For so long I had held Henry's potential like a card hidden up my sleeve. That card was lost to me now, as was Henry, whom I had planned to keep one way or another, whether by my side or Justine's. As it always was, the choice had been made for me by others.

"It is so lovely to be home." Justine sighed happily, staring into the crackling fire.

"Lovely," I echoed, closing my eyes and remembering the thrill and satisfaction of other flames. I had proved my cunning and capability were as much as I had always hoped. And now I had my reward.

I shivered against a sudden imagined chill.

I slipped through the doors and took my place at the dining table. Judge Frankenstein did not even look up at me.

"I have good news," I said as the maid placed soup in front of me.

The boys had already eaten. Ernest was old enough to eat with us now but preferred to dine with William and Justine. I would have preferred that, too, but was never given the option. I had to maintain my standing in the home.

Judge Frankenstein did not ask what my good news was, so I pushed on. "Victor has written that he will be returning home within a month. He is eager to be reunited with me." I allowed a feminine blush and ducked my head. "With all of us."

"Good," Judge Frankenstein said. The force of his voice surprised me, and I looked up to find him glaring intently at me over the papers I recognized from Monsieur Clerval. Victor's father stretched his lips beneath his mustache into an imitation of a smile. "That is good."

I fought the urge to recoil from the patently false expression. Was that how I looked when I pretended at happiness? No. I had far more practice than he did. And his smile was underwritten with desperation. It was the look of a street performer, hopeful and enthusiastic on the surface, patiently calculating beneath.

Did he think Victor would petition Henry about discharging our debts? Henry had fled the continent to get away from us. He would certainly do us no such favors. Or perhaps Judge Frankenstein thought Victor's return would allow him to consult with his son on how best to eliminate the household's only immediately disposable excess—myself.

He had no idea I had already won. Victor's return would forever seal my fate and keep me safe from Judge Frankenstein's harm. I returned his smile, and we spent the rest of the meal in miserable silence, companions in lies and deception, trapped forever under the same roof.

I had won indeed.

THIRTEEN

THAT ALL THIS GOOD OF EVIL SHALL PRODUCE

"We should have a party to celebrate Victor's return!" Justine said, leaning over William to help him with his letters. "Excellent! If you turn that *E* the other way, it is perfect! You are so smart."

Ernest, lounging on a nearby sofa reading a book about Swiss military victories, looked up. His thin lips turned down in a pout. "I would much prefer a party celebrating whenever he decides to leave again."

"Ernest!" Justine said. She communicated so much reproach with a single word that he flinched, abashed.

"It has been two years." I drummed my fingers against the mantel where I leaned by the cold fireplace. "Surely you can barely remember him!" It was early May, three weeks since we had left Ingolstadt. I had in my pocket a brief letter from Victor, who would arrive in one week. He had been true to his word. Perhaps when he was home I would feel less unsettled.

I thought I saw movement outside the nursery window. I rushed to look, but I was mistaken. It was just the blackened and tortured remains of that tree long ago destroyed by lightning. Why they had never torn it out, I did not understand. Something about it now struck me as obscene. It was like leaving a corpse as a monument.

"Do you think I am bigger than him now?" Ernest stood and threw back his shoulders.

"Than *he*," I absently corrected him. "And no."

I turned my back on the window and its false threats. Ever since Monsieur Clerval's visit, I had been haunted by the feeling of being watched. Perhaps it was Judge Frankenstein's new habit of surprising me at meals he had never customarily taken with me. Or the way he seemed to be staring at me whenever I looked up. But there was also the sense that if I simply turned around fast enough, I would catch a face at the window, staring in at me.

I never did.

"I think you probably will be taller someday," Justine said. Evidently I had hurt Ernest's feelings with the truth.

"Good," Ernest said. "I know I will be stronger. And I know how to fight. Victor never bothered learning that."

"Are you planning to challenge him to a duel?" I asked, laughing. But my laughter stopped when I saw Ernest rubbing the forearm that bore his scar. Whether the action was conscious or unconscious, I did not know.

Ernest looked at me too closely, much the way his father had begun to. "You have been spending an awful lot of time with us. You never used to."

"Perhaps our time away taught me to miss you." I crossed my eyes and stuck my tongue out at him as if he were still a little boy. "Or perhaps I am just bored."

"Must be truly bored to spend time in the nursery." He flopped back down on the couch, his careful posture abandoned. "I cannot wait to leave this house. This stupid house with no neighbors and nothing to do. I will row away across that lake and never come back."

"Do not say that," Justine reprimanded with gentle sadness.

Ernest sighed, sitting up again and crossing the room to her. He revealed his lingering childhood by throwing himself into her lap. Justine hugged him tightly and mussed his hair. He had been young when his mother died, but he was old enough to remember her. I wondered if he preferred Justine. I certainly did.

"I will always come back to see you," he said. "I promise. And I will write you every week."

"We have worked so hard on your penmanship, it is the least you can do," she said teasingly, though I could see her holding back panicked sorrow at the very thought of his permanent departure. "But you are not leaving yet! The military can wait until you are grown. Give us a little more time, dear Ernest."

"I am not going to be a soldier," William declared, continuing his march of poorly formed *E*'s across the parchment. Justine was too permissive, letting him use good ink and paper for his practice.

"What will you be?" Justine said, turning her attention back to him and releasing Ernest to go back to lounging.

"A dragon."

"That is a deeply practical aspiration," I remarked dryly. "Your ambition will serve you well."

William blinked his heavily lashed eyes at me, confused. "What?"

"Cousin Elizabeth means you can be whatever you wish." Justine ruffled his curls. For her, his dimpled smile appeared.

Was it wrong to envy a five-year-old child? As the third son of the family, he would have means but lack pressure. He truly could be whatever he wished. Perhaps he could even change into a fire-breathing hell-beast. Wealthy men did whatever they wanted, after all.

Though from what I had heard, if Monsieur Clerval had his way, none of the Frankensteins would be wealthy.

"I want to go shooting," I said to Ernest, who regarded me with surprise.

"Really?"

"Yes. I would like to learn. And I think you are old enough to teach me."

"Me too!" William said. Justine glared at me across the room, shaking her head vehemently. She grabbed William around the waist and guided him back to his seat.

But Ernest stood undeterred, his face alight with anticipation. "I will go and—"

The maid knocked on the door, peering meekly in. "A letter for you, Miss."

I stepped forward, but she shook her head. "For Miss Justine."

Justine never got letters. She appeared as puzzled as I about who would be writing her. I wondered if perhaps it was Henry. Another stab of jealousy pierced my heart, but I let it go. I had wanted both Victor and Henry for my own. It was inevitable I would lose one. I could be glad just to hear that Henry was doing well in England.

Justine opened the letter with a distracted smile, still paying more attention to William's disastrous writing. But as she read, the color drained from her face. She looked up, searching for me. I rushed to her just as she stumbled and fainted, insensible, in my arms.

"What is it?" Ernest demanded, fear raising his voice to a piercing whine.

I nodded toward the sofa. Ernest helped me get Justine placed comfortably there. Then I retrieved the letter that had fallen to the floor. I scanned the contents.

"Oh! Her mother died. Last week."

"God rest her soul," Ernest said sadly, crossing himself in imitation of Justine.

If God has any sense, he will damn her worthless soul for how she treated Justine, I thought.

* * *

After Victor left for Ingolstadt, with Henry occupied working for his father, Justine was my only friend. She took her role as governess to the boys as seriously as Victor had ever applied himself to his studies. I might have brought her to the Frankensteins out of an impulse to save her, but she turned out to be the best thing possible for the younger brothers. The death of their mother saddened them. But in beautiful, bright, infinitely loving Justine, they had more of a mother than their own had ever been.

One day not long after Victor's departure, the cook took ill. With no one to go to town to collect supplies, I eagerly volunteered and insisted Justine come with me.

She wrung her hands. "What about the boys?"

"Justine, you have not left this house since you got here! Surely you deserve an afternoon off. The maid will look in on them, and Ernest is old enough to be in charge for a few hours. Right, Ernest?"

He looked up from his one-sided game of chess. "I can do that for Justine! You should go and—" He paused, his face screwing up in thought as he tried to come up with something a woman might enjoy. "You should go and buy some ribbons!"

"Three ribbons!" William added. He had recently turned three and was obsessed with the number.

Justine laughed. She kissed Ernest and kissed and hugged little William far longer than a few hours' absence demanded. Then, finally, I got her out of the house and across the lake.

My last trip to Geneva had yielded me Justine. I had no hopes for an equally fortuitous trip this time, but it was a relief to be out of the house. Victor had just written of getting settled in Ingolstadt, telling me of his professors and his rooms. I had imagined it so fully I felt as though I were actually there.

But I was not. I was still here.

Geneva, at least, offered some distraction. Justine dutifully bought three red ribbons so she could show them to Ernest as proof that his idea was good and count them with William. She also found some candy for the boys, though why they deserved any extra kindness from the woman who spent all her waking hours being kind to them, I did not know.

We were in the middle of the market picking out vegetables when a shrieking demon flew into Justine, knocking her to the ground.

"You monster!" the demon screamed, and I realized it was Justine's mother. "You killed them!"

Justine struggled beneath her mother, the woman's hands like claws tearing at her face and her clothes. I dropped my things and yanked her away from Justine.

"Madame!" I shouted. "Calm yourself!"

Justine's mother's chin was covered with spittle as she continued shouting the most profane accusations. "You sold yourself to witches! The devil claimed you as his own the day you were born! I knew it! I could feel it! I tried my best to beat it out of you, but you won! You won, you wicked creature! Damnation on you!"

Justine was sitting on the ground, crying. "What did I do?"

"Nothing!" I answered.

"You killed them!" her mother screamed. "My precious babies, my beloved children. You killed them!" She tried to push past me once again, and I could scarcely restrain her. By now she had raised such a commotion that several men hurried over and helped me hold her in place. She writhed and contorted, throwing her body every which way before finally collapsing.

"My babies!" Justine's mother cried. "You killed them. They are all dead, and it is your fault. You left us. You left, and they died. God will remember, Justine. God will remember that you betrayed your own blood and became a rich man's whore to raise other people's children. God will remember! Your soul is damned! Hell has marked you for its own since the day you entered this world!"

A constable had joined the fray and directed the men to carry Justine's mother to the town hall, where they could sort out what to do with her.

"I am sorry, mademoiselle," he said, dipping his head to me. I helped Justine up.

"What was she talking about?" Justine trembled, clinging to me.

"Nothing. She is mad." I wanted to get Justine out of there, to get her back to the house. I should never have brought her with me. No wonder she had not wanted to leave that side of the lake and our seclusion there.

"Poor woman," the constable said. "All three of her children caught fever and died last week. We do not know what to do with her." He inclined his head again and followed the men taking Justine's mother away.

"Birgitta and Heidi and Marten," Justine whispered. She fell against me and I held her. "They cannot be dead. They cannot be. When I left they were all healthy. If I had known, I never would have— I could have helped them. I could have stayed and helped. Oh, she is right. I am the most wicked and selfish creature. I valued my own comfort over my family. My mother always knew, she always saw, and—"

"No," I said. I pulled Justine close, squeezing her to me, my voice harsh and determined. I would not comfort her, not in this line of thought. I would argue the point forever. "Your mother is a monster. If you had stayed, she would have beaten the light right out of you. You would have died with your siblings. I cannot imagine a world without you in it. You were not wicked to leave. It was God's grace, keeping you safe so you would not leave us."

Justine sobbed into my shoulder. I turned her toward the lake, and we stumbled together back to our waiting boat, all her pretty red ribbons left behind on the street like scarlet streams of blood.

Justine's orphaned status weighed heavily on me as I remembered her past and considered her future. Included in the letter about her mother's death had been a note explaining the delay in delivery. Her mother had specifically requested Justine not be notified until *after* the funeral. It had been her dying wish to spite Justine and deny her even the opportunity to mourn. Imagine wanting to mourn a woman who deserved no such tribute!

I insisted Justine take the next two days to herself—whether to spend them in bed, or walking the countryside alone with her thoughts. I knew she needed space to heal the final wound her mother had inflicted.

Unfortunately, that left me with William. Ernest was old enough to manage himself, but he was unsettled by Justine's absence and thus hovered around me like a gnat, pestering and useless but ultimately harmless.

The first day was spent with William clambering through the entire house, getting into everything. He begged to see my room, where he had never been allowed, then proceeded to ask me if he could have every shiny thing he saw. He was a magpie, this child. To get him out, I agreed to lend him my gold locket with a miniature portrait of his mother inside. I had never loved it, had certainly not asked for it. It was too expensive to give into the care of a five-year-old, but I would have given far more for even ten minutes' respite from his constant demands. Victor would be home in just a few short days, but that did not help in the meantime. I could be charmed by the children in minute doses; being in charge of their care was overwhelming. I could not imagine Victor being willing to take over.

On the second day, at a loss for ways to entertain William, I suggested Ernest accompany us on a walk. A very, very long walk that ideally would end with William exhausted into lethargy for the evening. To my surprise, as we were finishing our preparations—picnic packed and boots laced—Judge Frankenstein appeared.

"It is a lovely afternoon," he declared gravely, as if passing judgment on the weather were part of his authority. I was glad, for the weather's sake, that it did not meet his condemnation.

"Yes. I am taking the boys out for some fresh air and exercise while Justine rests."

"That is good of you." His lips pulled apart, and his mustache lifted like a curtain to reveal his teeth. His teeth, unused to the spotlight, were stained dark from years of wine and tea, though I suspected higher quantities of the former. "I will join you. It will be nice to go out together. As a family." He weighted the last word like a gavel dropping.

Wary but cautiously pleased, I gave him my best smile. One that would be given an encore and a standing ovation, unlike his own. "That will be lovely."

Thus, my walk took me through the woods with the three Frankensteins I had never had any use for. And . . . it was not awful. Judge Frankenstein was mostly silent, save to remark on the qualities of this tree, or the stately nature of that rock, or the general uselessness of that flower.

Ernest, ever aware of his father's presence, worked hard to walk with as much decorum and maturity as he could. But even he was unable to resist the warm spell of the glorious spring day. Soon he was chasing William, eliciting shrieking giggles and demands for vigorous play.

I laughed, watching them. There was something to be said for children after all. There was a deeply restoring and restful happiness watching a creature like William discover the world. He was all curiosity and joy. There was no fear or anxiety in him. Had I ever been that way? I did not think so.

Madame Frankenstein would have been proud of how well I had done in settling their family. Ernest and William had grown up safe. Victor had been ushered past his difficulties. I had even found a replacement mother far more suited to the task of raising William and Ernest than I ever would have been.

I could take pride and satisfaction in this life. I *would* take pride and satisfaction in it. I was determined to. I let the bright sun and brighter laughter warm me. I would finally release all the strain and fear I had worn like a shawl.

We found a pretty meadow near where the forest gave way to our closest neighboring farm and set up the picnic. After eating, I pulled out a book, and Judge Frankenstein lay down on the ground and closed his eyes for a nap. It was a shockingly vulnerable and casual position for him to adopt.

And it was aggravating. If he had not been there, I could have done the same. But I did not have the luxury of relaxation in public. At least I had a book. I shooed the boys away, instructing them to meet us again before the sun got too low.

As afternoon dipped toward evening and I worried over what I would do to entertain William the next day, Ernest came back. He was sweating and out of breath, his face hopeful and then falling as he swept his eyes over our little picnic site.

"William is not here?" he asked.

I closed my book and stood in alarm. Judge Frankenstein, who had woken a few minutes before, also stood. "What do you mean? He was with you."

Ernest shook his head. "We were playing hide-and-seek. It was William's turn. I counted to fifty as he asked. I searched and searched—I looked everywhere—but I could not find him! I hoped he had come back here as a trick."

I sighed in exasperation. If we delayed much longer, it would be dark before we returned home. Heavy clouds gathered on the horizon, promising a tremendous storm. All the brilliant grace of the day was gone. I was tired and cross and sore from sitting on the ground for so long.

"William! The game is over!" I sounded too annoyed. He would not be lured out by that. With Ernest and Judge Frankenstein at my side, I changed tactics as we fanned out through the trees and looked.

"William! Oh, William! I have a pocket full of candy for the first person who finds me!"

Ernest adopted a similar ploy. Judge Frankenstein merely shouted the boy's name, which was, I supposed, as much as we could ask from a man who had never done anything to care for his own children.

Ernest doubled back to check our picnic place again while Judge Frankenstein and I ranged in larger circles around the area William had last been seen. My voice grew hoarse, and I decided William would be forced to sit in the playroom all the next day with nothing to entertain him.

The sun was at the horizon, rain clouds quickly overtaking it all, when a howl of agony and terror came from behind me.

I ran toward the sound, pushing through clawing trees and branches that barred my path. When I broke through to the meadow that still held our abandoned picnic, I saw Ernest, kneeling on the ground with his head bowed. Before him, laid out on the blanket, was little William, fast asleep.

I did not know how he had beaten us back here and managed to fall asleep, but—

Why had Ernest made that sound?

Why had he not just called for us?

Why was William lying so still?

I stumbled forward. "He is sleeping," I whispered to myself as a charm, willing it to be true. "He is sleeping."

Dark bruises like a collar around his neck, his face peaceful.

I dropped to my knees beside Ernest. He collapsed into me, animal sobs wrenching from his throat. I could not cry, or move, or do anything but stare at little William. He was sleeping, and he would never wake again.

FOURTEEN

WHAT CAN WE SUFFER WORSE?

I COULD NOT SAY how I was pulled from William's side or returned to the house. Once securely back in my room—for death is, and always has been, the occupation of men—I was left alone to my astonished grief. Ernest, only eleven but suddenly a man, and Judge Frankenstein joined the local men to search the forest for William's murderer.

Who would have done such a thing? For what purpose?

Either the murderer had found William after he had wandered back to meet us, before we found him, and killed him there—

Or, a degree worse, if hell has degrees—

Someone choked the breath from his body and then *placed him on the blanket for us to discover.*

I could not cleanse from my mind his ruined neck, the ink-dark bruises that marked his parting from this world. *The end,* they had written in fingerprints across his unblemished skin. But why? Why murder a child? I had been in that meadow, as had Judge Frankenstein, asleep and vulnerable. Why William?

My hand drifted to my throat, and dread sank its terrible claws into my soul.

The necklace.

The child had been wearing a necklace of gold that I, in my impatience to distract and quiet him, had given him.

I would have pretended to question whether it was motivation enough for someone to kill a child, but I knew better. My caregiver on Lake Como certainly would have murdered me if there were any profit to be had in it. I had no doubt. And somewhere out in those woods was someone equally callous, equally uncaring of the value of a life when compared to the value of a bit of gold.

I tasted acid at the back of my throat. I knew exactly such a person. I had stabbed his wrist with my hatpin.

All the times I had felt watched since returning here rushed back as I ran from the sitting room and out to our barn. Two men stood guard, dripping water from the pouring rain. They tried to bar me entrance, but I pushed them aside and ran in.

Judge Frankenstein turned, along with the constable and several men I did not know. They shifted to block my view of William's carefully laid out body. As if I had not already seen it. As if I would ever be able to unsee it.

"I have murdered him!" I cried, the guilt of it a millstone around my neck. This child, whose life I never cared enough about, but whose care had been given to me by his dying mother—he would have been better had he never met me.

"What is the meaning of this, Elizabeth?" Judge Frankenstein said, catching me by the shoulders and shaking me. "You were with me the entire time."

I wished I could slap him. "A necklace! William wore a necklace. A gold locket that opened to reveal a portrait of his mother. I let him wear it. It is my fault."

The men turned and, as respectfully as they could, searched the tiny body. "It is not here," one said.

The constable nodded grimly. "I will send word for them to look where his body was found to make certain it did not fall off. And we will alert every merchant in the area to be watchful for someone trying to sell it."

Judge Frankenstein led me from the barn and back to the house.

"You cannot blame yourself," he said, his voice hollow and without any force.

"I can." I did not care about disagreeing with him. I could not tell him the full truth, though the weight of my guilt threatened to drag me beneath the sodden ground. Because I was certain it had been the charnel house devil. Somehow, he had followed me here. Motivated by greed or revenge, he had murdered that innocent child and taken the gold lure.

But I could not say! I was sealed in most damnable silence! If I gave them a description of the man, I would have to say why I thought it was him. Judge Frankenstein did not know about my trip to Ingolstadt. But I would admit it, if that was all the trouble I would bring down on my own head.

It was Victor I worried about. Always. Because if I led them to the vile charnel house man, they would discover why I had met him. They would follow the connection to Victor. And all my work to protect his reputation would be undone. His madness revealed. His own brilliant future aborted as cruelly as William's young life. And, if he was committed to an asylum, my future aborted, as well.

I could only pray they found the man and killed him before he could talk.

Judge Frankenstein interrupted my thoughts. "You did not murder the boy."

"I might as well have hung a target around his neck. You know the greed of men."

He sighed, hanging his head. I had never thought him an old man, but his years dragged him down and showed in every movement as though the night had robbed him of twenty years of his life. He escorted me to my room, then patted my hand. "I will write to Victor. You need not recount the horror to him. Get dry and try to sleep."

He shuffled away. He tried to close my door quietly, but it hung askew. The wood scraped and groaned against the frame until finally it shut.

And then I realized my punishment was only beginning. Because I had not yet told Justine that her William—her precious charge, whom she loved more than his own mother had—was gone. I could not bear the thought, but the idea that she should find out that she had slept peacefully when her William had been taken away was too awful. She had to be told.

Scarcely able to catch my breath, I went to the servants' wing of the house. There was no answer when I knocked on her door. I eased it open to find her bed made and unslept in. But it was night now, and raining. Where was she?

It was selfish of me, but I was relieved. I had tried to do the right thing. Let her have one last night of peace, one last night of happiness. I stumbled back to the other wing and passed up my room in favor of Victor's. I crawled into his bed, the welcome oblivion of sleep claiming me from the new horrors of my waking life.

I lay, unable to move. One eye was closed, pressed against the dirt. The other rolled wildly, but all it could see was sky between brilliant red leaves. I made a strange, high, keening cry that I could not form into words. I could not speak, could not move, could not see anything other than the uncaring sky and the dying leaves.

Then there was another noise.

A tearing, ripping sound. The horrible grating of metal against something unyielding. A sawing sound in fits and starts, in time with the heavy breathing of some other creature. And then the wet slop of things sliding out and hitting the ground.

That was when I realized:

The noises were coming from me.

Still I could not move, could not scream, could not do anything other than lie frozen, listening to my own dissection.

I would wake up, bathed in cold sweat, my heart racing but my voice silent. I was too afraid to open my mouth, too terrified I would only be able to produce the same dying cry as the deer.

On those nights, I would pad down the hall and slip into Victor's room. He would shift sleepily to the side, holding out an arm and letting me nestle into him. I would feel my stomach, run my hands down my ribs. I was still alive. I was fine. Victor was there, and he would protect me.

When I slept at his side, I never had nightmares.

The sun was nearly at its zenith when I was jarred back to consciousness. I clamped my mouth shut over the strange cry I had been making.

I felt my stomach, desperately ran my hands over my ribs.

I was fine.

I was fine.

I tried to still my breathing, but then the previous day's events crashed down, transitioning the dread and terror of my nightmare into the dread and terror of my reality.

Bleary-eyed and numb with grief, I made my way down to the dining room. I still wore my dress from the day before, my stockings somehow lost in Victor's bed. I had never before entered the dining room barefoot. The floor was cold and hard beneath my feet, gritty with dust and dirt that needed to be swept.

Judge Frankenstein sat at the table, his meal untouched in front of him and his head in his hands. I took my place across from him.

He looked up in surprise. "Elizabeth."

"Do you know where Justine is?" I could barely stand to be in here at all. Not when I needed to finish my most horrible task. "I have not told her yet. I have to tell her. She was not in her room last night."

He frowned. The maid came in to see if I wanted food. I could not imagine wanting anything for my body, ever again.

"Check Justine's room," Judge Frankenstein ordered. "See if she has returned."

The maid curtseyed and left. I wanted to ask Judge Frankenstein if there had been any news. If they had found the charnel house man. But I was certain if anything had happened, he would have mentioned it by now. He would not have been sitting alone at this table.

"Damned girl has been listening to everything," he said, frowning at the door the maid left through. "I should dismiss her. Who knows what tales she will take back to town. Meanwhile, my boy—my baby—" His shoulders shook, and he dropped his face back into his hands.

Though I had long considered him my foe, I saw now only a man who had lost too much over his years. He had already buried the baby born between Victor and Ernest, and his own wife. Now he would have to add to the family plot, when doubtless he had expected his would be the next stone marker.

"Judge Frankenstein, I—"

"Call me Uncle." He lifted his face and wiped his eyes. "Please. I have so little left. My hopes are all on you now."

"Uncle," I said, the word strange and false on my tongue, "May I—"

"My God!" The maid ran back in, breathing fast, her eyes wide with some twisted combination of panic and elation. "Merciful God in heaven, I have discovered the murderer!"

Judge Frankenstein frowned, but when she did not back down, he stood and followed her out of the room. I trailed them, my own heart racing. Had the charnel house man returned for more prizes? When she stopped outside Justine's room, though, I froze in panic and dread. Had he murdered Justine? Was he in there with her now?

"Here," the maid said, rushing inside. Justine, her hems covered with mud and her coat still on, was sprawled across the bed. I wilted with relief, but also with confusion at her state and why the maid had brought us here. I felt her forehead. She had a mild fever, and her hair was damp.

"Look!" the maid pointed in triumph.

Next to Justine on the bed was the glittering gold accusation of guilt.

My necklace.

"How can you believe this? It is absurd!" I was holding Justine's arm, engaged in a tug-of-war with the constable. He kept his eyes on the floor.

"Please, Mademoiselle, she needs to be taken in."

Justine was crying. "I do not understand. Elizabeth, what is happening? What are they saying about my William?"

"You killed my brother!" Ernest was backed up against the far wall, staring in horror and hatred at the woman who loved him best in the whole world. "You killed him!" He collapsed into sniffling sobs. "Why would you do that?"

Justine tried to stumble to him, swaying and nearly falling. The constable used her shift in balance to pull her away from me. Another official I did not know jumped between us.

"She did no such thing!" I shouted, trying to push past the man.

While I was blocked, the constable rushed Justine down the hall. "She cannot account for her whereabouts," he said.

"She is not well! She cannot even stand!" I twisted free and darted after them. "This is absurd! She loved him!"

"William," Justine sobbed, losing her strength and falling to the floor. Her arm was wrenched where the constable had not released his grip. Another officer—where were all these men coming from? Where had they been when William was in danger? Why were there seemingly dozens now, as though Justine were a threat?—grabbed Justine's other arm, and they continued to drag her away.

Someone grabbed my arm, and I turned with my other hand raised, ready to strike.

It was Ernest. I stayed my blow. He was still crying, and I saw a resemblance to Victor in his enraged visage. "She stole the necklace! That is evidence!"

"That is not evidence, you stupid child." I flinched at the hurt that managed to break through on his face. I dropped to my knees and looked up at him. He was a child, but somehow I felt that if he believed in Justine, it would be proof of her innocence. And I knew how badly it would hurt her to hear that Ernest had believed this false and terrible accusation. "She knows I would have given it to her if she had so much as asked! She had no reason to steal it! She lives here. She could have taken anything at any time."

"Then why did she have it?"

"Perhaps the maid was framing her," I snapped. The men had paused in the entry hall, and I stood to give chase, stopping short only when one stepped into my path.

"Why?" Judge Frankenstein asked. "What motivation would the maid have? She loved Justine, as did we all. And she was here all afternoon with the cook. Neither of them had any reason to fear accusation, or a need to deflect blame."

Ernest jumped in, parroting what he had heard from the constable, who was already building a case against Justine. "And why would she spend the night in a farmer's barn not a mile from where William was murdered?"

"She was sick with grief over her mother! Who among us can claim to act rationally when faced with the death of family? Neither of you is!"

Ernest turned his back on me, trembling with anger. "You are defending a *murderess*. She killed my brother. She might have killed me, too."

"Ernest!" Justine called. He ran from the room. Justine's sobbing intensified. "Ernest, please! He is so upset. Where is William? William needs me. Elizabeth, please. Where is William? I will take care of William while you go and help Ernest. Please bring me William. He is fine, I know he is. He has to be."

I shook my head, covering my mouth so I would not cry.

"Elizabeth." Her eyes were wild and feverish. "Please. Help me. Tell me where William is. Tell me why they are saying— Tell me it is not true."

I could only stare at her. I saw the moment the truth finally broke through her haze. The moment she finally grasped that William was beyond her care, forever. The light in her eyes, so frantic, died. She dropped her head and fell to the marble floor.

"Let me help her!" I shouted. Judge Frankenstein took my elbow in a tight grip, and I could only watch as the men lifted Justine and carried her out the door. "Let me help her! She is innocent!"

I turned to my captor, glaring up at him as my tears cooled on my cheeks. "You know she is innocent."

Judge Frankenstein shook his head. "There is evidence both for and against her guilt. We must trust the courts to rule justly and fairly. It is all we can do. If she is innocent, they will discover it. And if she is not . . ." He raised his free hand and then lowered it. It could have been a shrug, but it looked like the motion of the terrible lever that operated the gallows trapdoor. "Then they and God will see to her punishment."

I shoved my arm forward and then ripped it back, breaking his grip. I ran outside, but I was too late. They had already bundled Justine into a boat and were out of my reach.

I needed to get to her. I ran to the dock, but the only boat left was occupied by a man we sometimes hired to row us across. "My apologies," he said, and he did look sorry. "They said not to let you cross right now."

I let out an animal scream, shocking him. Then I ran into the trees. I knew what Justine would want. She would want me to go to Ernest, to take care of him.

What did I care for him? He had believed her guilt with the barest of evidence! How could he? How could any of them!

The trees grabbed at me, twigs and branches like claws. My dress caught repeatedly, and my hair tumbled free. I ran until I reached the hollowed-out willow tree where I had read Henry's last letter to me. How would things have been different if I had not been the cause of Henry's departure? How would things have been different if I had not selfishly gone to Ingolstadt to chase Victor and secure my own stability?

I curled up in the tree, burning with hatred and guilt and secrets. Judge Frankenstein had said the truth would come out. But how could it, when I had worked so hard to obscure it?

I awoke with a start. I scrambled free from the tree, pushing against its confines. How had I fallen asleep? The night—for day had passed me unaware—was hungry and vicious, another storm punishing the land for our failure to protect the innocent.

Lightning lit my way and rain lashed my face. I ran toward where I thought the house was, all sense of direction scrambled in my disorientation. I stumbled and fell. My hands and knees slammed into the ground. I let my head hang heavy. I had brought all this down on us. And then I had fallen asleep, while my Justine was somewhere in a cell! I had to get to her. I could not help William now, but I could help Justine. I had to fix this somehow, because one truth remained: if I did not, no one would.

Lightning flashed. Thunder rumbled. I lifted my head.

"Damn you!" I shouted at the skies. "Damn you for watching and never helping! I curse you! I curse you for ever creating man, only to let him destroy the most innocent among us, over and over and over again!"

Movement drew my attention and I whipped around, certain it was Judge Frankenstein and that he had heard my blasphemy. I lifted my chin, defiant.

But the figure blacker than the night was not my benefactor. I lunged toward him. It was the charnel house man. I would kill him myself, keeping Victor's secrets, avenging William, and freeing Justine!

Some animal instinct halted my violent intent, and I froze.

It was not the weasel of a man I had encountered in Ingolstadt.

I dreaded another flash of lightning for what it might reveal of the person in the trees watching me. He stood at least seven feet tall, a hulking and unnatural creature. Fear drained my fury.

"What are you?" I demanded. I had seen it before. Was it a manifestation of my guilt? My own wickedness, formed by my mind and projected outward? *Was* it the charnel house man, swollen to devilish proportions by his evil?

And then, in a flash of purest white, the monster was revealed. This was no creature of my mind's making. No creature of God's making, either. Neither my mind nor God's could have conceived of such a perversion of humanity.

I screamed and turned to run. My foot caught on a root and I tripped, hitting my head on a rock.

Blackness claimed me.

FIFTEEN

LOVE OR HATE, TO ME ALIKE

I SMILED AS I awoke, lured from my depths of slumber by the scent I found most comforting in the world: ink and book leather and the dust of parchment.

"Victor?" I asked, starting to sit up.

It was a mistake. Pain roiled through me. My stomach swam, and I froze, lest moving again create a new wash of agony.

Why did my head hurt so? What had—

William.

Justine.

And the monster.

"Victor?" I whispered.

"I am here."

I heard a heavy tome close. I peeled my eyes open to see Victor looming over me, concern narrowing his features and drawing his eyebrows close to each other. "We keep reuniting over sickbeds. I think it is a tradition best ended now."

"When did you—"

"Two nights ago. We have had this conversation already." He took up my wrist to feel my pulse, then placed the back of his hand against my cheek. "Three times."

I lifted my hand to touch my forehead, but he caught it and held it in his own. "You have a large bruise and a small cut, which, fortunately, I was able to stitch up myself. It should be easy to hide beneath your hair. What possessed you to go running in the woods in the midst of a tempest?"

"Justine." I tried again to sit up. Victor sighed in exasperation, but propped pillows behind me and helped me get upright. When I had been still long enough for the pain to subside into manageable amounts again, I pushed on. "Ernest thinks her guilty, and your father will not intervene! But now you are here." I closed my eyes in relief.

Victor was here. He would fix this.

"The evidence is quite damning." But I could hear in his voice that he did not think her guilty.

"It is entirely circumstantial! She spent the night in a stable to take refuge from the storm."

"And the necklace?"

I looked up at him without a smile. "You and I both know how easy it is to place an object in a convenient location to shift blame onto an innocent party."

Rather than being offended, Victor gave me a rueful smile. "That was playing. We were children. And who could want to harm Justine? You told me yourself she is an angel on earth. Does she have any enemies?"

"No! None. The only person who bore her ill will was her own mother, a wicked harpy of a woman who died last week."

"Well, that certainly removes suspicion from her, then."

"Victor!" I snapped.

He looked mildly abashed. "I am sorry. I know it is a terrible time.

But I cannot deny I am happy to be reunited with you. Even under such circumstances."

I sighed and closed my eyes again, bringing his hand to my lips and kissing his palm. "There is . . . something I have not told you."

"What?"

"In Ingolstadt. I visited some addresses I found in your—" I caught myself. I had pretended I had seen nothing of his laboratory. Hopefully he had been so delirious at the time, he would believe my next lie. "I found on a paper on your table. One of the addresses was a charnel house. The man there—"

"Dear God, you went there?" Victor finally sounded horrified. "Why would you do that?"

"He was awful! And he said you owe him money. He tried to grab me. I stabbed his wrist with my hatpin. Is it possible he followed me here, saw the golden necklace on William, and—"

Victor interrupted. "He was still in Ingolstadt when I left."

"How can you be sure?"

Victor leaned over me, peeling back my eyelids to examine my eyes. "Your pupils are returning to normal. That is good. I know he was there because he was part of the debts I had to settle. I told you as much before you left. So he was not here, *and* I do not owe him anything."

I did not know whether to be relieved that I had not drawn the murderer here, or upset that I could not produce a suspect other than Justine.

Victor put his finger on my chin, tilting my head down so he could check the wound. "Now, tell me what happened in the forest. Why were you out there? What caused your fall?"

I sighed, wishing I were still asleep. "I ran out because I was upset with your father and Ernest for not defending Justine. And I did not want to mention the charnel house man as a suspect until I had spoken with you about him."

"I am glad you waited. It would only have distracted from the investigation."

I nodded, then instantly regretted the motion. Sparks danced in my vision, reminding me of the lightning. "I did not mean to stay out there. But I fell asleep, and when I awoke, the storm was in full force. I was running home when I saw someone. Some . . . thing."

His hand twitched, and I opened my eyes to see him staring at me with wide-eyed intensity. "What did you see?"

"You will think me mad."

"I have known madness, Elizabeth. I see none of it in you. Tell me."

"I saw a monster. Like a man in form and shape, but no man created by God. It was as though a child had crafted a figure out of clay—disproportionate, too large, unnatural in both shape and movement. I cannot describe it except to say it was *wrong*. And I do not believe it is the first time I have seen it."

"A monster," he repeated. He spoke slowly, his words perfectly even, like the ticking of a clock. "You hit your head *very* hard."

I scowled at him. "After I saw it! And now I am certain I saw it watching me in Ingolstadt, and again on the journey home."

"And you said nothing?"

"I thought it a dream." If the charnel house man had never been here, then it was some other presence I felt, some other nagging sense of having been watched since Ingolstadt.

"Does it not make more sense that it is still a dream? A product of your injury and your extreme upset? Maybe inspired by something you might have seen—an image? Or a nightmare?" He spoke carefully. He was holding something back from me. I could see it in the way he seemed to look everywhere but into my eyes.

"I am not the one who falls delirious into fevers! I have never dreamed anything like this. How would I have even conjured such a . . ." I paused. I had not had time to connect the two, but now that I could separate myself from the sheer panic and terror of being in front of the thing, I realized I *had* seen something like it before.

A drawing.

In Victor's notebook.

Did he know I had seen his notes? Was that why he had suggested that the product of my injured mind had been inspired by an image?

Or was there some other reason he was being evasive? "When you were sick, when I found you," I said, hesitant, as I sorted through what I wanted to reveal and what I wanted to hold back, "you said 'It worked.' Your experiment worked. What was it?"

Victor's face briefly contorted in rage. I flinched and he turned his back, picking up a book and then setting it down. When he finally spoke, his voice was so measured and calm I could hear every hour I had spent teaching him to control himself. "It does not matter. Whatever I said, I was out of my mind. Nothing I did in Ingolstadt was successful."

I did not want to push. I did not want to risk one of his fits when he was so newly restored to me. But I could not let this stand, not when Justine was threatened. "Are you certain? Sometimes when you have your fevers, you forget things. Things that happen just before you fall ill. Things that happen before you are confined to your bed. Is it possible that—"

Victor set the book down with a sigh. "I want you to rest. I believe you that Justine is innocent. I will investigate this and haunt the courts until they free her. Her trial began this morning. Now that you are awake, I will return to it."

"This morning!" I pushed up, but my head swam. I could not stand, as the room swayed around me. Victor gently but firmly guided me back down to the bed.

"You are in no state to attend. You could injure yourself further."

"But I must testify on her behalf."

He sat at the desk and pulled out a quill, dipping it in my inkwell. "Tell me what you wish to say, and I will present it as character evidence."

It would be better if I were there in person. I could picture exactly how I would look testifying: My golden hair like a halo around my head. I would wear white. I would cry and smile at exactly the right times. No one would be able to doubt me.

But if I went as I was now, I would look crazed. Victor was right. I could not help her in this state.

So I poured out my heart for the letter. Justine was the kindest friend, the truest person. She had loved William as her own child from the moment she met him. Never had a governess cared so much about her charges or taken such delight in nurturing them. After the death of Madame Frankenstein, Justine had stepped into her place and provided William with the most compassionate surrogate imaginable.

"Oh, Victor," I said, sadness competing with pain. "We have not even spoken of William yet. I am so sorry."

He finished the letter and then carefully blotted the quill and set it down. "I am sorry he is dead. It is a waste, losing him so young. But it feels more like something that happened to someone else. I barely knew him." He turned, searching my face for either my response or a clue to how his own should be shaped. "Is that wrong?"

I had guided him so much in how to react to things, how to shape his expressions, how to be sympathetic. But I had nothing to offer him now. "There is no wrong way to feel after something so violent and terrible," I said. Of course Justine had been insensible. It was overwhelming, and so strong and big a feeling that it felt . . . unreal, in a way.

"Death touches us all in different ways," I said finally. I closed my eyes, my head already aching so badly that I longed to fall back asleep. Victor was probably right. Perhaps a combination of the storm, my upset, and the blow to my head had lifted Victor's gruesome drawing out of my memory and placed it, in terrifying size, in my mind. I had, after all, been plagued by nightmares my whole life.

Though I had never before seen those nightmares while awake.

"Death is never allowed to touch you." Victor traced his fingers along the spill of my hair across the pillow, and then walked from the room.

Most nights, when the children around me had fallen asleep, all scabbed knees and biting teeth and freezing feet, I slipped out of the hovel and crept to the banks of Lake Como.

I had made myself a burrow there, in a depression beneath the overhanging roots of a massive tree. When I climbed inside and curled into a ball, no one could find me. No one ever tried to, of course. If I had stayed there and never come out, my passing from the world would have gone unnoticed.

Some nights, when even my child's heart knew that what I had been asked to endure was too much, I would stand on the edge of the lake, lift my face to the stars, and scream.

Nothing ever called back. Even among the creeping things of the lake's night, I was alone.

Until Victor.

The next morning I awoke early, ready to go to the trial. Victor had returned with a mixed report. The evidence remained circumstantial, but public opinion was against Justine. Testimony of her mother's violent madness had been offered. It provided a family history that painted Justine in a bad light, competing with my character witness.

"What is your father's opinion?" I had asked Victor.

"He insists the law will make it right. I think he is too overwhelmed by William's death and the potential of Justine's betrayal to commit himself to either side."

I was not too overwhelmed. I would stand in front of them all—judge, jury, damnable townsfolk—and force them to see that Justine was incapable of such an act. If only I had a suspect to present to them, other than my nightmare monster. I wished it were real, that I would find some evidence of it.

What bleak and dark days, that my hope was in favor of a monster existing!

I opened my door to find Victor with his hand raised, ready to knock. "I am ready," I said. My head still hurt fiercely, but I could walk without losing my balance. My pale countenance would only amplify the blush of my cheeks and the blue of my eyes. I would be perfect testifying. "Take me to the trial."

Victor's countenance was heavy, his eyes mournful. "It is over."

"Why? They cannot have made their decision already!"

"They did not have to. Justine confessed."

I staggered backward. "What?"

"Last night. She confessed to the murder. They are hanging her tomorrow."

"No! That cannot be. She is not guilty. I *know* she is not."

Victor nodded. My voice was rising in tone and intensity, but his remained calm and steady. "I believe you. But there is nothing we can do now."

"We can talk to her! Make her retract it!"

"I already spoke to my father. The courts would not accept a retraction at this point. Once a confession is made, it is taken as irrefutable proof."

A sob ripped from my chest, and I threw myself into Victor's arms. I had only pictured having to fight to get her name cleared. I had not imagined *this*. "I cannot lose her," I said. "Why would she confess? I must go see her. Right now."

Victor went with me, helping me into the boat. The ride across the lake was miserable, increasing the pain in my head with every dip and wave. As we hurried through Geneva, I was certain each window contained the face of someone who wanted to see Justine pay for a crime she never could have committed. I wanted to throw rocks through all the glass. Tear out their window boxes of lying, bright flowers. I wanted to burn the whole city to the ground. How could they not see her innocence?

And how could she claim guilt?

When we finally reached her prison cell, I found her in mean condition. She wore black clothes of mourning, and her chestnut hair, always so carefully pinned, was tangled around her shoulders. She was curled on a bed of straw, her ankles and wrists manacled to long chains.

"Justine!" I cried.

She rose immediately, throwing herself at my feet. I dropped to my knees on the cold stone floor, pulling her to me. I stroked her hair, my fingers catching in the snarls. "Justine, why? Why did you confess?"

"I am sorry. I knew how much it would hurt you, and I am sorriest of all for that. But I had to."

"*Why?*"

"The confessor—he was here whenever I was not in the court, hounding me, screaming, shouting the same things my mother said. And I had no one here for me. I began, in my despair, to fear that my mother had always been right. That I was a devilish girl, that I was damned. The confessor told me that if I did not admit my crime I would be excommunicated, that hell would claim my soul forever! He told me my only hope was to be right by God. So I confessed. And it was a lie, which is the only sin I have to weigh on me. To avoid damnation, I have committed the only crime of my life. Oh, Elizabeth. Elizabeth, I am sorry." She wept, and I held her.

"Victor," I said, looking up at him. "Surely the confession cannot stand."

He had his back turned to give us privacy. He did not turn around, but his voice was quiet. "I am sorry. There is nothing that can be done."

"I will fight them, then! I will do whatever it takes! I will not let them hang you. Do you hear me, Justine?"

She calmed some and lifted her face. It was lined with tears, but her eyes were clear and lucid. "I do not fear to die. I do not want to live in a world where devils can take such perfect, beautiful innocence without punishment. I think I prefer it this way—to go on to my sweet little William so that he is not alone."

The absurdity of her acceptance rankled my soul. She had been so convinced of her wickedness by her cruel and depraved mother that she would let a man convince her to confess false guilt simply for the sake of some invisible soul's well-being!

I would lose my Justine *for nothing.* Would lose the one person I had tried to save in the midst of a life spent selfishly trying to make certain I stayed safe myself. The one person I loved because she made me happy, rather than because my security depended on her. And she was going to die because I had decided to help her that day in the streets of Geneva.

"I cannot live in this world of misery," I said, the words harsh as they ripped from my throat.

"No!" Justine took my cheeks between her hands, the cold iron of her manacles brushing my jaw. "Dearest Elizabeth. My beloved. My only friend. Live, and be happy. Honor me that way. Remember me by having the life I dreamed of for you, the life you deserve."

I deserved no such thing.

"We must go." Victor nodded to the waiting guard.

"No," I growled.

"Go." Justine stepped away from me, smiling. A ray of light from the window beamed down and lit her from behind as the angel I had always known her to be. "I am not afraid. Please do not come tomorrow. I do not want you to see it. Promise me."

"I promise you that I will prevent it. I will stop this."

Justine trembled. "Please, this is all I ask of you. Please promise me you will not be at the scaffold."

"It will not come to that." I would not say it; I could not say it. If I agreed, I was agreeing that it would happen. And that I could never do. But the hurt and need were so raw on Justine's face that I could not deny her.

"I promise," I whispered.

"Thank you. You saved me." She smiled, and I watched her over my shoulder as the guard escorted Victor and me out. Finally we turned a corner and my angel was lost to view.

The judge would not see me.

Judge Frankenstein would not intervene.

My agitation was such that, the next morning, the Frankensteins rowed across the lake with both the boats so that I could not possibly get to the city and enact some "regrettable" course of action. Victor tried to stay behind, but I shouted at him to go if he could not save her. If they could not save her, they should have to bear witness.

* * *

I was alone.

I wandered to the edge of the lake and collapsed to my knees. Then I lifted my face to the heavens and screamed. I screamed my rage, and my despair, and my intolerable solitude.

Somewhere nearby, a creature answered my call. I was not alone. The other cry contained the soul-deep sense of loss I could scarcely breathe around.

I curled into a ball around myself and wept until my senses left me.

SIXTEEN

SO FAREWELL HOPE

I LOST A WEEK to the madness of grief. I would see or speak to no one. I hated them all for being alive while Justine was dead. For being men and being unable to save her.

William's death was a tragedy.

Justine's was a travesty.

When I finally came down from my room with enough strength to at least pretend not to hate everyone in the house, I found Ernest packing.

"Where are you going?" I asked, though I could not actually care.

"School in Paris. Father thinks it best I leave for a while." His lip quivered as he struggled for bravery. He had lost so much in his young life—his mother, his baby brother, and now the governess he had loved and trusted. I wished I could comfort him by insisting on her innocence once again, but would that have helped? He could either rage at the presumed betrayal by someone he trusted or despair at the betrayal of the entire world in failing to protect her in her innocence.

It was easier to rage than to despair.

"Where is Victor?"

"I do not care," Ernest snapped, tears filling his eyes. Had I been like Justine, I would have rushed to him. Taken him in my arms and comforted him as a mother.

Had I been like Justine, would I, too, be dead?

I drifted away to leave Ernest to find his own path through grief. I certainly could not guide him, as my own grief trailed in my wake, threatening to rise and strangle me.

I found Victor in his bedroom. He was pacing, muttering to himself. Before he noticed me, he opened and shut and threw several books. He was agitated, his eyes rimmed in red and accented by dark circles.

"Victor?" I said.

He turned, jumping as though expecting attack.

"Elizabeth." With a deep breath, he closed his eyes and attempted to release some of the tension I could still see throughout his body. He trembled, shaking out his hands. Then he opened his eyes and really looked at me. "I am sorry."

We had not spoken since Justine's execution. "I know." And I did know. He alone remained steadfastly on my side, believing me about Justine's innocence though he barely knew her. "Will you come with me today, to visit her grave?"

He flinched. "There is no grave."

"What?"

"I offered them money. But she died a condemned murderess. They would not bury her in hallowed ground."

My heart broke anew. I knew what such a thing would mean to Justine. She had lived in a constant effort to be right before God. She had even died because of it. "What did they do with the body?"

"It was burned. They would not give me the ashes."

I closed my eyes and nodded, dropping this injustice into the sea of horrors already drowning me.

"I have been thinking," he said. Then he ran his fingers through his hair. His eyes darted constantly to his window, either looking for something outside or yearning to be there himself. "But I cannot think here, in this house. I am going for a walk through the mountains. I may be gone a day or two. Please do not worry. I hope, in the majesty of their embrace, to find some clarity."

I wanted him here to comfort me, but I did not know how to be comforted. So I nodded and let him pass by. He carried a leather satchel.

He did not smell like ink and paper.

Later that afternoon, I prowled around the exterior of the house, glaring up at it. I had offered this place to Justine as a sanctuary. It had betrayed her.

I had betrayed her.

A spray of violets was growing beneath Victor's window. Justine had always loved violets. I stomped through the other plantings to get to them. Whether to tear them up or to admire them, I had not decided. But I paused when something caught my eye. Beneath Victor's window were footprints. I slipped my own booted foot down into the depression in the mud.

The foot was easily twice the size of mine, larger than any I had seen before. There were no impressions of shoes or boots, but neither were there toes. I would have thought something had been dropped there, but the placement was exactly as though someone had been standing beneath his window, looking in as I was now.

They were footprints, but too large. Too large by far.

Monstrous.

I rushed back inside. Judge Frankenstein was wandering through the first floor. His shirttails were untucked, and his hair was sticking up on the back of his head. "Have you seen my pistol?" he asked. "I wanted to go shooting, and I cannot find it anywhere."

Victor. The satchel he had carried with him out of the house.

A growing anxiety gripped me with viselike intensity. I had *not* imagined the monster in the woods. And Victor had seen it, too. He did not say—he could not say! But if the monster had been here . . .

William.

No wonder Victor had been so certain of Justine's innocence! I hated and pitied him in equal measure. I had hidden my own suspicions to avoid revealing secrets. And *my* suspicions were of an actual man. Who could stand before a judge and jury and claim a monster murdered the child? Of course he could not speak the truth. Even knowing his genius as I did, I, too, had thought Victor mad upon seeing his notes. I had burned down a building to keep the world from judging him.

And if I felt guilt, I could not imagine how he must have felt. Because if I was right, if there was a monster, I knew its origin. Why it had found us here. Why it had hurt us, of all the people in the world.

Had it been following me this whole time? I remembered the thing in the chute as I burned the building. The open door. I had nearly killed it then; I was certain of it. Would to God I had been successful!

How it had found me at the boardinghouse, I could not—

The card! I had made cards of my address at the boardinghouse. One had fallen out on the doorway of Victor's laboratory, and in my haste I had not picked it up. Could a beast read, when so many men could not? If it could, I had led the monster right to me.

And then it had followed me back here.

Victor might have created it, but I had brought it to our home. And now Victor had gone away, alone, into the mountains. With a pistol. He was trying to end this, to protect us all. But I had seen the monster. Victor was no match for it.

I would lose my Victor, too. It was more than I could bear. I grabbed a cloak—Mary's, another reminder of Ingolstadt and all the tragedy it had rained down upon our heads—took the sharpest knife from the kitchen, and rushed to the path that led from our home to the mountain trails.

I did not pause to question myself. I knew I could still be wrong. Prayed for it, even. Prayed I would find Victor alone in the mountains. That my head injury was leading me to absurd and even laughable conclusions. That, in my desire for revenge, I was making a monster where only an unknown man had acted.

I did not care. I would not risk it.

The monster—if it existed—would never take a loved one from me again.

It was bitingly cold in spite of the summer sun. The farther into the mountains we went, the closer we grew to the glacial plains. Huge sheets of ice covered miles, ancient and so compacted that the cracks shone deepest blue. The terrain was treacherous and slick, capable of claiming unwary hikers. Victor and I had been forbidden to venture this far when we were children.

But we were no longer children. I was drawing near to fifteen, Victor and Henry almost seventeen. Justine, with us a month now, had turned seventeen the day before. Though she had tried to keep her birthday quiet, I would not hear of spending the whole week as we always did. After pleading with Madame Frankenstein, I received permission for a special day trip to the glaciers.

We rose before dawn, setting out a company of four friends. Henry and Justine got along well. Though Justine was quiet and shy, Henry's ease with happy conversation drew her out until they were laughing.

I considered their dynamic with appraising thoughtfulness, always with an eye on the future.

Victor walked fast and steady, as though the day trip were something to be accomplished rather than enjoyed. I laughed at him, taking his hand and skipping merrily beside him until he shook his head in exasperation. But I had managed to tease a smile from him, and his manner lightened.

The journey through the valleys to the glaciers took all morning and into the afternoon. We stopped frequently to admire pretty cascades, to nibble some of the food we had packed, or to rest. The day was as beautiful as any I had lived. The blue of the sky, the deeper blue of the glaciers, the sheer size of the mountains and scope of their majesty, allowed me, too, to step outside my constant worry and simply be. *I truly understood for the first time the meaning of the word* sublime.

Though we were supposed to return home by evening, we lingered, everyone loath to abandon the fun and freedom of our excursion.

It was a mistake. The light left faster than we had anticipated, and watching it go, we knew we could not navigate the treacherous glacial plain in the dark.

"There!" Justine pointed. A dark shape slumped against the white of the plain. We crossed to it, slipping and sliding. Though we should have been worried, we could not quite manage it. I felt safe with Victor and Henry and Justine. I knew we would be fine.

The shape turned out to be an old shack, the purpose of which we could not guess. But inside was a dusty pile of wood and a dented stove. Delighted with our stroke of luck—providence, as Justine declared it—we settled in for the night.

None of us slept. We sat, shoulder to shoulder, our legs stretched out across the floor nearly touching the opposite wall. Justine was to my left, Victor to my right, Henry to his. I was in the middle of the three people I loved best.

The only three people I loved at all, if I was being honest.

The night was cold and long and still somehow the brightest and warmest I had ever spent.

In the morning we stumbled down from the mountain, hungry and giddy with lack of sleep, laughing over our misadventure. It had been a day without fear, a day without study. A day without pretending. I would carry that day in my heart, locked up tightly where nothing else could touch it.

As the afternoon slowly faded, I despaired of catching up to Victor on the mountain. I hated to come up here alone on such a bleak and terrifying mission. All my happy memories of the day we had spent hiking were being replaced by cold dread and seething anger.

Hours passed and I found not so much as a footprint. I was about to turn back, when far ahead, on the glacier, I saw a figure moving faster than should have been possible across that deadly terrain. I ducked behind a massive boulder lodged in the ice. My heart raced. I was torn between screaming and laughing. I struggled to contain my delirious emotions.

It was the monster.

There was no other explanation. And though my soul curdled at the thought of such a creature existing, it also meant I had not been hallucinating, and that Justine was beyond a doubt innocent. Because there was no question in me that that thing, that unholy creation, was what had killed William.

I clutched my knife—and then all my exultant triumph at being right crashed around me like ice falling from the eaves of a house. If the monster could move like that here—and was as tall and powerful as I had seen it to be—what did I hope to accomplish with my kitchen knife?

My zeal to protect Victor had not been accompanied by a similar portion of sense. I should have told his father. Should have raised the alarm in the city, gathered a militia with swords and torches. Even a pitchfork would have been a better weapon than my sad little knife.

I peered around and watched as the monster drew closer and then stopped. In spite of the speed of its movement, there was something awkward and ungainly about it. Its feet did not bend as they should. It ran on the pads of its feet, like an animal. The knee joints were too high, the femurs too short. The arms, too, did not move naturally with the body, remaining still at its sides as the legs did all the work.

I shuddered to think what the monster would look like up close in the daylight—what seeing it in full truth would reveal. How could Victor have created such a thing? How deep must he have been in his own tortured mind to ever conceive of it?

As though summoned by my thoughts of him, Victor approached the monster. It waited in place for him, letting Victor struggle across the ice. I wanted to jump out. To shout for Victor to shoot from that distance. But he was wiser than I. Pistols were good only at short range, accuracy and power traded for convenience and stealth.

I trembled, waiting for the monster to attack. Wondering how I would help when it did.

Instead, it remained motionless as Victor walked up to it. Victor shouted, his words muted into unintelligibility by the wind. I could see him screaming, raging at the monster. Why did he not just shoot it?

But . . . what good would a bullet do against the sheer bulk of the thing? Even wounded, it would be more than a match for Victor. He was no smarter than I, with my knife. Apparently Victor had reached the same hopeless verdict. His shouting subsided, and he shifted, turning away from the monster. Doubtless he could not bear to look at it.

After several minutes of this—Victor appeared to twitch occasionally, to nod or shake his head as though they were in conversation—Victor's shoulders slumped. He rubbed his face, running his hands through his dark curls. Then he pointed away from himself, back up the mountain, and hung his head.

The monster . . . left.

It turned and loped away, straight up the icy plain, covering in mere minutes a distance that would have taken me an hour.

His shoulders still lowered, Victor began the long, slow walk back toward the house. What had I just witnessed? What had transpired between man and monster?

Whatever it was, I was certain Victor had not won.

I did not try to beat Victor down the mountain. Trusting that he would not check my room that night, I gave him a large head start and then followed. My entire frame trembled with cold and exhaustion. But my brain burned with questions. In the morning, I would confront Victor.

I would have the truth.

All our lives, I had never pushed him to give me a full story. I had let him maintain his dignity, let him dwell in the gift of my grace. But I could not do that this time. Not after what I had seen. In order to protect him, I had to know the truth of all things.

Whatever power this monster had over him, I would discover it so I could break it and free Victor.

And then I would kill the creature.

I collapsed into my bed just before dawn, as physically tired as I had ever been in my life. When I awoke that afternoon, I dressed in all white. It was my uniform. My costume, as Victor's Elizabeth. I wanted to remind him who I was—that I was his, that I had always been his, and that he could trust me with whatever terrible secrets he sought to protect me from.

When I went down to the dining room, I found only Judge Frankenstein.

"Where is Victor?" I asked.

He looked up from his papers. I recognized some of the sheets from

Monsieur Clerval. Judge Frankenstein slid them beneath a leather book. "He asked me to give this to you." He passed me a sealed letter in Victor's cramped and efficient handwriting.

I opened the letter and then sat in the chair, wounded and shocked.

Victor was gone.

PART THREE

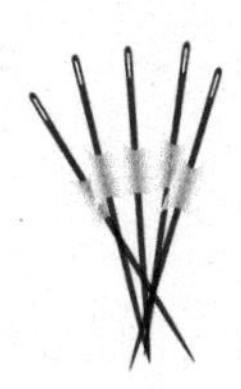

LONG IS THE WAY
AND HARD,
THAT OUT
OF HELL LEADS
UP TO LIGHT

SEVENTEEN

WHICH WAY SHALL I FLY

I STEPPED OFF THE boat, the passage along the coast of England up to Scotland as rough and wild as the night around us. The wind tore at my long black veil as though demanding I reveal myself and my intentions.

I tucked it more firmly in place.

"Madame? Your trunk is here. Shall I call a carriage?" asked a tiny, stooped porter.

"Yes, thank you." I waited, hands clasped primly in front of my black dress. A carriage rumbled close. My trunk was loaded, and I settled into the back.

"Where to, Madame?" the porter asked as he closed the door.

"Inverness," I replied.

"So far? Would you not rather spend the night and leave in the morning?"

"I do not like being questioned." My voice was as cold as the late Scottish spring.

The porter nodded, chastised, and passed along my instructions. I was on my way. And it had all been so much easier than I thought.

My Dearest Elizabeth,

I am sorry to leave you so soon after being reunited. I would not do it under any other circumstance, but there is a complication from my past that compels me to resolve it.

I go to England, where I will work. I also hope to find Henry. As Henry is still retrievable, I shall do all in my power to retrieve him for you. I hate him; I always shall. But perhaps I was wrong to banish him from our lives.

When my business is finally resolved, I will return to you, I hope triumphant in all things. And then our life together can truly begin as it was always meant to.

With all the affection of my soul,
Victor Frankenstein

"Foolish boy," I muttered, resting my head against the hard wooden back of the carriage. I took out my notebook and replaced his letter. Next to it, I had the rest of the letters that had arrived before I left. And I had made notes of all I knew and suspected.

Victor had, in some combination of genius and madness, created a monster from body parts of dead things.

That monster had followed me to our home for revenge.

It killed William.

It implicated Justine.

It somehow threatened Victor such that he immediately fled.

I could only assume that I had been the subject of the threat. The monster had had ample opportunity to kill me or to create mischief that would lead to my destruction. And yet, though I had even come face to face with it in the forest, it had never touched me. This meant it was capable of higher levels of thought. Of planning. Of subtle machinations for revenge.

And it clearly still wanted something from Victor. What better way to convince Victor to do its bidding than to demonstrate its ability to destroy anyone at any time, and then threaten to do it to me should Victor not answer its horrible demands?

Noble Victor!

Stupid Victor.

Running here to lead the monster away from me. Where he would once again be alone and un–looked after, subject not only to the monsters in his mind but also to the monster hunting him! He thought he was protecting me, but he was the one in need of protection.

The carriage passed the grimy buildings clinging to life at the docks. People moved through the dark. Some furtively, advertising their fear. Some aggressively, stalking the night as predators. And some aimlessly, anonymous and vulnerable in the dark. A monster could walk among them and they would never know. Just as I could button myself into the clothes of a widow and suddenly be free to move invisibly through society.

It took more than that, of course. I had sold every gift the Frankensteins had ever given me, and several things that probably were not mine to sell, as well. By the time Judge Frankenstein realized I was planning something, I was already gone.

What wrath I would return to, I knew not, nor did I care. He was not my concern. Victor was the only person left whom I loved. I would not let the monster take him.

In my trunk I had my funds, my own set of pistols, and my widow's clothing. I knew the monster feared fire—it had fled the burning building. I would find Victor, and then we would devise a trap to burn the hellish thing from this earth.

I reread the next letter, though I knew them all by heart now.

My Dearest Elizabeth,

London is a dreary town, and I loathe its smoke-choked buildings and refuse-choked streets. Henry was here but has since moved north to Glasgow. Probably to wander the highlands, spouting poetry and crying. I would express how pointless I think it all, but doubtless you, knowing my heart, can anticipate and imitate what I would write. I will save the ink.

My own business still weighs heavily on me. I find London too crowded, too teeming with wretched life to focus. I will follow Henry to Scotland and there, I hope, discharge both my responsibilities to myself and to him to satisfactory conclusions.

With all the affection of my soul,
Victor Frankenstein

We stopped only to refresh the horses. My surly driver—in English I could barely understand despite my extensive study of the language—insisted he did not usually conduct women places in the middle of the night. I promised him more than generous compensation, which notably improved his mood.

We made good time. The countryside here, lit by the light of the moon, was all gentle hills. I missed the security of mountains, the solid and jagged definition of the horizon. Here, the hills rolled on until darkness- or distance-obscured. I felt exposed and unprotected. Perhaps that explained the military aggression of this tiny island country: they could never feel the edges of their land, so they pushed forever outward.

I had lost so much time preparing to chase Victor. The bulk of my journey here—down rivers and across the continent until I found a boat to take me up the coast to Scotland—had taken a fortnight. A fortnight agonizing and waiting, poring over my journal entries, reviewing what I knew and what I suspected. Never writing what I feared most, lest committing it to paper would make it come true.

The final letter I had received—and I prayed none had come since I left—guided my course.

My Dearest Elizabeth,

I write with bad news. I have found Henry in Inverness. I scarcely recognized him.

We will not be reconciled in this life. I have turned my back on him forever. I am sorry. I could have, perhaps, made more of an effort for your sake. I have taken a cottage nearby so that I can finish my own work.

It is cold and dark, the wind eternal and wretched, but for you, I would endure anything. I feel as if you are with me, by my side. My time here is agony. I am haunted by past failures. They whisper to me at night and plague my dreams. I will not fail again. I will protect you always.

With all the affection of my soul,
Victor Frankenstein

I arrived in Inverness sometime before dawn, too early to venture out. A cozy private room was secured by waking an angry innkeeper, and I sat by the fire, relieved to be behind stone walls but still feeling the motion of carriages and boats.

The flames illuminated Victor's words as I again studied the three letters that had found me before I left. I had already delayed so long! I prayed I was in the right place. And I prayed my courage would not falter. I would find Victor the next day, and feared and hoped—in equal measure—that doing so meant I would find the monster, as well.

EIGHTEEN

HIS DARK MATERIALS TO CREATE MORE WORLDS

I BRIEFLY CONSIDERED LOOKING for Henry, too, but he was under no threat from the monster. That was one benefit to his estrangement from us: the monster had no reason to find him, no purpose in targeting him. I hoped dearly that someday Henry would reconcile with us. But for now he was safe, and that was enough for me. And he was also blissfully unaware of Justine's death. I envied him that.

Did I, though? Would I prefer to know she was gone from the earth, or to go on under the false belief that she was well?

I thought I would rather believe her well than know the truth. But I had no such luxury.

Thus it was that my first stop was the local post office. It was a charming stone building in the shadows of Inverness Castle. If I had been on holiday, I would have been delighted by my surroundings and taken the morning to stroll and discover. The buildings here were nearly all dark stone and thatched roof. In place of Geneva's carefully cultivated gardens, their yards were wild and creeping riots of plants.

But I was not on holiday and did not so much as let my eyes linger on the castle. The postmaster was already awake and sorting through his parcels when I walked in.

"Can I help you—" He paused, peering to try to pierce my veil to ascertain my age. Unable to do so, he added, "Madame?"

"I have had a letter from my cousin, Victor Frankenstein, that gives Inverness as his most recent address. I am afraid I have terrible news, the type which is best delivered in person. Can you tell me where I might find him?"

He scratched his head beneath his cap. "Well, that *is* a funny thing. I was just now gathering all Mr. Frankenstein's letters to have them sent along."

My heart and spirits leapt. He was here, then!

"Give me the address, and I will deliver them myself," I said, trying to sound both friendly and forceful at once. I even held out my hand in expectation.

"That will be a bit of a challenge." He gave me a gap-toothed grin. "Mr. Frankenstein has moved along to the Orkney Islands, which are a day away by horse—if you have a good horse—and almost as long by boat."

I swayed, my travel-weariness crashing back down after the cruel and taunting surge of hope.

The kind postmaster must have sensed my upset. "But as I was saying, I was about to send them along. By boat. My brother has business near the Orkneys and was going to deliver them in the course of his day. I am certain he could be persuaded to take a passenger along with the parcels."

"Oh, thank you!" I clasped my hands in front of me and bowed my head. "I have come so far with such terrible weight, and I fret with every minute lost."

He patted my shoulder with what I assumed was paternal kindness. I had never received such a thing, and it filled me with the oddest sense of sadness over what I had missed. "There, there. We will get you to your cousin before nightfall. I can ask George to travel straight there and drop the rest of the parcels off on the way back instead."

Full of emotions that defied categorization, I threw my arms around his neck. "Thank you, sir. You may have saved a life."

I released him to find him blushing as he fixed his cap. "Well. I will go get George and send you off."

I packed a light bag, leaving the rest of my things at the inn in Inverness with a fee to ensure they were stored safely. George, a wiry man whose face was lined with decades of sun and kindness, was silently companionable, leaving me with my thoughts. They were mournful, anxious, distracting company, but the gentle motion of the boat as he guided it along the line of the shore, the cool wind, and the occasional salt spray of the ocean did much to soothe me.

The Orkneys, he told me, were a lonely group of islands jutting off the northeastern coast of Scotland. Victor's new dwelling was on the barest of them all, with only two or three cottages there.

"Orkneys are for folks who do not fancy seeing anyone," he said. Then, after a pause, he added, "Or being seen themselves."

I eyed Victor's letters hungrily. Who else was writing to him? Had his father written to warn him of my approach? I had not told Judge Frankenstein where I was going, but surely he could guess.

George caught me gazing at the bundle of letters as we shared a simple lunch of cheese and bread. He turned to the prow. "I will be looking this way for quite a while, Madame. I would have no idea if you were to, say, open your cousin's letters to search for news of home. My brother would not approve, so I cannot say I do, either. But I also cannot say anything about what I do not notice."

"Thank you," I said, tears in my eyes from the sun and the wind and the kindness found in such unexpected places.

There were several letters. Two of which, I was surprised to see, were from Henry Clerval's father.

Victor,

You have not answered my letters. I blame my son's abandonment of his family and his duties on you. Your father tells me you have gone on to England to convince Henry to return. As it is your fault he was driven away from his responsibilities, the burden of restoring him to us is yours. Do not think any past friendship will compel me to discharge the debts of your father. I will wring blood from the stone of Frankenstein Manor if I must.

Find Henry and send him home, and perhaps I will find some forgiveness.

Fredric Clerval

Victor,

I have seen your most recent letter. You are a liar and a fiend. I have hired a detective to find both you and my son. If my son has been ruined through association with you, I will take everything your family has ever owned and find a way to make you pay for the corruption of my son in the courts, as well. You will find that my wrath can reach you even on the moors of Scotland.

Fredric Clerval

I had never known Henry's father well, but I cringed to think of what news the detective would bring back. It would not end well for poor Henry. If Monsieur Clerval was this harsh to Victor, I doubted he would show any kindness to his son.

Another letter was from Judge Frankenstein. I opened it with trepidation.

My Son,

I do not know what possessed you to leave us in the midst of so much trouble. It was poorly done. Regardless, you should know that Elizabeth has gone. Where, I do not know. She left without warning.

We need her back. I cannot lose her. Not after everything else. Please return home and help me find her.

Your father,
Alphonse Frankenstein

I set down the letter, shocked. I had expected accusations, condemnations. Instead, I found only desperation to have me back. I felt the first pang of guilt toward the man who had allowed me to become part of his family. He had lost so much, and I, ever ungrateful, had not even told him where I was going.

I resolved to make peace with him when I returned. And that would be done with Victor, safe, at my side. It was the kindest thing I could do for Judge Frankenstein.

The second letter was more recent and postmarked from London, which shocked me.

Victor,

Fredric Clerval has taken some notion of revenge in his head. I cannot dissuade him from seeking you out. I fear for what mischief he might create for you on foreign soil, where I have no influence. I have followed him here and will endeavor to find you before he does.

If you see that idiot son of his, tell him to write his damned father a letter.

Alphonse Frankenstein

Judge Frankenstein and Henry's father! Both in England, perhaps getting close to Scotland now. I did not know whether that made things easier or harder for me. I hoped it did not affect me at all. Neither of them had any idea the forces of life and death Victor was wrestling with.

Only I could help him.

It was twilight when George steered the boat up onto the rocky shore of the tiny island Victor had claimed. One other boat was there, though it looked as though it had not been used in some time.

"I do not want to cross back in the dark," George said. "Makes navigation tricky. Will you be all right?"

I nodded, wishing he could see my warm smile beneath my veil but preferring anonymity. "I will. And I can take the letters up myself so you do not have to delay. Thank you so much for your kindness today, George. I am forever indebted."

He ducked his head, tipping his cap. "I hope things go well for you."

"I hope so, too." If Victor was not here, I faced a long, uncertain night on a cold, inhospitable island. I turned to the steep and jagged tumble of black rocks. There was a barely visible trail that wound its way up to a narrow plateau. I followed it, stepping carefully in the fading light. The first cottage I saw—though *cottage* was a generous word for something that looked more suited to being a chicken coop—was empty and, much like the docked boat, held no evidence of recent inhabitants.

The second was dark, as well. I peered in the windows. There was a cradle by the cold fireplace, no books or pens or anything that made me think it was Victor's.

I walked on. The island was not large, but I could have been wrong in my judgments. Perhaps the first cottage *had* been Victor's. Or I had come to the wrong place and missed him yet again.

Just as I was certain my entire life would be spent in pursuit of Victor, I passed an outcropping of lichen-splotched boulders and saw a third cottage. This had a cramped living space and a larger wooden outbuilding attached to the rear wall. Though the whole thing leaned from decades of relentless wind, it seemed sturdy enough.

There were no lights here, either, but I rushed forward with more hope. The cottage was at the highest point of the island, and the wind whipped me with vicious force. It whistled through the rocks, singing a mournful and solitary song. I nearly lost my veil, and as I turned to catch it, I saw on the horizon of the sea two lonely boats bobbing far offshore—my only company for the night.

Bracing myself for disappointment, I opened the door to the cottage. Inside, I found a sparsely furnished space: a stove, a cot, a table with one chair. On the table was a journal. My heart pounding so loud I could hear the blood pulsing through my veins, I stepped across the slate floor and looked down. The last lingering light of day revealed Victor's handwriting.

I had found him.

Letting out a trembling sigh of relief, I resolved to sit and wait. His things were here; he would be back eventually. And when he returned, I would tell him I had discovered the truth and wanted him with me. We would fight this monster together, as we should have from the beginning.

But I wondered—what was he doing out here? Did he hope to lure the monster to such a secluded spot? To keep it away from me, or to destroy it?

The outbuilding could contain anything. Or it could be empty. But I suspected with growing excitement that it held a trap for the monster, or some other means of destroying it. That must have been the work Victor referred to.

I took the lamp from the table and lit it. As I went back outside in the shrieking wind, the flame nearly went out in spite of its protective glass globe. I pushed open the door to the outbuilding and was immediately assailed with strange chemical scents I both recognized and was repulsed by.

It was another laboratory, I realized, a split second before I saw what was on a metal table in the center of it.

Or rather, *who* was on a metal table in the center of it.

NINETEEN

SHOULD GOD CREATE ANOTHER EVE

Justine lay as though sleeping, but there was something terrible in the stillness of her face. Truly relaxed, it lost the shape of her life, her happiness, her soul.

It was Justine, and it was not.

It was only a body.

But it was *her* body.

I wanted to run from this place. But I could not run from Justine, not when she needed me. Because she needed me still.

How could Victor do this? How could he violate her so completely? She lay beneath a short sheet, her head and shoulders exposed and her feet bare. I twitched to cover them so she would not get cold but could not bring myself to touch this . . . thing. This thing that had been my beloved Justine.

It was a foolish impulse to protect her from the cold anyway, and knowing it would not matter made me feel all the worse. What he had done to preserve her body thus I did not know, but there were stitches up and down her arms, across her shoulders, down to her chest beneath the sheet. The greatest concentration of work was done immediately below and above her neck. On her throat was no evidence of the rope that had cut her tragic life short. I wondered what the rest of her, covered by the sheet, looked like, then gagged and turned away so I would not have to look at what had been done to her.

How had she ended up here? For what purpose? The explanation crept upon me, rising along my spine until it settled like a sickness in my brain.

The monster had not implicated Justine merely to punish Victor.

It had framed Justine as a means of getting her body.

This must have been what the monster was talking to Victor about on the mountain! A demand for Victor to create it a mate as horrible as itself. But why would Victor agree? He knew that what he had created was an abomination. I did not doubt that, from the little he had told me while he was sick and delirious. So why would he be willing to do something this wretched for that creature?

And then I realized: The monster had already killed. It would do so again. And doubtless it had watched long enough to know how to manipulate Victor. The monster had threatened to harm me. No wonder Victor had ranged so far to conduct his devilish experiments! He had to draw the monster away from me.

We had cost Justine her life, and now we had cost her body its rightful peace in death.

Wild rage consumed me. I lifted the lamp above my head to burn this sacrilege done to her body. But the sight of the light catching in her chestnut hair, still shining and lovely in death, stopped me.

I sat on the frigid floor, where the edge of the table blocked my view of Justine save one lock of her hair that hung over the side. What would Justine want?

She would want to be alive. She would want to be with William. I could not give her any of that. All I had given her was death. And even that was a cursed and threatened state, thanks to me.

Justine deserved better. She had not attended the burials of her mother or her siblings. She had been denied the chance to grieve. And she had been denied her own body's Christian burial. She deserved one, as proper as I could manage. I did not want what was left of her mortal frame to remain forever on this blighted island.

And I would *not* allow the monster to have her in any form. I did not care if it threatened my life, or even if it killed me. Victor would disagree, but my safety was not worth this steepest of costs.

Justine would rest in the peace she should have had during life.

I formed the vaguest of plans. There was a boat docked on the shore. I would take it. After I had cared for Justine, I would come back for Victor.

I wrapped the sheet around Justine, covering her face. I was not strong enough to carry her, though I longed to cradle her to me like a child. There was a wheelbarrow in the corner of the makeshift laboratory. I cleared it of the chemicals and tools that rested inside, then moved it to the table and maneuvered her body into it.

It was no easy task pushing the wheelbarrow down the steep and rocky path. Several times it nearly overturned, and I feared I would do yet more violence and disrespect to Justine's body by tumbling it over the rocks. But I managed to transport my precious cargo safely down to the dock, where the lonely boat bobbed in the waves.

I set her body inside, mindful of her head. Mindful that such attention to her feelings no longer mattered, but not caring. I laid my own cloak over her body, covering her completely. I hesitated before untying the boat, though, something tugging my attention back to the island. Justine's body was safe. But as long as there was a laboratory, the monster could find a way to force Victor to do its will. And Victor would be pushed down this most heinous of paths. I could not forgive him for Justine yet, but I could protect him from further crimes against nature and goodness.

The wind was at my back as though urging me to hurry. It whispered danger in my ears, tugged my veil, tangled through my hair to pull me along. It need not have urged me so. Once decided, I would not have let that laboratory continue to exist for anything in this world.

I did not want to enter it again, but with Justine's body gone, it looked merely like a chemist's or a surgeon's room. If I had not known what hellish purposes the instruments served, what unnatural terrors those chemicals unleashed on the world, I would have been entirely uncurious.

I lifted the nearest glass bottle, intent on spilling it across the metal table so that the fiendish platform might burn in some form. Then I heard footsteps grinding across the rocky trail.

Toward the house.

I had come here to rescue Victor. But now that I had seen what he was doing—what he would have done, had I not discovered it and prevented him—I could not face him. My revulsion and anger would be plain on my face. Knowing what I did about his motivations and his obvious distaste for the work, I could perhaps forgive him eventually. He did what he did out of love and a desire to protect me.

But the cost!

Even now I could picture him carefully cutting open Justine. Filling her veins with some substance to take the place of the blood that had fed every blush of her lovely cheeks. Opening her chest to see the heart that had beaten with such love and devotion, now a dead thing until he was ready to force it violently back to life.

What would come back? I wondered. Surely Justine's soul had long since fled this mortal plane. Free of the cruelty that had separated it from body, off to join her beloved William to care for in death as she had in life. Would this resurrected Justine be a shadow? With her mind and heart, but without anything good or lovely to animate them?

Perhaps that was why the monster had had no qualms about murdering a child. Victor could create life, yes. But he could not give it a soul, a higher morality, that thing which separated us from animals. That was why his experiment had both succeeded and miserably, devastatingly failed.

I dimmed the lamp, hoping Victor did not note its absence. I did not want to confront him until I was settled in my own emotions. Otherwise, how could I carefully guide his? Peering out the thick, warped glass of a small window, I saw that he carried his own lantern, and willed him not to come in here. My hopes were answered as he instead entered the cottage. It shared a wall with the outbuilding, and I could hear the muffled sounds of a body settling into a space.

And then I heard new footsteps. Louder by far, and syncopated with a rhythm no human stride would make.

I might have rationalized away my fears—We were so remote! How could the monster have come here?—but the desolation and harshness of this island seemed by its very form to have warned me that I would find only unholy things here. I knew the monster was with us. I cowered, pressing my ear to the wall. If the monster looked first to check on the progress of his unwilling mate, I would be discovered. I shuddered with relief as I heard the door to the cottage open once again. It was selfish of me to wish the monster on Victor, but I was in far more danger.

"Abominable demon." Victor's voice carried through the wall. "Why are you here?"

The monster answered, its tones so low I could not understand the words.

"Never will I create another like you, equal in deformity. Leave my sight forever."

There followed a conversation that, because of some shift in position, I could not make out. Victor was enraged, and the garbled and tortured voice of the monster was impossible to interpret. I imagined he shrieked and growled, grunting his wishes and forcing Victor to glean some meaning from them.

Finally, Victor shouted, "Devil, cease! Do not poison the air with your filth. I will have nothing further to do with you. I am no coward to bend to your threats. Leave me. Nothing can bar me from my decision."

My heart soared. Though I had removed Justine, it was evident Victor had already repented of his willingness to do the creature's bidding. He would not have brought her back to life, even without my intervention.

And in that moment, I understood in part what had driven Victor in the first place. Because as soon as I knew Justine would, of a certainty, not be brought back . . . I wondered if she *could* be.

If I knew I would get her back—even without a soul, with just her heart and mind—would I ask him to do it?

It was more tempting than I cared to admit. I, who had struggled so, who had loved so little in my life, could be tempted to break the very laws of God. Could consider tampering with a creative force that had obviously bent itself to destruction. How much worse must it have been for Victor, who had the actual ability to call forth life? How much harder to resist the temptation to defy the natural bounds of our mortal coil?

But we both knew the cost, even if I would pretend I did not. I had already resolved it. If I confessed to Victor what I had seen, he would have to explain to me what he had done to Justine's body and what he might have done further. I did not want to speak of it.

Ever.

Victor could keep this secret. I would leave it to him so that I could forgive and love him still.

The door to the cottage flew open, and as that barrier was broken, I could at last understand the monster. To my shock, his voice, though deeper than any man's, was accompanied by speech as eloquent as any I had ever heard.

"Your hours will pass in dread and misery! Soon the bolt will fall which must ravish from you your goals forever. You have stripped me of everything save revenge—revenge, henceforth dearer than light or food! I may die, but first you, my tyrant and tormentor, shall curse the sun that gazes on your form, which hides so much. I, the monster, who shrinks now from sight, while you walk freely! Be careful what you do, Victor, for I will watch with the patience of a snake."

"Leave!" Victor said, as cold and eternal as the wind buffeting the island. "Your mere presence offends me."

"I go. But remember, I shall be with you on your wedding night."

I shuddered, dread seizing me. This proved that I remained the monster's target. Victor was not yet free of its demands, nor ever would he be.

But as long as Victor had something the monster wanted, he was safe. Assured of that, I sank against the wall. Victor was safe. I might be living under an unseen blade hovering ever ready to cut my soul from my body, but so long as I had breath, I had the same goal as the monster: revenge.

I sat for some time considering the laboratory. With Victor in the cottage, I could not destroy it. And I was not ready to face him. He still thought me an angel, still thought he had protected me by keeping me unaware of all this. I did not know how he would react if he knew that was not the case. Doubtless he was already close to his breaking point, which could trigger a blind rage or a delirious fever.

I could only hope he would suspect the monster had taken Justine's body after Victor refused to resume working his dark arts on her. Victor needed to believe I was innocent of any knowledge of his actions. Would that I could erase all I had done and seen!

Just as I was determined to creep back down to the dock, I again heard the approach of footsteps. My breath caught as I anticipated the monster's return. But no. There were several sets of footsteps. Someone pounded on the door to the cottage.

"What is the meaning of this?" Victor asked.

"We are arresting you in connection with the disappearance of Henry Clerval. And we want to question you about several mysterious deaths in the area."

"This is an outrage!" Victor said. "I cannot be held accountable for the actions of that fool. I certainly cannot be arrested for them!"

I prayed that he would not fly into a fit. If he lost control, it would only prove to them that they were right in their suspicions. I longed to run out and tell them the truth: that Henry Clerval was brokenhearted, not missing, and that any suspicious deaths were doubtless the work of the fiend, seeking everywhere to sow his murderous chaos and make Victor's life a living hell.

But how could I make my case without sounding like a madwoman?

"Tell me where my son is!" a voice demanded. Henry's father. So he had found Victor. There were some scuffling noises and a metallic clink, though nothing that sounded like a struggle.

"Look in that building," one of the men directed. I froze, then darted behind the door. It opened inward, perfectly shielding me. A dark figure peered inside. All that greeted him was an empty table and the lamp I had thankfully dimmed.

He backed out and closed the door. "Nothing in there."

"Nothing?" Victor exclaimed, his voice getting higher. I trembled, fearing what might come next. But he began to laugh. The sound had an edge to it that was worrisome, as bitter and howling as the night. At least Victor did not seem to be fighting them.

I collapsed against the wall with relief. If they had come but an hour earlier, they would have found Justine's body! Doubtless they would have assumed evil on Victor's part. I had not saved him from the monster. But I had saved him from himself and from the false judgment of the world. Though he was not entirely innocent—he *had* created the monster that had done these things—he was no murderer. His crimes were pride and ambition, stepping beyond the boundaries God set for the world. How did one punish those? The monster, surely, was punishing him enough.

The footsteps departed, taking Victor's laughter with them.

I weighed my options, agonizing over my next course of action. Should I follow them? Plead Victor's innocence?

And then *I* laughed. The monster, in its evil spree of violence, had created the safest refuge imaginable for Victor. It had no hope of getting to Victor in a prison cell. And I knew from the letters I had read that Victor's father was already in the country. He would find Victor and easily secure his release. After that, they would travel home together, again preventing any mischief from the monster, which seemed loath to be seen by anyone but Victor.

I had not destroyed the monster, nor had I directly rescued Victor. But my trip here was not in vain.

After giving the men enough time to get their boat off and out of sight, I went back down to my own sad cargo. I practically crawled down the trail, hiding and looking behind myself for fear the monster was still on the island and would surprise me. But no one accosted me. I was alone.

I rowed back to the mainland in the dark, grateful that the fates had at last shown respect for Justine by calming the wind and giving me glassy waters. At the nearest visible town, I pushed us onshore. The spire of a church called to me. It was the work of a miserable hour carrying Justine's body there, and then another few hours digging a grave with a stolen shovel. But the ground was soft and wet with recent rain.

I could not dig in the middle of the graveyard, but I did on the nearest border, beneath weeping boughs of a tree. Graveyards had never held any horror for me—though now I knew death was not as permanent a state as I had thought—and I relished the peaceful work of honoring my best friend's earthly remains.

I held her body, placing a last kiss on her forehead. That was the one kindness amidst all this horror: I was able to say a proper goodbye to my truest, dearest Justine. Then I lowered her into her grave and let the earth claim her.

It was far less than she deserved but the most I could offer her. I gathered a bunch of thistles that were her favorite color and left them on the freshly turned dirt.

Morning dawned as bright and clear and terrible as glacial ice, and with it, my path:

The monster had promised its revenge on Victor's wedding night. That meant I would know an exact time and place where I could expect it to show itself. And then I could end its sorry, hateful existence once and for all.

I would be ready.

TWENTY

FLESH OF FLESH, BONE OF MY BONE

Dear Elizabeth,

You cannot imagine my relief—and Victor's—at hearing you are once again safe at our home in Geneva. I do not understand why you left but require no explanation. My joy at your return is enough to soothe all injuries.

You were probably quite surprised to come home and find my letter relating that I am in England. Circumstances necessitated that I travel here to defend Victor from baseless accusations of wrongdoing, leveled by Fredric Clerval.

I am sorry for your sake and for Victor's that Henry grew to be such a disappointment, but I resent him for creating such trouble for us. I wonder if perhaps it was his plan all along as jealous revenge for Victor's greater brilliance. Their family has been against ours all this time!

With Victor's freedom secured, we are even now traveling back to Geneva to be reunited with you. Ernest remains in Paris at school, which is best for the time being. Let him grow and learn in peace, free from the spirit of mourning that naturally and inescapably suffuses our house at this time.

But my hope—long-cherished by my departed wife—is that you and Victor will soon bring happiness back by celebrating a most blessed event.

I am grateful for your delicacy in broaching the subject of a marital union with Victor. You are ever thoughtful to offer him his freedom should he view you more as a companion than a future wife. But I assure you that he cherishes nothing more than the thought of spending the rest of his life with you. He has told me repeatedly how determined he is that you two never be parted.

As such, we will proceed with a marriage as soon as possible upon our return. I am eager for the day you join our family legally as my daughter. We will travel with as much haste as God and the elements grant us to see that it is so. You can anticipate us within two weeks.

Victor shares my joy, though a lingering fever from his brief confinement prevents him from writing to you himself. He sends his love and devotion, and I send the warmest regards of my heart from a father to a daughter.

With all other regards nobly
and lovingly sent,
Alphonse Frankenstein

I set down Judge Frankenstein's letter. My entreaty—delicately and carefully worded—for Victor to return and marry me had succeeded.

And thus the date for my vengeance would be set.

I knew I should feel sorry that I looked forward to my wedding day not as a blessed moment to be forever united with the family who had sheltered and raised me, but as a day for bloody reckoning, when I would make that forever-damned monster pay for what it had taken from us.

I did not feel sorry.

Perhaps in another life, under other circumstances, knowing that Victor and I were to wed would fill me with relief that my place in the world would at last be secure, with all the legal protections the Frankenstein name would offer. Never again would I fear that I would be abandoned, that everything they had given might be taken away.

Certainly only a few months earlier, receiving such oddly loving sentiments from Judge Frankenstein would have given me cause for celebration and happiness. Perhaps, if he had thus expressed himself *ever* in all our years under the same roof, I would not have chased after Victor and brought the monster back with me.

But I suspected it was that same monster and its devastating evil that had effected this change in Judge Frankenstein. Had he not lost so much, would he bother clinging to an orphan of no family, no fortune? Losing those things he loved most must have broken his heart enough that I finally found purchase there.

So be it. I did not doubt that Victor would want to marry me. I had always been the only girl in the world who mattered to him. If he was to marry anyone, it would be me. But I *had* feared that Judge Frankenstein would reject my claim on Victor. I was grateful to have his and Victor's official approval, and to learn that they shared my desire for speed.

I had never been the type to imagine a wedding or what it would mean to be a wife, other than having binding protection. I tried now, envisioning something simple. Beautiful. But in my imagination, Justine was at my side, and Henry at Victor's.

I had lost that ideal. And so I would push through, little caring about the wedding itself. It was the wedding night I had to plan for.

With no other women in the house to help me besides the maid, with whom I had no relationship, I was free to arrange the barest, most utilitarian wedding ever planned in the long history of the Frankenstein name. I scheduled a priest to marry us at the chapel nearest the edge of Geneva bordering the lake. I invited no one.

My one extravagance was a notice sent out to all the regional publications I could find, advertising the upcoming union of Victor Frankenstein and Elizabeth Lavenza.

The trap was set. And I was both bait and poison.

Once my plans were settled, I had nothing to do but wait. It was agonizing. I knew Victor and his father were making their slow and steady way home to me. And I knew that somewhere out there, the monster was doing the same. I was in the midst of a great spider's web. Whether I would end up as the spider or the fly was yet to be determined. All I knew was that the strands that held me here had been woven since my childhood on the shores of Lake Como.

We were, all of us, bound in this deadly and horrible dance, until we died or triumphed.

A few days before I expected Victor and his father to return, I received another letter. But it was not from them.

It was from Mary, the bookseller in Ingolstadt. And it was addressed to *Elizabeth and Justine*. Another person who dwelt in a beautiful fantasy in which Justine still lived. I could not so much as bring myself to open it. Could not linger in words that assumed Justine was alive, that assumed the world was good and fair and as it should be.

And I could not think of Justine without remembering the stitches, the neck repaired from its injuries so that it could once again draw breath from dead mouth to dead lungs.

Despite some time and distance from having discovered Justine's body, I had not moved any closer to forgiving Victor. I wanted, instead, to understand. He still tried to keep me in the dark about his monster. How deep his shame and horror at what his own hands had wrought on the world must be!

But in helping to destroy the monster, I would no longer be able to feign innocence, and he could no longer deny the truth. Once it was dead, Victor would have nothing further to hide from me, and we could speak plainly. It was another reason any thought of delay was unsupportable. With the monster's death, so too would die any secrets between Victor and me. We would have only each other, a truth too terrible to be believed by outsiders binding us more permanently than any priest could.

I yearned for the freedom I anticipated.

Freedom from the monster.

Freedom from secrets.

Freedom from the fear of having nothing.

When at last they arrived home, I met them at the dock. Victor, gaunt and worn but with eyes burning as brightly as they ever had, disembarked and officially offered me his hand. I gladly accepted.

The ceremony was over almost as soon as it began. I wore white, as Victor had always preferred. He wore a suit, taken in at the last minute to fit his ever-leaner frame. He brushed his lips across mine after we were made man and wife. I kept turning toward the door, expecting the monster to darken the threshold and come roaring in to tear us asunder.

The door remained firmly closed.

Victor and I walked through the morning sun to the boat that would bring us back home. Though I doubted the monster would reveal itself in daylight, my every muscle tensed, anticipating attack.

Only when we were safely in the boat in the middle of the lake did I relax enough to take in my surroundings. I could not have said what we agreed to in the chapel, or whether I had smiled even once. I might have felt sorry, been certain Victor deserved more. But we were in this miserable state because of his monster.

Still, I smiled at him as he rowed our own boat back across the lake to the house, where Judge Frankenstein and a handful of strangers to me would have a reception in our honor. Victor did not return the smile, and I could not manage mine for long, either.

"You do not seem happy, Victor." I debated calling him Husband, but that felt as unreal as a house without Justine and William. This whole endeavor was something I longed to wake up from. I ached to find Justine and Henry laughing in the boat with us, celebrating. To return home and let William and Ernest have too much cake. To luxuriate in being a wife, in being a Frankenstein.

Instead, I was slowly rowed back to a house empty of anyone I loved, hoping for a visit from a devil.

Victor looked up from where his gaze was fixed, troubled, on the horizon. "I will not be settled until I can at last claim victory over a problem that has drawn me low and caused me much agony. I have once again been ripped from my progress by stupid men."

I wished he would speak plainly. He knew I had seen the monster, though he pretended it was the result of injury and a fevered mind. But if I pushed, he was likely to shut down entirely and not speak. And if I revealed that I knew the monster's attack was imminent, he might arrange for me to be locked away somewhere to keep me safe. I could not let that happen.

"It is my hope that soon we will be able to leave this wretched state behind forever," I told him.

His expression lifted and he laughed. "That is exactly my intention. Soon all this will be resolved, and we can live as we were meant to." Then he fell back into his weighted silence, and I dared not disturb him again. He was closer to anger than anything else, doubtless on edge, dreading the same attack I hoped for.

I watched the house approach. Though the day was brilliantly sunny, I was seized with a premonition of doom. What if the monster was already in the house? I was not ready to face it! I did not know if I would ever be ready. I had spent so much time in anticipation of this confrontation. Now that it loomed, I found myself regretting the steps that had brought me here. Each pull of the oars moved us closer to our destruction.

"What is it?" Victor asked. "You look frightened."

I joined him on his bench, tucking myself against his chest as he rowed. The steady beat of his heart was calming. "I want to keep you safe."

I could hear his annoyance. "Nonsense. It is *my* job to keep *you* safe." All aggravation left his voice, which became as cold and steady as the mountains watching over us. "And I will. I promise."

Inside the house, though I braced for attack, I found only Judge Frankenstein and several men I did not know. They stood in the dining room. Pale roses, the edges of their petals already brown, wilted in the center of the table, surrounded by food that was sweating condensation. No one ate anything. Why he should have invited strangers to our wedding party, I had no idea. But I had never understood him. I wanted them gone so I could retreat to my room and organize my supplies. I had been stockpiling oil and matches, as well as long branches I had fashioned into torches. I planned to hide them throughout the house so that wherever the monster surprised us, we would have a weapon handy.

"And here she is!" Victor's father said. "Elizabeth Lavenza, raised as my own all these happy years, and now united with the Frankenstein family in marriage."

The men looked at me as though I were being examined, then nodded, apparently satisfied. A heavyset gentleman with white hair and black eyes spoke. "We will have the assets accounted for so that Victor may gain access to them at any time. Please write ahead should you wish to obtain any of the funds. But the villa at Lake Como is now in the Lavenza name and available."

"I would like to have the funds made available immediately"—Judge Frankenstein paused—"for their new life together, of course."

"Yes," the portly gentleman said. "Of course." His eyes narrowed thoughtfully. "But, in keeping with the inheritance rights the court agreed to, they will remain in the Lavenza name and pass only to her heirs. If no heirs are provided, the Lavenza fortune will be reclaimed by the Austrian Crown."

I looked at them in confusion. I had prepared for attack by a monster. I had not prepared for whatever strange news this was.

Judge Frankenstein nodded, though his jaw twitched in irritation. "I have a detailed account of the money we have spent raising her. I am sure it is within bounds to request compensation."

"What are they talking about, Judge Frankenstein?" I asked.

"*Father*," he corrected me, smiling possessively.

"You can submit the list in writing, and your claim will be evaluated." The speaker settled his hat on his head. "Or you can resolve it privately, now that she is your daughter. I recommend the latter. It will take less time."

The men shook his hand and took their leave. A fly droned lazily, the only thing enjoying the meager feast on the table. There was no air in this room, no current or breeze, despite the high ceilings and the wall lined with windows looking out onto the green of the forest. I wanted to be out there. The glass was not a protection from the elements—it was a barrier. A cage, designed to allow a view of freedom and beauty without ever touching it.

Was the monster just outside, watching us? Did it long to be in here, exulting in its bloody revenge, while I longed to be out there?

"You have come into your inheritance," Judge Frankenstein said to me, taking a glass of wine and toasting us. "It was to go to you at twenty-one, or upon the occasion of your marriage."

I sat down at the table, overwhelmed. I should have been making my preparations for defeating the monster. I could not understand what Judge Frankenstein was saying. "Inheritance? From where?"

"From your father, of course. The Lavenza family fortune."

"But—" I looked up at Victor, who raised his eyebrows to let me know he had no idea what his father meant, either. "I thought he died in prison. In truth, I thought he was a myth. I had nothing when you found me."

"You had your name." Judge Frankenstein drank deeply, setting his glass down with a satisfied sigh. Then he paused, looking quizzically at me. "Do you mean to say all this time you thought we took you in without knowing anything of who you truly were? That we were foolish enough to accept the word of some filthy hag in the woods?"

I had no answer, as that was precisely what I had thought.

His incredulity increased. "You thought I would agree to marry my oldest son to a girl of unknown origin? A foundling child? *Elizabeth.* You have more sense than that."

I let out a strangled laugh. He was right. I did have more sense than that. That was why I had tied myself so tightly to Victor, why I had chased him down to bring him back. I knew I could not depend on the kindness of his father. I could only depend on the love and loyalty of Victor to shield me from abandonment.

But apparently I had grossly overestimated even my low accounting of his father's generosity. Of course he would not have kept me all these years without reason. Of course Madame Frankenstein's dependence on my help with Victor was not justification enough.

"Has there always been money?" My voice was meek out of long practice. If I had known—if I had been aware that at the age of twenty-one I would be secure on my own, without needing anyone else—

What would it have changed?

Judge Frankenstein ripped a leg off the whole roast chicken before us, tearing some of the meat away with his teeth and then wiping the grease from his mustache. "No. Only the potential for it. I have spent many years in a legal battle with the Austrians who seized your father's estate. It was not easy to secure your inheritance, even after your father died in prison. All my trips abroad were to appeal your case in person. But this has happened just in time. I nearly had to rent out this house—imagine, me! A grasping landlord! My father already sold off much of the land, and I could barely squeeze more money from what remained. Now that you are part of the family, your husband will take charge of your finances. And you can begin to repay our years of kindness."

"Father," Victor said, distaste dripping in his voice, "if it is Elizabeth's fortune, she can discharge it however she sees fit."

I reached over and gripped his hand. Now Judge Frankenstein's true reason for being so graciously joyful over my return was obvious. He did not care about *me*; he cared about the money my name brought.

Victor had not known. He had never worried about my name or my origins. He had always loved me for myself. All my machinations and manipulations filled me with shame. He had been far truer to me than I had been to him. I had wanted him because he kept me safe. But he had wanted me only because I was his Elizabeth.

I looked up with tears in my eyes. "I love you, Victor Frankenstein."

He brushed my cheek and then kissed the spot where he had cleared a tear. "Of course you do. And I love you, Elizabeth Frankenstein."

It was the first time the name had been mine. It did not feel the way I thought it would. But nothing that day had.

Victor cleared his throat. "I do not relish the thought of spending our honeymoon here. And in a stroke of luck, we have just been given a villa on Lake Como as a wedding gift! Imagine how much space we will have. How much privacy." Victor directed me up from the chair. "Go pack your things, my wife. We need some time away from these walls."

Judge Frankenstein stood, his face purpling with anger to match his wine. "We need to discuss the finances."

Victor shooed me with his hands. "On our wedding day, we need only consider our own future."

"Ungrateful boy!" his father roared.

Victor turned to him, smiles replaced by a cold radiating so powerfully that even I shuddered, though his wrath was not directed at me. Victor slammed his fists on the table, rattling the chipped finery. His father startled, nearly tripping over the chair behind him. He sat heavily in it instead.

I put my hand on Victor's back, stroked his neck to calm him. Part of me wanted him to lose control, to throw one of the violent mad fits of his youth. To terrify his father even further.

To hurt him.

But Victor responded to my touch, taking a deep breath and stilling. "I know what you think of me," he said to his father. "What you have always thought of me. You have never truly seen me, have never seen what I am capable of. You looked only for fault, only for weakness. The unimaginable heights of my genius, unrivaled, unrestrained, have made you nervous and petty. You would have me gentled. You would have me do nothing with my life but provide you with more money to feed your own appetites and pleasures. And you would use Elizabeth to do it." Victor leaned forward, and Judge Frankenstein shrank back, that old fear fully resurfaced. He had gotten too used to a tame Victor. "You have no power over us, old man. And if you ever try to control me again, you will understand at last what *true* power is and who wields it in this family."

He turned away from his father, his face still a cold mask, terrible in its alien lack of emotion. I saw only a second of it before he fixed his gaze on me and my Victor was returned. "Well," he said, "shall we go to your old home?"

I had assumed we would be fighting the monster here, but with this new information, everything was put off balance, dizzied and confused. A trip by boat, some distance between us and this house; his father; that monster—

"Yes," I said, taking his hand once more. "Take me home."

TWENTY-ONE

HIM WHOM TO LOVE IS TO OBEY

Our journey was by boat, taking us down the Rhone toward where it connected to Lake Como. The river was swift but placid, the countryside enough to fill the breast with stirrings like religious euphoria. The green and gold of the land promised a wealth of happiness and health.

But I could not stop my thoughts from spinning with Judge Frankenstein's revelations and the alteration they cast on my life. Such was my agitation that the monster and its promised attack were pushed to the furthest reaches of my mind. The river carried me swiftly from my past—and back toward my past.

If I had been in full possession of my senses, I might have delayed our return. Lake Como was not a kind place for me. I had no happy memories there. My life had been hunger and pain and suffering. I had always viewed Victor as my savior for taking me away from it.

And now, to celebrate our official union, we were returning. Victor, at least, seemed soothed by our journey. His intense agitation and distraction dissipated. Each league no doubt filled him with relief as it put us safer from pursuit. Fish leapt from the water, keeping pace with the boat, and he laughed and pointed. But he saw that I could not mirror his ease.

He took my hand. "You are sorrowful. If you knew what I have suffered and what I may yet endure, you would endeavor to let me taste the quiet and freedom from despair that this one day, at least, permits me to enjoy."

I did know! I knew full well. He was the one in the dark, both about my knowledge and about the ancient childhood anxieties this trip dredged up.

Still, I would not forget that he had never known, never cared, about my wealth. And he had stepped in to prevent his father from seizing it before I could gather my wits and explore my options for keeping it from him.

It was not that I did not want to help the Frankensteins.

It was that . . .

No, perhaps it *was* that. Madame Frankenstein, with her tepid, conditional kindness, was dead. William, beautiful child, also gone. Ernest would find his own way in the world, never counting on an inheritance as a second son. And Victor was mine, regardless of his family fortunes.

I had known so much strain growing up, constantly fearing that if I failed, I would once again be set out in the world with nothing of my own. And Judge Frankenstein, knowing otherwise, had never offered me comfort or assurance, preferring me to think myself entirely indebted to his generosity. Even this marriage, which could have been delayed until I was at least eighteen, had been presented to me as my best option, when he knew full well that at twenty-one I would have the funds to be independent.

I closed my eyes, trying to sort through my feelings. What life would I have chosen, had I known?

But it was an exercise in madness. I had never known. I had demanded the swift marriage myself as a trap. And now binding me to

Victor were not only a life and love, but the terrible secret of his monster. I had not chosen this life, but I would stay true to those in it who had chosen me. I would stay true to Victor. I would stay true to the memory of Justine.

I opened my eyes and smiled weakly at Victor. It was enough to assuage him, and he returned to admiring the landscape.

"A fresh start is exactly what we need," he said. "Here, away from the past. A new life together as we build toward what I have always promised you." He put his arm around me and drew me close. "You can paint. I can resume studying. We will have seclusion and peace. Enough time that I can correct the failures of the past."

I, too, was hopeful. I had arranged the marriage for a speedy confrontation with the monster. But as we entered the waters of Lake Como, all my childhood vulnerability, fragility, and fierceness fell on my shoulders like the light misting of rain we were under. It coated everything, quickly soaking me through.

I was not yet ready to face the monster. I would accept this respite and try to sort through who, exactly, I was as Elizabeth Frankenstein on the shore of Lake Como.

The interior of the villa—as familiar to me as a long-ago dream—was cloaked in white cloth and dust, everything shrouded as if for burial. I wandered through it in a daze. I touched various objects in hopes of sparking some memory, some concrete connection to this life that had been restored to me.

I felt nothing.

Victor left me in a bedroom while he explored the rest of the villa, doubtless looking for a library. In the morning, we would go into town to find a woman to hire as cook and housekeeper until we knew what my finances were and how much help we would need.

I wondered if any of the people I found in town would be one of my long-lost foster siblings. I would be certain to hire an old woman. I did not need to fear my family here. I was not their victim anymore; I was a married woman. I owed them no kindnesses and would deny any claims made on me.

I stood at the window, watching the sunset break through the dissipating rain clouds for one brilliant orange farewell to my wedding day. I had planned on this day's being one of vengeance and fire. The monster had planned the same. But I was not where I was supposed to be, and thus nothing could disrupt our wedding night.

A new horror descended on me, though this was less a mortal terror and more a humiliating fear.

Victor was my *husband*. We had shared a bed countless nights growing up. But now we were man and wife: I, at seventeen, a woman; and he . . .

I dared not turn around. The bed behind me felt as though it were growing, taking up more and more of the room, lurking like the monster itself in anticipation of claiming me.

I had wanted to wed as a means to kill a monster. All my plans had centered on spending my wedding night in a fight for my own life, and for Victor's, as well. I had never once considered a wedding night on which we were safe and relatively free.

I was hit with a sudden longing for a mother. Not any mother I had ever known—the horrible woman here who I sincerely hoped was dead, or useless Madame Frankenstein—but a mother like what I imagined a mother should be.

A mother like Justine.

A longing for my friend punched through me with physical force, and I collapsed to the floor. Escaping Geneva had not let me escape the ghosts of my past.

I could not simply stay here, safe. Painting. Sitting at Victor's side as he studied. We might have left Geneva, but I had not left behind my purpose. I pulled out my journal, desperately reviewing what I knew of the monster and what I had written about it.

The words on the pages led my mind inexorably to the memory of William, lying dead. I wished I had never seen him, never branded on my memory the cold body, the closed eyes, the terrible bruises on his neck. Even now I could see them, each mark of a brutal finger written on the skin with blackest violence.

I pictured the monster: picking him up, silencing his scream, placing its enormous hands around his—

I set down the journal and raised my fingers to my neck. Something was wrong. I could feel the edges of my certainty fraying.

The prints of the fingers on William's neck were not misshapen, not massive. They were as slender as my own hands.

Which meant that the monster had not murdered William.

Someone else had slowly squeezed the life from the boy. Someone else had carefully taken the pendant. Someone else had found Justine and planted the pendant on her when she was asleep. Someone else had engineered the sequence of events perfectly so that—

I let out a choked sob of horror.

Someone else had engineered the sequence of events perfectly so that he could have Justine's body.

"Victor," I whispered.

"Yes, my love?" he answered, a dark silhouette in the doorway.

TWENTY-TWO

HAIL HORRORS, HAIL INFERNAL WORLD

ALL MY MANY YEARS of tailoring my emotions to fit others' needs, of making certain I showed only what was expedient, of training myself to be someone else's, failed me.

I was unable to pretend.

"Victor." My voice trembled as the scaffolding of my life fell away to reveal a ruinous and terrible mausoleum where I had sought to build a home. "Did you kill your brother?"

"Which one?" His question was genuine; there was no teasing in his voice. He entered the room and sat on the bench at the foot of the bed, crossing one leg over the other knee.

I gasped out a choking laugh of shock and disbelief. "*Which one?*"

He raised an eyebrow, as though I were the one being confusing. "I have two dead brothers. I suppose I did kill Robert, but it was an accident. I was just curious."

"Who is Robert?" My mind whirled as it tried to fill in the past with this new information.

"My first brother. The one who died as an infant."

"I am not talking about that! I have never asked you about that!"

He frowned at my shrill tone. "I know. Because you understand me."

I stood, buzzing and numb at the same time. I was going to fly apart. I clasped my hands tightly in front of myself to keep them from shaking. "I am talking about William. Did you kill William?"

He said nothing, blinking several times as his eyebrows drew close together. I had always loved that expression, loved the thoughts that churned mysteriously behind it. Now I wanted to carve it from his face.

He finally spoke, with the careful, soothing tone I had always used on him. "I was not yet back in Geneva. And Justine was found with damning evidence."

"I taught you how to plant blame!" I jabbed a finger toward him in accusation. "And you agreed with me that Justine was innocent! You were as convinced as I that she was not guilty! It was because you knew the identity of the murderer. All this time, I thought that you knew and could not say because no one would believe you that the monster existed. But you knew and could not say because it was *you*!"

He sighed, pinching the bridge of his nose. "You were never supposed to see the monster. I am humiliated."

"You are humiliated? That is your response?"

He shook his head and turned, as though considering walking out the door. But he took a deep breath, steeling himself. "I can see that this is upsetting you. I knew it would. Why have you insisted on chasing after the things I keep hidden for your own benefit? You are my angel, Elizabeth, and I have ever endeavored to keep you ignorant of the less savory requirements of my work."

I staggered back, leaning against the wall lest I fall to the floor. "So you did. You murdered your child brother. And then you framed my dearest friend so that she would be killed for it."

His eyes flashed, and all ease left his posture. "*I* am your dearest friend."

The enormity of my culpability threatened to overwhelm me. "Did she— Did you pick her because I *loved* her?" A new realization stole my breath. "Did you kill Henry, too? Is that why no one has heard from him since he left for England?"

"Henry is alive, and the world is much more wretched for his presence in it. And as for my motivations with Justine, do not be *petty*," he snarled, his very denial confirming he had killed her out of jealousy. "I needed a healthy young body. My previous attempt was chaotic. I had to work with so many parts. Unsure of my technique, I made everything larger so it would be easier to see and manipulate. I used animal pieces to adapt for size and shape. I thought it would be wonderful. Something new. But it was an abomination. I could not repeat that mistake. I needed to refine the process. To perfect it. To work with a single body, or as close as I could get, instead of so many different ones."

"I saw her." A sob escaped me. Even now I saw Justine, carved with Victor's violent quest for control. When I thought of her, I more often saw her dead face than her beloved living one. Victor had taken her from me in memory now, too. "I dug her grave myself."

"*You* took her?" His fists clenched, white skin pulled taut over the knuckles I had kissed to remind him to release that tension. The hands I had held and looked to for protection. The hands that had strangled William and framed Justine! He took a step toward me. "How dare you follow me! You were told to stay. I gave you every opportunity to be innocent. If you are upset, it is your own fault."

"I thought I was protecting you! I thought the monster was stalking you, and that I would save you!" I waved my journal at him, then threw it to the floor. "I wanted to protect you as I thought you had protected me. But it was all you. You had her on a table like a slaughtered calf! You snuffed out the brightest, purest light in the world so you could possess the *flesh* of it."

He snorted derisively. "You overestimate her value. She was simple.

Not even intelligent. What would she have contributed to the world if she had lived another decade, three, even four more? Nothing. And now her body is wasted. In death, she was to serve the highest purpose there is."

"She loved your brothers! She raised them!"

Victor brushed his fingers dismissively through the air. "Anyone can teach a child. Governesses are interchangeable. You had no qualms about getting rid of Gerta."

"We did not *kill* Gerta!" I hesitated, then covered my mouth in horror. Gerta had gone, had disappeared an hour after Victor left me. We had never heard from her again.

Victor had solved the problem for me.

His look of condescending annoyance would have frozen me previously, made me immediately change course. Even now I flinched from it. His lip curled. "You cannot complain that you dislike the method, when so many of the methods were of your own design. You made it clear from the start you did not care what I did so long as you did not have to know the specifics. It was our agreement!"

"No. No, no, no. I never asked for this. I never wanted this." I longed to pace, to curl into a ball, to run screaming at him and strike him. Instead, I stood there and stared at the boy I had always known, the boy I had thought I knew better than myself. I was looking at a stranger, yet I understood every flicker of emotion on his face. It was too much for me to reconcile.

And still I did not understand. "Why would you do *any* of it? Why would you take Justine like that? Why would you even think of creating a mate for the monster?"

He frowned, tilting his head in confusion. "Why would I give anything to that loathsome creature? As soon as it took its first breath, I knew I had fallen infinitely short of my goals. You have seen it. You understand. It was an abortive mistake, a repugnant error. That it has continued to haunt me, watching me, threatening me, is my own punishment for failing so spectacularly in my pursuit of perfection."

"What perfection can you hope to find in death?"

He lifted his eyes to the ceiling and gave a minute shake of his head. "You do not understand. You have never understood these things. You, who can appreciate the beauty of the world so easily without ever wanting to go deeper—I have done all this for you. To save you."

"To save me from *what*? The greatest suffering of my life has been in the last few weeks, and has been at your unseen hands!"

He moved toward me in an explosive burst. I shrank back against the wall. He was between me and the door. His anger was mounting, but he still seemed in possession of himself. I was here to soothe him, after all.

I would never soothe him again.

He grabbed me by the shoulders, shaking me with the strength of his terrible grip. "Suffering is temporary! And so are you! I almost lost you. You would have died, leaving me here *alone*. When I saw you on your sickbed, inching ever further out of my reach, I swore I would never let that happen. You are mine. You belong to me. And I will be damned if I let the sickening frailty of *flesh* take you from me. Do you think I enjoyed what I had to do? I hated it. But I had to do it. All my work, all my sacrifice, has been for a single purpose: I am going to defy death. I am going to steal the spark of creation from it, to make life eternal, untouchable by corruption. And I am doing it for *you*. When I succeed—and I will succeed—then you will count yourself the most blessed creature on God's earth, because you will no longer be subject to Him. I will step into that place. I will be your god, Elizabeth. I will re-create you in my image, and we will have our Eden. And it will never be taken from us."

"You are mad." My voice trembled, but I could contain my fury. And

I could wield his own as a weapon against him. He was already on the edge of losing himself to his blind passions. I just needed to push him. "I feared you were mad when I saw your laboratory in Ingolstadt. I protected you by destroying it. I should have known that the danger was what you carried inside—in your mind, in whatever you have where a soul should be. You are mad, and I will have nothing to do with your sick perversion of Eden. You say you created an abomination? You *are* one, Victor. You made a monster because that is all you are capable of being yourself. I am finished with you."

I braced myself for one of his rages. I was counting on it. He would lose his ability to function rationally, devolving into a pure destructive force. I could escape then. I would run to town and summon the constable. If he struck me, it would help my case.

But Victor only sighed. He released my shoulders, then walked to the door, closed it, and locked it. His actions were so much the opposite of what I had expected that I simply stood watching. If he had attacked, I would have fought back. Instead, he leaned against the door. He looked so cross, I had to tamp down my instinct to divert his attentions and make him smile instead.

"This is not how I wanted tonight to go. I need more time. I am not ready for you yet. I will not risk any accidents or failures when it is your turn. I would have been so close, but, thanks to your *help* when you burned my first laboratory, I lost my journal and all my notes. And then I lost any progress I had made on the body in the Orkneys."

I trembled with rage. I was ready to attack him now. *"Her name was Justine."*

He let out a noise of impatience. "You still do not understand. I knew you would not. You were never strong enough mentally or emotionally for this task. You will just have to be patient. After you are changed, perfected by me, I know you will finally be grateful."

I laughed, a harsh sound, like the carrion bird I had found that day in his laboratory, pecking at his trunk filled with terrible violence and worse intent. "We are finished. I will never stay with you. I will fight you. I will stop you. You are truly insane if you think for one second I will ever show you any kindness or gratitude again."

He took a deep breath. When he looked down at the carpet, I lunged. I threw myself at him with all the rage and pain I possessed. I clawed at his face, aiming for his eyes. He caught my hands and twisted them, throwing me to the floor. He put his knee into the small of my back before I could rise. I tried to hit him, but he pinned one arm behind me, the other trapped beneath me. I struggled, screaming. But as slight as Victor was, I was no match for him.

I fought with fury; he, with the cold determination of a murderer. Only one of us was aware of how far they could go. I pressed my face into the rug, squeezing my eyes shut. I could not win this fight. I would have to figure something else out. I would have to be smart. Maybe I could—

"We have always been a team," Victor said, increasing the pressure of his knee as he shifted, doing something I could not see. "Once again, you have provided the solution I needed. You went to such lengths to hide my work, knowing that anyone who saw it would think me a lunatic. Would immediately imprison me for my own safety." He laughed. Then he cleared his throat, and his tone of voice changed. "My poor beloved wife. On our wedding night, too overwhelmed by the death of little William at the hands of the woman she chose to care for him, Elizabeth's mind broke. You will see, sympathetic doctors, this journal in her own hand. Look at her writings about journeys she never took. No one in England, Inverness, or anywhere will recall a young woman named Elizabeth. She imagined the whole thing! And the monsters—creatures of darkness and death—that she sees in the world around her! Oh, how it breaks my heart! But I know she will be safe in this asylum. She will be safe, and secure, and patiently locked away to anticipate the day I am ready to retrieve her." He set something down on the floor by my side, then gently stroked my hair. "Do you think I should talk more about what you have been through? Perhaps lingering on your guilt over trusting Justine when she was clearly plotting to murder William? If only Henry were here to write it for me like one of his pathetic plays . . . Well. I will practice."

I wanted to twist my head, to bite his hand where it still stroked my hair. But that would look like evidence in his favor. I would need my wits about me in order to argue my way free from this when he brought in the constables. I could try to run as soon as he released me, but I feared that would support his case more than mine. And where would I run to?

No. I would be calm. Dispassionate. I would explain his history and temper, try to provoke him again into a rage. I would be—

A sharp jab stung my neck, followed by a rushing, burning sensation. It flooded the veins there and traveled through my body.

"Sleep." Victor's lips brushed my ear as he stroked my hair. "Sleep, and know that I will take care of everything."

TWENTY-THREE

SO SHALL THE WORLD GO ON, TO GOOD MALIGNANT, TO BAD MEN BENIGN

When I awoke, I was bound to a bed.

A nurse leaned over me, lifting my gown to place a chamber pot beneath me.

I gasped. "What are you doing?"

"Just do your business," she said with a long-suffering sigh.

"Madame, please!" I struggled to move, to no avail.

She leaned over into my line of sight. She was thick with age, and broad shouldered. Her eyes were neither kind nor unkind. They were tired. "If you do not piss right now, I will leave the pot under you. It will bruise your fair skin, and you will cry. I will not care. And if you struggle, you will spill your own shit and piss all over your bed, and I will forget to change your sheets. Do you understand?"

Her tone was without anger or malice. And I did not know how to reply—what could I say to convince her? How could I best manipulate her into releasing me?

"Yes, of course," I said meekly. "But could I sit up, please?"

"Two days bound to the bed to make certain you will not injure yourself. Do as you are told, and then we will talk about letting you piss sitting up."

Horrified, humiliated, I found I could not release so much as a drop.

She left the chamber pot beneath me.

It bruised, as promised, though my soul and dignity suffered far worse damage than my skin.

Three days I lay bound to that bed. Sometimes I heard weeping. But that was almost a comfort, because the rest of the time I heard nothing. I could only turn my head side to side and see blank, whitewashed walls. I was alone, save the brief visits of a nurse.

The second night, the longest night, I repented of my wish to hear things. A woman nearby screamed, and screamed, until my throat felt raw and aching on her behalf. How she continued I did not know.

How could any of us continue like this?

After three days of doing everything the nurses asked, they unbound me. I was taken into the asylum master's office. I did not know what country we were in, but the doctor and nurses all spoke German. The walls were paneled in dark wood, the desk and his chair massive and foreboding. A simple stool was placed in front of it. I sat, perched on the edge, with my back straight and my chin held at a demure angle.

They had not let me brush my hair, nor had they given me anything other than the shapeless gray shift I had worn since I had woken up.

"Good afternoon." I smiled primly. "I am so grateful for a chance to speak to you. We have a terrible misunderstanding to clear up."

The asylum master did not so much as glance up from where he was writing a letter. He was pale and crinkly, and I suspected if I touched his skin it would hold the indent of my finger. His thin lips were pursed into a single cross line.

"You see," I continued, "I should not be here."

"Hmm," he said. "I have seen your writings and have testimony from your husband otherwise."

I laughed in embarrassment. "Oh, but he did not let me explain! You see, I was writing him a story."

"A story?" He finally looked up from his letter.

"Yes! A novel. I wanted to surprise him with it. He has always loved scary stories, so I was writing a story of a monster. I am humiliated that anyone else read it."

His mouth stretched into a smile. "My dear child. Do you really think claiming that what you were writing came from your imagination does anything to prove your sanity? Indeed, if anything, it further confirms how much you need our help."

I shook my head, my heart racing. "No, no, I can explain. I—"

"You have suffered tremendous loss. And being a tender young woman, the thought of being a wife was too much. You need quiet. You need a place where you are safe, where your mind is not tormented or challenged. I promise we will give you every opportunity to settle your hysteria."

I wanted to stand, to shout, but anything I did or said would only be evidence against me. My lips trembled, but I did my best to give him a sad smile. "Am I permitted to write letters? To have visitors? I would like to see—"

Who? My father-in-law? Judge Frankenstein would not care one whit about my placement here, so long as he could still access my inheritance. He only needed me alive for that. Ernest was too young to be of any help. Henry was in England, and if his own father could not track him down, certainly my letters could not reach him.

And the day I saw Victor again would be the day all was lost forever.

I had no one. I had only myself. I let tears brim manipulatively in my eyes and turned the full force of my angelic beauty on him.

He was not even looking at me.

"Take her away," he said. Two nurses came and hauled me roughly by each arm. I did not resist.

"When can I go outside?" I asked the next morning. I had been confined to my room ever since my meeting with the asylum master to allow time for my "*nerves* to resettle."

The nurse setting down my breakfast tray grunted. She was not the same nurse who had promised me bruises. She was younger, but the same brutally uncaring determination was written across the slope of her shoulders. "Being outside is too much stimulation for you. Be good and in a week you can join the other girls for evening meals."

"But I—"

"Be good," she grunted. Then she left.

When, after a week, I was allowed out of my tiny, windowless cell, I sat as ladylike as I could manage on the cold benches of the central visiting room. There were no visitors. I was surrounded by women sitting in similar fashion, each of us still moving as though we wore collars up to our chins, long skirts, and corsets, instead of loose gowns made of coarse gray material. We were not allowed hairpins for fear we would injure ourselves, so even my hair was long and undone. I felt unmoored, exposed, with nothing between my body and the air but this singular layer.

They had stripped us of everything we were taught made us women, and then told us we were mad.

Still. I would prevail. I prepared my case carefully, meticulously, in my mind. At my next meeting with the asylum master, I would convince him of my sanity and Victor's guilt, and then I would be released. I had been good, as instructed. I would be exactly what I needed to be in this horrible place, and I would win my freedom.

Someone snickered next to me, and I turned my head to see a woman lounging in an almost profane manner on the floor.

"It will not help you," she said, gazing up at me. Her hair was a mess, her nails bitten down until they were rimmed with dried blood. But her expression was sardonic and intelligent.

I did not want to engage with someone so clearly not in possession of her wits, but I had not spoken to anyone besides the uncaring nurses in a week, and I longed for communion of any type.

"What will not help me?" I asked.

"That." She jerked her head toward my perfect posture, my hands folded demurely in my lap. "You cannot convince them you are sane by behaving the way you think they want you to. They do not care."

"It is their job to care."

She snorted, stretching out, lifting her arms over her head languorously. "It is their job to do what they are paid to do. And what they are paid to do is keep us in here. Keep us alive. That is the sum total of it. Do you know why I am here?"

I did not have to be good to *her*. She did not matter. "Because you are possessed of a spirit that makes you lie on the floor in polite company?"

She cackled. "Oh, I like you. No. I am here because I tried to leave my husband. I packed what I could carry, and I walked out in the middle of the night. He spent ten years beating me, cursing me, pulling my hair, and spitting at me. He would fly into jealous rages, accuse me of cuckolding him, of mocking him behind his back, even of stealing his manhood's strength while he slept so he had none left when he wanted to enjoy me. And *I* am mad for trying to walk away from that."

She sighed, looking up at the cracked ceiling, the exposed beams mimicking the bars across the singular window in the room. "I did the same as you for the first while. Behaved. Tried to demonstrate how undeniably sane I was so I could be released. It took me two years to give up." She grinned, winking at me. "The last eight years since have simply flown by. So whenever you are ready to give up, there is a place on the floor right next to me."

She patted the scratched and scored wooden planks companionably. Then she smiled maternally at my obvious horror. "Ask the other women what they are in for and you will find more of the same. Though Maude does cry and sleep an awful lot. And Liesl—well. You should be glad your husband cared enough to purchase a private room for you." She gave me an appraising look. "Why are *you* here?"

I could feel my back curving, my shoulders slumping. For two *years* she tried to convince them of her sanity, and all she had against her was an attempt to flee a horrible marriage. For all my work learning how to be what others needed, I had not realized I was already perfectly suited to this asylum. I was *exactly* who they wanted me to be. Who Victor's father and mother had groomed me to be. Who Victor had created me to be.

I was a prisoner.

All my life of surviving, of being someone else's Elizabeth, had led me here. And what was I left with? Who was I when I was not performing for someone else?

Even now I realized I had a false, pleasant smile on my face. For whom? For what? So this woman on the floor would not judge me? So the nurses would think me sweet?

I slowly released the smile, let my face be as still and unanimated as Justine's when she lay dead on that horrible table. Let myself default to my most natural state. Wondered what, in fact, that state would be.

The woman on the floor watched me, curious. "Well?"

"My husband," I said, the word foul and poisonous on my tongue, "experimented on and then cobbled together dead body parts to create a monster. Once that was accomplished, he went on to murder his brother and frame my best friend for the murder so that she would be hanged. Then he tried to use her body to practice his dark science on, in preparation for eventually changing me from living to dead, and back again to a new form of being that would never corrupt or die or be parted from him. I told him I was not interested in being his wife under those particular circumstances."

The woman's eyes were wide, and she scooted several inches away from me, pushing herself along the floor.

"So." I smiled, the expression that had been my instinct all these years feeling false and at the same time more true than ever as it cut meanly across my face. "We are here for basically the same reason."

Over the next month, despair settled around me like snow falling on the ground, covering my dreams of vengeance. Then despair covered my dreams of life itself, until all that remained was a blank white plain of nothingness.

I would be in here forever.

But I always caught myself when I began despairing at that thought. Because being in here forever would be preferable to Victor's alternative.

He was out there, somewhere, murdering victims to perfect his technique. I could not even count on that obscene monster to find and kill him, as it had had ample opportunity before and never followed through. Victor had been haunted not by the monster's threats, but by his own failures.

So Victor was free, truly and fully, and I was in here. I would remain until Victor was ready for me. And then, because he was a man and I his wife, they would hand me over to him, and he would finally have full power over both my body and soul.

And no one would help me.

And no one would care.

I continued to pretend to be good, because I knew of no other way. The woman from the floor had spread rumors that I was truly insane, and no one spoke to me. I did not mind; I had no use for friends among the other prisoners.

I watched carefully. The cell doors were always locked. A nurse escorted me to my only meal with other people. We went down a hall that connected to the large common room. The doors leading out were guarded. Nurses worked alone, but they never left individually—always in a pair. So any idea of overpowering a nurse and stealing her uniform was out of the question.

I had no weapons. No means of obtaining one. Even if I were to devise an escape, what would I do once I got out? I could not go back to the Frankensteins, could not go back to Lake Como. I would be what I had always feared: cast out, penniless, destitute. The walls that bound me went far beyond this asylum.

Each day was the same, an infinite parade of degradations and torture accomplished by unyielding women and overseen by the condescension of uncaring men. If not mad already upon internment, surely no mind could withstand the torment of this hell.

I focused on avoiding laudanum, though I also longed for the release of it. Surrounded by blank-eyed, foggy-minded prisoners, I was both repulsed and envious. Was that how we endured? How we survived? It was how I had lived my whole life: willfully ignoring and erasing truths around myself.

I held off; the nurses did not care so long as I was manageable. But without a goal, without something to achieve, I could feel any resolve or strength I once thought I had slipping away. Soon, doubtless, I would let laudanum claim whatever time I had left before Victor was ready for me.

I had begun talking to the nurses, though they were rough and unkind and never spoke back. But I had to do something to occupy myself, and we inmates were not permitted much conversation at supper. I wanted to unburden my mind. To strip away all the falseness I had clothed myself in, until I stood, naked and unformed, truly myself.

Most days I spoke of Justine. Of my guilt. Of her goodness. I circled ever closer to the truth, a wound still too raw to touch. When I finally spoke the truth, I would give up. I would take the drugs. And I would look for whatever blank forgetfulness I could find.

The forty-fifth morning of my captivity, I lay on my cot with my eyes on the ceiling, trying to find pictures in the cracks of the plaster. The nurse came in with my food. Breakfast and dinner were choked down in solitude so we would not have our delicate nerves overtaxed by socialization.

I glanced at her, avoiding eye contact. The nurses interpreted a direct look as threatening; it was a guaranteed way to be bound to the bed for a day or two. I had begun to develop calluses on my wrists and ankles. Besides, I had just ended my monthly courses, during which I had not been permitted to leave my bed at all so as to avoid *taxing my strength*. I did not want to spend any more time than I had to in here.

But in my furtive peek, there was something in her clever dark eyes beneath the stiff white cap that reminded me of someone I had once known. Or maybe I just longed for a friend. Any friend.

I did not deserve a friend. I was ready to tell the truth. I closed my eyes, finally letting the memory play out as it had actually occurred.

"Can I tell you a story? Justine loved this story. But this time, I will tell it the way it really happened. I always lied to Justine. I wanted the world to be more beautiful for her. The world is ugly. Uglier now, without her. Anyhow. Here is my story:

"I needed Victor. I needed him to love me. So I climbed a tree and brought down a nest of robin eggs as blue as the sky. He picked up the first egg, holding it to the light of the sun. '*Look. You can see the bird.*' He was right. The shell was translucent, and the silhouette of a curled-up chick was visible. '*Like seeing the future,*' I said. But I was wrong. The future would be revealed in a few more moments.

"He lowered the egg and used his knife to crack it open. I cried out in shock, but he ignored me. He peeled back the egg, grimacing as liquid spilled out onto his hand. He never did like to get messy. Digging up the bodies must have been hard on him. That is probably why he choked little William. No blood.

"So Victor pulled the chick free. He let out a trembling breath, and I realized he was scared. He looked up at me—and because I did not want to lose this chance at a new life, I nodded for him to keep going. '*I can feel its heart,*' he said. The chick shuddered and shivered and then went still. He peered at it, pulling its tiny claws, its wings that would never unfurl. '*How did the egg keep it alive? And where did what made it alive go, I wonder, when its heart stopped? It was alive, and now it is just . . . a thing.*'

"'*We are all just things,*' I answered, because I had never been more than that to the people who had raised me. Victor looked thoughtful. He held out the chick to me, as though I would want to hold that little piece of death.

"I took it. He watched me closely, so I acted as brave and curious as he had been. I acted as though we had not done a terrible thing. I said, '*You should cut it open, see where its heart is. Maybe then you will know why it stopped.*'

"Victor looked how I had felt when I discovered the nest: like he had found a treasure."

I sighed, numb with the release of finally telling the rest of the story.

Of all Victor's crimes, of the murders I now knew he had committed, that tiny bird haunted me the most. Perhaps because it was easier to think of a bird than of Justine, or of William. But probably because I had been complicit. I had *made* myself Victor's that day. I had chosen to look directly at whatever he did, unflinching, unjudging. I continued that for the rest of our childhoods together. I never asked what happened to Ernest's arm in the cottage. I just dealt with it and took care of Victor.

I never asked, and he never told me, and we both assumed we were protecting the other. Was it any wonder he thought I would continue as his forever, after bloodying my hands at the moment of our meeting?

That was, I thought, the moment I ceased being Elizabeth and became *his* Elizabeth. And now I could be neither.

"God in heaven," the nurse said. "What have they done to you?"

I sat up in shock at being spoken to. I *did* know her face after all, but in the bleak haze of the asylum it took me a few moments to process it.

"Mary?" I asked, incredulous.

She sat, tugging off her white nurse's hat and setting it on the bed next to me. "You have been a difficult girl to track down."

"How long have you worked here?" My mind spun, still unable to process the appearance of someone from my old life, here, in my new hell.

"I do not work here, silly thing. I tried to get permission to speak with you, but they would not allow it. So I stole their laundry instead. It is hard to get out of this asylum, but decidedly easy to get in."

I raised an eyebrow. "So easy, I did it while sleeping."

"I preferred a method that would allow me to leave when I was finished." She frowned, studying my face. I was suddenly conscious of how I must look. My hand darted to my hair to smooth it down, but she shook her head. "I am sorry," she said, "for what has been done to you.

I suspected that you were Victor's accomplice, but now I think you are yet another of his victims."

I leaned forward, grasping her arms. Too hard, I was sure, but I could not stop myself. "You know about Victor? About what he has done?"

"About his murders? Oh, yes. I have figured it all out."

"Have you seen the monster?"

Mary frowned at me, and I instantly regretted my words. She would think me truly insane and stop talking to me!

But she continued. "After you left, I did not hear from my uncle. It worried me. One day a fisherman had been dragging the river with nets and pulled up a number of bodies. Seized with a premonition of dread, I went to the charnel house, where they were being kept until someone could determine where they had all come from."

"Did you meet that horrible man? The one who looks like a weasel?"

She shook her head. "No. They said the man who ran it had disappeared not long after you left. I went to see the bodies, but I had been misled. It was not bodies so much as it was *parts* of bodies. Arms. Legs. Torsos. One body had the head and torso intact. Even its jacket was still in place. The face had been ravaged by its time in the river, bloated and picked at, unrecognizable and so horrible I will never forget it. But I knew the jacket. I reached inside and withdrew a tiny gold-filigreed book of scripture that my uncle always kept. The pages that he loved had dissolved in the water, leaving only the empty shell of it."

She paused, looking haunted. "The empty shell of the book, the empty shell of my uncle. It was him."

Mary stood, pacing the tiny room. "They would have assumed the parts were other bodies that had been decomposed until they came apart in the water. But my uncle's condition prompted them to look closer. Because above where his ravaged face should have been, the top of his skull had been neatly, surgically sawed off."

She finally stopped, looking at me with her chin raised. "They found all the bodies downriver from Victor's residence, which had a chute running directly from the second story to the river. I know he is well connected, and I know how precarious my own situation is as a single woman. I already cannot collect on what is owed my uncle because men simply refuse to see me. If I were to accuse Victor of murder, I would lose any credibility left to me through my uncle's name. So I cannot go after Victor without risking all I have left. That is why I looked for you. It was not easy. But I was determined. You know more than you had ever said." Her lips twisted wryly. "And your presence here confirms it. So please, I beg of you. Tell me the truth. Tell me all of it."

I stood, taking her hands in mine. Her pretty face was braced against pain, and there was a determined set to her jaw. This new revelation made me sad for her. It also forced me to revise what I had assumed yet again. How many times would I be wrong about Victor's activities and motivations? I had not known, had never dared to suspect he had killed before William and Justine. I assumed his murders had started with them. My old reflex of turning away from the worst of him had not been abandoned, apparently.

But of course Victor would want only the best materials. Of course he would not be satisfied with flesh long dead. He had moved from the graveyard to the charnel house to picking his own supplies.

No wonder Frau Gottschalk had locked the doors so insistently. No wonder rumors of what happened if you were out at night alone plagued the city. There had, in fact, been a monster in Ingolstadt.

Henry, I remembered with a sharp stab of panic. But Victor had told me Henry was still alive. And he had not been lying, had had no need to lie after confessing to the murders of his brother and my Justine. I had not failed Henry, then. Perhaps through my conniving unkindness, I had saved him alone of those I loved!

I wiped beneath my eyes, startled to find my face wet with tears. "I did not know until now Victor was murdering people in Ingolstadt.

I swear to you. If I had suspected, I would *never* have protected him," I told Mary, then paused. Was that true? I did not know. Not for certain. It was so hard, sorting through what was left of me when I cut off the parts that existed for others. I did not think even old Elizabeth would have been able to overlook the murder of strangers. But she did not need to. She had deliberately and willfully looked the other way, as always.

Mary's sharp, unyieldingly intelligent gaze had forced me even back in Ingolstadt to be honest. Perhaps if I had stayed with her, I would have come to these truths sooner.

I shook my head. It did not matter now. Nothing mattered now. "I could have investigated more thoroughly. But I thought the bodies were stolen from graveyards and purchased from charnel houses. I thought that he had lost his mind, that I was protecting him from the censure of the world, not from justice well deserved. I should not have rushed to help him. I am so sorry. Please know that being complicit has cost me everything I love in the world."

She gripped my hands, her clutch almost painful. I leaned into her touch, starving for it.

"I am not sorry," she said. "I am *furious*. And you should not be sorry, either. He has taken too much from both of us. From the world. He cannot be allowed to win. Will you help me?"

I laughed bleakly, looking around the box that held me. "I cannot even help myself."

She reached under her skirts and removed a second nurse's uniform hidden there. Nurses always left in pairs. The two of us could walk out of this nightmare.

"Elizabeth Lavenza." Her black eyes narrowed with intensity. "It is time to kill your husband."

TWENTY-FOUR

AND STUDY OF REVENGE, IMMORTAL HATE

The moon herself hid her face from our violent intent, shrouded in clouds as though ready for burial. The gates of Geneva were closed, but we had no use for the city, no desire for witnesses.

Mary and I sat side by side, rowing our way across the lake that long had been the border of my home. Now it carried me to my dark purpose: to end the boy who had brought me there. Waves blacker than the night slapped at the sides of our boat, gusts of wind carrying spray to our faces. I imagined the lake baptizing us, consecrating us for our unholy task.

Surely nature abhorred Victor.

A low rumble of thunder passed through the valley, echoing off the mountains in the distance. The waves grew choppier, the wind stronger. Hanging on the gusts was the distant, lonesome cry of some beast in agony.

My heart had made the same cry too many times. I turned my face from the unseen creature's pain. I could not shoulder anyone else's, not even that of a poor dumb beast.

Tonight, I would kill Victor. Tonight, I would destroy the last remnants of the foundation I had spent my entire life building. Would I be left to sift through the rubble, to see whether anything I was, was worth salvaging? Or would I fall, too?

A brilliant streak of lightning illuminated us in the center of the lake. We were in the midst of a rising maelstrom. Rain slashed down with cutting force, soaking us in seconds. Still we pulled on the oars, undeterred from our deadly design.

"The pistols will not work!" Mary shouted. I could barely hear her over the storm. "They have gotten too wet!"

I nodded. We each had a knife, though we had hoped to be able to use the pistols. I remembered the ease with which Victor had overpowered me. It filled me with shame. Had I fought harder, or faster . . . But if the bodies found in the river were any indication, Victor had had a good deal of experience capturing and subduing people.

We finally made it across the churning lake. We slipped over the dock, buffeted by the storm. The night had given itself to violence. A tree crashed to the ground with a tremendous crack and we both jumped, barely dodging the branches. The wind pulled my hair from the pins Mary had given me, and long wet strands whipped my face with stinging blows.

The house was waiting. None of the bedroom windows glowed warm; only the entry hall held a hint of light. Another flash of lightning threw the building into perfect relief, and I noticed one detail that had changed in my absence: a long pole, topped with a metal orb and wrapped with coils, now rose from the roof over the dining room, soaring far above the sharp peaks of the house.

"He made another laboratory," I whispered. But the wind and the rain stole my words. I grabbed Mary's arm and pointed, screaming my observation in her ear. She nodded grimly, wiping water from her eyes. I gestured to the back of the house, where I knew we could climb the trellis and pry open a loose window in my bedroom.

I entered my old home like a thief in the night. I was there to steal the life of its heir. I set my feet on the richly polished wood floor on which generations of Frankensteins had trod. My soaked skirts dripped a steady puddle of water that would damage the wood if left unmopped. As a child, I would have cleaned it immediately, wishing to leave no trace of myself and no opening for censure.

I leaned over and wrung out my hair all over the floor.

After my time in the asylum and our nighttime travel here—Mary and I had slept during the day, hidden in a barn—the room was a riot of visual stimulation. I had always liked it as a child, but now I saw the garish roses on the wallpaper as pale imitations of reality, like everything in this cold house. The windows were draped with heavy cloth, which blocked both light and the view of nature's majesty. Next to one window was a painting of the same mountains one had only to step outside to see.

Perhaps that was why Victor was so desperate to imitate life with his own twisted version. He had never been able to feel things as deeply as he should; he had been raised in a home where everything was pretense and no one spoke the truth.

Not even me.

I had accused Victor of creating a monster, but I had done the same.

Mary clambered in next to me. She looked around with a raised eyebrow, taking in the velvet stool, the gilded vanity, the hulking four-poster bed. Every covered surface was a different fabric, a different pattern. Anything that did not work in another room had been given to me. I did not know whether I was dizzy because of anticipation and nerves, or because I was no longer acclimated to the chaos of Frankenstein castoffs.

"How did you manage to sleep in here?" she asked, throwing our now-useless pistols onto the bed. The door was open, fortunately, so we would not risk its loud release from its frame.

"I did not sleep much." All the nights I had sought Victor for comfort from my nightmares trailed in my wake as I walked like a ghost through the house where we had grown up together. We passed the nursery, where I had vowed to him I would never love the baby his mother was carrying more than I loved him. Where Justine had spent most of her happy hours. Where William had grown, joyful and careless.

We passed the library, where I had soothed Victor and felt so triumphant for coaching him on how to hide his rage and hatred from others; then passed the door to the servants' wing, where he had implicated Justine using my own technique.

Everything I had known of him, everything we had shared, rose like the dead before me, rotted through to show the horror of what festered beneath the skin.

"What about the father?" Mary whispered as I furtively checked the kitchen. It was empty. The maid and the cook must have been in their rooms, though they had not yet readied the house for the night. Or perhaps Victor, in his pursuit of privacy for his studies, had dismissed them.

I prayed that they had actually been dismissed, and not *dismissed,* as unfortunate Gerta had been.

"At this time of night, Judge Frankenstein will have already retired to his bedroom. If Victor raises an alarm before . . ." I paused, knowing what had to be done but loath to admit it aloud. "If his father finds us, I will speak to him. He has a financial interest in keeping me alive."

"Then I will be certain to stand behind you." Mary smiled grimly.

I pointed to the double doors leading to the dining room. I had to guess that that was where Victor was, based on the location of his metal device. He certainly would not be sleeping—not when there was work to be done.

The doors were closed. On them, carved and stained and polished, was the Frankenstein family crest that I had so often run my fingers along over the years. The shield that protected them was my shield now, too, according to the law. I was Elizabeth Frankenstein, married into this diseased and broken family tree. Which somehow made me even more their possession than I was when I had depended on them for everything.

I thought of the woman in the asylum, locked away for daring to want a life free from pain and abuse. How mad she must have been indeed for dreaming such a thing was possible.

Bleak sadness soaked and chilled my anger as certainly as the rain had chilled my clothes. What hope was there in a world such as this? Was Victor really so wrong to look for ways to circumvent the demands of nature? Because if we had grown to be this way as a society through nature, surely nature itself was as corrupt and malformed as Victor's monster.

I had tried to warn Mary about the monster, but I could see that she did not believe me. It was just as well. She already believed in the real monster and was prepared to face him.

"Are you ready?" Mary whispered. She pulled out her knife.

I nodded, cold down to my soul and trembling as my pale fingers wrapped around the handle of my own knife. I wished we were there with an army at our backs. Wished I knew someone, anyone, who would believe us about Victor's true nature. Wished this desolate responsibility fell on anyone but me.

So do all guilty wish to foist their burdens onto others.

I pushed the doors open, brandishing my knife and bracing myself. Mary screamed, and I whipped around, looking for her attacker. But then I saw what had made her cry out: she was screaming at the horror of the scene before us.

Victor stood with his back to the windows. Between us was the table where we had eaten, the table I had often squirmed at, wishing we could leave his father's presence. It had been covered by a metal sheet, and on that lay a body. Judge Frankenstein's sightless eyes stared up at where the ceiling and roof had been cut away to make an opening for the metal rod courting the storm's lightning. Towels and sheets had been discarded along the floor to soak up the rain.

Victor looked up at me and frowned. Rain dripped from his hair down his face. It almost looked like he was crying.

Victor never cried.

"What are you doing here?" he asked. Mary raised her knife. He cursed, pulled out a pistol, and shot her. She staggered back, falling through the doorway and onto the floor.

"No!" I screamed, turning to help her.

"Stop!" Victor commanded.

"Shoot me," I snarled.

"I do not want to shoot you," he said, exasperated. "I keep this pistol in case the creature returns." I ignored him, kneeling at Mary's side. Her shoulder was bleeding freely.

"He did not hit anything too important." I pulled a tablecloth off a table in the hallway. The table had always held flowers several days past their prime, their scent cloying and fulsome. The flowers there now were so old, they were covered in fuzzy black mold. The vase tipped off and shattered on the floor. I used my knife to cut a portion of the tablecloth and pressed it to her wound, using another strip to tie it off.

"Of course I did not hit anything important." Victor stood over me, with the pistol trained on Mary. "That would be a waste of good material. But if you do not do what I say, I will shoot her in the head. I do not have much use for her brain. Drop your knife."

I dropped it. He kicked it away with disdain. Mary's had been lost in her fall; I did not see it anywhere.

"What are you wearing?" Victor scrutinized my clothes with as much horror as that with which we had viewed the body on the table. I still wore the nurse's uniform, with a cloak buttoned at my neck. "Go and change immediately."

I was aghast at his priorities. "I have just escaped from the asylum where you trapped me, have come here with the express purpose of killing you, and *you want me to change my clothes?*"

He kicked Mary viciously, and she cried out in pain. "We do not have time to argue. If lightning strikes, I need to take immediate advantage. Any delay will ruin the whole process and render the body unusable. And then I will have to prepare another one." He gestured meaningfully at Mary. "So go and change."

He waited until I was moving, then nudged Mary roughly with his foot. "Into the laboratory, please."

I tensed to pounce on his back, hoping to throw him off balance, but he angled himself toward me so he could watch my progress while keeping the gun trained on Mary. She was pale, her clever features pulled tight with pain. She was in no condition to fight him. Her injured arm hung limply at her side.

She turned her back to me as though she was cringing. Her limp arm hid the knife, tucked in her hand and half up her sleeve.

"Go and change, Elizabeth," she said. "He is right. You look dreadful." She walked into the dining room and sat heavily in a chair by the door.

I raced through the halls and upstairs to my old bedroom and put on one of my white dresses; it felt like preparation for a ritual I wanted no part of. All our rituals as humans seemed to revolve around birth and death—marriage being the exception, though my wedding had been a ritual intimately connected to death, given my choice of partner.

I had no weapons in my room other than the useless pistols. But Victor did not know they were useless! I tucked one into the broad, heavy pleats where my skirt met my waist at my back. If I minded the angles I presented to him, he would not see it.

Taking a steadying breath, I marched back to Victor's new laboratory to be reunited with my husband and my deceased father-in-law—who might not be in that state much longer. I had not cared for him in life; I did not care to be reunited with him after his death.

"Much better," Victor said, barely glancing up from where he was reading gauges and measurements on his array of instruments, the use of which I could only guess at. "You may sit. I have to concentrate." He gestured with the gun toward a chair on the opposite end of the room from Mary. I moved to sit beside her instead, and he cocked the hammer of the pistol. "You may sit *over there.*"

Mary watched him with more curiosity than fear. "Did you kill him?" She was using exactly the right tone to keep him calm. We had already disrupted his process, and he was liable to snap at any moment. It was what I would have done—what I *should* have done. Gotten him talking.

"Hmm?" Victor seemed confused about whom she was referring to. Then he looked down at the naked body of his father. Incisions, black and neatly sewn up, went down each pale limb and in numerous tracings across his broad chest. The throat, I saw, bore old markings.

He had been strangled.

"Yes," I answered. "Victor killed him."

Victor followed my eyes to his father's throat and tapped it thoughtfully. "The key is not to crush the windpipe. That is a challenge! I learned that lesson in a frustrating sequence of events I do not care to relive. You have to squeeze hard enough to cut off the supply of blood to the brain until they pass out. And then you simply continue until they stop breathing. I tried a lot of other methods, but they were too messy or too destructive to the materials. I lobbied for Justine to be executed in some other way, but they would not listen to me, and I could not tell them why. It took so much time to replace her neck and throat. I might have succeeded if I had not had to waste all that effort." He glowered.

"How many have you killed?" Mary kept her tone conversational, not accusatory. "Do you keep trophies, other than their body parts?"

Victor flinched, a look on his face as though he had smelled something unpleasant. "I do not *enjoy* it. I regret the necessity of the killing. I tried for some time working with reanimating tissue that had been dead for longer. But the deterioration was too much. The connections I needed for the current to enervate a whole body were broken down. Fresher material was required." He paused, holding a vial of noxious-looking yellow liquid. "I did not think I could do it. The first time was awful for me."

"For him, too, I imagine," I said.

Victor surprised me, his lips twitching with a smile that previously would have felt like a gift. "His suffering was brief. I had to live with the high price of my ambitions. It has been a burden, I assure you." He rested the gun on the table, still pointed at Mary, as he injected the liquid into his father's milky, unseeing eyeball. I did not look away.

I would never again let myself look away.

"If you admire the stitchwork," he said to Mary, gesturing to the black lines of thread, "you should compliment Elizabeth. She is the one who taught me to sew. It is quite wearing on the hands, though." He took the gun again and lifted both hands, turning one empty palm up and considering it thoughtfully. "It is all quite demanding. This hand has to be capable of the most minute cuts. One slip, one twitch, and I can ruin an entire body's usefulness. Not to mention the strength required to strangle someone. I had never considered the sheer physical demands before I started. It was all lofty mental ideas, problems explored on paper." He sighed. "Such is the nature of science, though. At some point theory must be turned into reality, and there will always be more work than anticipated."

Mary tutted sympathetically. "It must have been exhausting, killing my uncle. He was not a small man."

Victor looked up at his pole, then turned another dial. "Who was your uncle?"

"Carlos Delgado." Her calm deteriorated in the face of his ignorance. "The bookseller! Your friend!"

He frowned, searching his memory. "Oh! Yes. I had just lost much of my material because of a trial amount of injection gone wrong. I needed a replacement immediately. He showed up at my door. It was bad luck, really. But tell me, did anyone look for him? No. No one ever did. All the men I took from the dark streets, the drunks, the foreigners, the vagrants looking for work. No one ever looked for them. And that is what brings me comfort. I gave them a purpose higher than they ever had in their lives."

"I looked for him!" She took a deep breath, deliberately relaxing. "I looked for him."

"And no one cared to help you, did they? I could have taken you, too, at any point, and never suffered the slightest inquiry." Victor did not say it meanly. He stated it as fact, because it was.

Mary turned to me. Her face was pale and her eyes shadowed. The binding I had put on her shoulder was already soaked through. "I am sorry to say, I do not have much faith that your marriage will be a happy one."

Lightning forked overhead. Victor looked straight up, hungry with anticipation. I stood, creeping closer. A bolt of the lightning lanced down and hit the pole with blinding force. The air crackled, all my hair standing on end.

Victor reached over to throw a lever. I shouted, waving my pistol to get his attention. At the same moment, Mary stood and threw her knife at him. It spun through the air and hit his forehead, hilt first. Stunned, he stumbled back.

The lightning passed.

The lever was left unswitched.

There was a sizzle and a putrid scent of burned flesh and hair as Judge Frankenstein's body was ravaged beyond repair by the current that Victor had failed to redirect.

"You have ruined it!" Victor screamed, leveling his pistol at Mary.

The windows behind him revealed a terrible dark shape running toward us. It crashed through the glass with an inhuman roar, slamming into Victor.

The monster was here.

TWENTY-FIVE

DID I REQUEST THEE, MAKER, FROM MY CLAY, TO MOLD ME MAN?

THE MONSTER, TERRIBLE IN aspect from far away, was even more horrible to behold up close. His hair, long and black, hung lank from his misshapen head. The lines of Victor's patchwork sewing made his skin ridged and puckered, portions of it different tones and a few sections withered like a mummy's.

His lips were black like tar over teeth as straight and white as any I had ever seen. The contrast, rather than being pleasing, made both seem more alien and repulsive.

He grabbed for Victor, his massive hands misshapen and clumsy. The fingers had been fashioned roughly, lacking nails, the joints all wrong. Victor ducked, darting under the monster's grasp and then leaping onto the table. He stood on top of his father's mutilated corpse. The monster grabbed the edge of the table with a roar, intent on tearing the whole thing apart.

As soon as the monster touched the metal, Victor leaned over and flipped the switch. Whatever power was lingering from the lightning strike, it crackled and sparked, directed now into the monster.

The monster seized, straightening to its full colossal height, and then stumbled backward before falling against the wall and sliding down to sitting, its long legs splayed at an impossible angle. The feet, each as large as my thigh, were bare, revealing stunted, club-like appendages that ended in massive wolfish pads.

Victor leapt carefully off the table, retrieved his pistol, and pointed it at Mary. It shook with rage in his hand, but I did not doubt he would strike true. I turned, panic choking me, to find she had fainted from loss of blood, or from the shock of seeing the monster. Satisfied, Victor tucked the pistol back into his belt.

"You can put yours away, too, Elizabeth," he snapped. "Either it does not work or you are incapable of shooting me."

I dropped it to the floor, all feeling gone from my extremities. I could not tear my eyes away from the monster. Now that he was still, my gaze traced his form, unable to linger on any one terrible feature. Everywhere the mind rebelled against the shape of him, rejecting something so close and yet so far from humanity.

Finally, I settled on his eyes.

Though he appeared incapable of movement, his eyes were alive with emotion. Yellow sclera surrounded irises that were shockingly, perfectly blue. And as I looked at them, I realized I had seen them before.

"Henry?" I gasped.

Victor kicked one of the monster's feet out of the way, stepping over the other. "Well. Some of him, anyway. I told you he was alive."

A sob escaped my lips, and I dropped to my knees as this, the last part of my heart, was cut from me. I had saved no one I loved.

I had damned them all.

"It is funny," Victor said, wrapping his hands in a towel and tugging the ruined remains of his father off the table with some strain. The skin had burned, sticking to the metal. "Even in that form, stronger and faster than any human, more capable of resisting the elements, *still* he is too kindhearted to kill me. But then again, it is not Henry's heart. I cannot recall whose heart it is.... Maybe it is her uncle's? Whosever heart it is, it is not up to the task of killing me. Miserable wretch! He fills me with the deepest disgust. To think that I, who reached so high, could create such an abomination even the devil's angels would turn away in fright." He finished yanking his father free and forcefully tossed the remains against the far wall. The floor was littered with glass from the window. It caught the lights of the chandeliers and lamps, gleaming in the puddles of rain still gathering. Judge Frankenstein's tortured and twisted earthly shell lay amidst the glass and the water.

"Do you love *nothing?*" I asked, able for now only to look at Victor. But even in the presence of the monster, Victor was far more monstrous.

"Only you." He stated it as fact. But his expression was angry, his tone sharp. "Another body, wasted! And more mess to clean up."

"I tried to protect you," the monster groaned. I looked at it, shocked. Why would it would ever try to protect Victor? But its eyes were fixed on me.

Henry.

The monster.

"I saw you. In the city of my birth. Where all else was shadows and fear, I knew your face. I had awoken in darkness and terror, rejected by my creator. I ran, hiding, not knowing why I elicited such terror but unwilling to expose myself to more hatred. I was as a newborn infant, and instead of love and comfort found only bitterest rejection. I had no sense of myself, though. How I had come to be. What I had been . . . before. I knew only what I had seen since my eyes opened in his laboratory.

"And then I saw you, and I *remembered.* Not everything. But I knew your face when my own was alien to me. I followed you. I wanted to warn you, but the idea of you seeing me and crying out in fear bound me like a coward. I hid as a creature of the night, observing. I revealed myself to Victor to threaten him. To let him know I was watching, would always be watching. I would not allow him his evil pursuits, and I would not allow him to hurt you."

It was not Henry's voice, or his face, but they were almost his words. I was ashamed at my revulsion. I would have given anything not to be repulsed by him. But he was an outward reflection of all the evil Victor had practiced on the world.

"And *I* tried my best to kill you," Victor said, checking some dials and refilling his vicious needle. "If I had not made you so damned strong, it would have been much easier. But I learned a great deal. I have had to comfort myself with that."

I did not know what to say—feared I would never again know what to say. Tears threatened to overwhelm me, and I envied Mary her insensibility. I longed to leave this room, this consciousness, to leave behind forever my awareness of these horrors, my full knowledge of all I had lost and would yet lose.

Victor had won.

He looked up at the sky, where a rumble of thunder too close for comfort signaled that his work for the night was not yet finished.

"One more jolt should do it," he said. "To snuff out that spark of life I should never have deigned to light in you." He frowned, staring down at his first creation. "It will be very difficult to leverage you up onto the table."

I looked at Mary, helpless. She was a perfect victim. Doubtless she was next for the table. I looked at the door. I could run. I could escape.

Victor sighed. "You really should be helping. I have always had to do most of the work. Run if you must. You do not want to see this part. You never did. But be assured of this: I will find you wherever you go. And when I do, I will be ready. You are mine. Nothing you can say or do will stop me from achieving my goal. Surely you, knowing me best in all the world, know that this is the truth."

Shuddering, I turned back to Victor. My savior. My husband. I did know that. And I knew that, out there, the world held no help or pity for me. I nodded.

Some of his anger dissolved. "I know the process seems horrible. But you will not see or feel those parts. It will be as waking from a deep sleep. And when you awake, you will be as this abomination is—stronger, faster, invulnerable to the elements. Free from pain and fear. But you will not be a corruption like him. You will be like a seraph from on high. You will be perfected. All your life you have lived in fear and worry. I will keep you safe from ever fearing anything again." He paused, and I watched as he deliberately softened his expression, put on the smile I had taught him to use. "I will let you look away. I will let you leave now and not observe any of my final trials. I take this burden on myself alone, to gift you with the result after I have waded through hell to deliver you heaven. Can you accept that?"

Defeated, exhausted beyond imagining, faced with the loss of my final friend and the impending destruction of my newest one, I raised my eyes to meet his. I would be strong. So much stronger.

"Will you let Mary go?" I asked.

He frowned. "She will be useful."

"Please. No one I know. Not again."

He sighed. "She knows about us, though. We will have to relocate. It will complicate things."

"We could go back to Lake Como. I could paint while you . . . work. I would look away. Wait for you to finish. We have time."

Victor's shoulders relaxed. The true smile that only I could ever coax from him lit his face like sunshine breaking free from the clouds. "I sold the villa and emptied most of your accounts." He gestured to a large leather trunk in the corner. "We can buy a new laboratory. Somewhere secluded. Somewhere I will not be interrupted again. Together." He opened his arms.

"I only ever wanted to be with you," I whispered. I stepped toward him, but I slipped, falling to the floor amidst the glass and the water. Victor rushed to me. He crouched down, reaching to help me up.

My fingers curled around a shard of glass. I jammed it into his side.

"Damnable bitch!" he shouted, staggering back out of my reach. The glass was still embedded in his side, sticking out of his torso.

I stood, another piece of glass cutting into my hand where I grasped it with all the strength I had left. I bared my teeth at him, a falser smile than the ones I had taught him to show. "I would have aimed for your heart, but there is only an empty space there."

He staggered toward the table to retrieve his pistol. I rushed to beat him there, but we both stopped short. The monster loomed over us.

"I am ready to kill you now, I think," the monster said.

Victor spun, grabbing me around the waist and grasping my hand so that the glass cut into it. He pushed my hand against my throat, holding the razor shard to the vein that supplied lifeblood to my whole body.

"If you move toward me, I will kill her!" I could feel Victor trembling, could sense that soon he would lose control. "I only need her body."

The monster threw back its head and let loose that same cry that I had heard before. The one my own soul answered. The cry of the lost, of the damned, of the soul that found no refuge on this earth.

I wanted to make the same sound.

But I had already decided I would be stronger. I did not need Victor's venomous resurrection for that.

"You cannot run with me," I said. "I will slow you at every turn. And if you kill me now, what is to stop the monster from killing you? He will have no reason not to. If you kill me and still manage to escape, my body will be too large a burden. By the time you have access to another laboratory, I will be so far decayed I will not be of use. You lose me, Victor. Any choice means you lose me."

His hand twitched, the glass cutting into my skin. A warm rivulet of blood stained my collar, bleeding down to dye my perfect white dress.

"You are mine," he hissed in my ear. "I will never stop. I will follow you to the ends of the earth. And then you will know my power, and you will worship me as your creator, and we will be happy together."

He shoved me forward. I stumbled into the table, where the remaining charge shook through my body, and, at last, blessed darkness claimed me.

TWENTY-SIX

WHICH WAY SHALL I FLY

"She is waking up," a woman's voice said.

I clawed my way back from the darkness, letting the agony of my body lure me toward consciousness. When I opened my eyes, Mary was sitting next to me, grinning.

"Did you get enough beauty sleep?"

I sat up, my head spinning. "Your arm!" I lifted my hand to her shoulder. It had been bandaged again; only a little blood had seeped through.

"I will survive. And so will Victor, unfortunately. You could not have stabbed him in the neck? Or in the eye? Or in the chest? Or in—"

I put my hand over her mouth. "Mary. I have not trained with glass shards. You will have to excuse my amateur aim."

She pushed my hand away and waited for me to stand. Once I steadied myself, I helped her get up.

And then I had to look at the monster.

Henry.

As though sensing my thoughts, he spoke from where he lurked in the darkest corner of the room, shoulders stooped and face turned away from us. "I caught you as you fell and absorbed some of the shock so it did not kill you. Victor got away. I could not get him in time and lost him in the storm. He took a boat, and I do not swim or trust your boat to hold me. I am sorry."

"It is not your fault. It is mine."

Mary clucked her tongue. "Now then. I hardly think you can take credit for Victor. You did not make him do all that he did."

"But I did not stop him."

"When would you have?" Mary walked over to the leather trunk, opening it. "Oh, this is nice. He will be quite unhappy to leave all this behind." She shut it again, then continued her exploration of the room. "Would you have stopped him when you were a child, depending on his family for survival? When you were locked in an asylum without any recourse for release?"

"I am not blameless."

"Not being blameless is not the same as being guilty." Mary smiled gently at me.

The monster shifted, trying to fold himself even smaller in the darkened corner. "Henry . . . ," I started, not letting myself look away from him.

"My name is not Henry. Not really. He is part of me, but I am not him."

"What is your name, then?" Mary asked.

"It was Henry. And I think it was Felix, as well."

"My uncle's name was Carlos."

"Then that is also my name."

"It is quite a long name," she said. "I think, because you are something new, you should name yourself."

There was a pause, and then the monster nodded. "Adam," he said. His voice rumbled as low as the thunder now receding from our mountain valley.

"I like it. Literary, with a touch of irony. It is a pleasure to meet you,

Adam." She busied herself with more snooping around the dining-room-turned-laboratory. I suspected she did it in part so she would not have to look at him. She had not believed me that he existed. Even in the room with him, I struggled to make sense of his form, disbelieving that it was real.

"I would be wary of the chemicals," I said to Mary as she lifted the still-full syringe. "You do not know what they do."

She scowled, as though her ignorance was more offensive than the chemicals themselves. She found a large leather folio full of loose papers. Her eyes widened as she opened it. "Victor forgot his research."

The monster—the man—Henry—not Henry—*Adam* reached into his own rough cloak. It looked as though he had fashioned it out of a boat's sail. From some pocket he withdrew a similar book. "I have his old one."

"Where did you get that?" I recognized it from the horrible trunk in Victor's first laboratory. And then I remembered. "You were there that night. I almost burned you to death." I hung my head in shame. "I am sorry."

"You did not know."

"No, I am sorry for so much more than that. I was not fair to you—to Henry—in life. His first life. But whatever part of you is Henry, I used you. Not as cruelly as Victor used you, but I let you remain in love with me because it made me feel safer. Not because I had romantic feelings to return. I do not know that I have ever had those feelings, or that I could. They seem a luxury of safety and security."

I paused, taking a deep breath and forcing myself to look at the monster. I would accustom my mind to him until my eyes no longer recoiled. I found Henry's eyes in the midst of that ruined face, and I focused on them alone. "I put you in the path of that demon. And I provoked him deliberately to get him to come home, or to allow you to marry me and secure my future that way. I did not care which way it happened, which meant I did not truly care about your feelings. I used you. And for that I am sorry. I will always be sorry."

"I understand now being trapped," he said, his words slow and measured, each delivered with precise care around a swollen and clumsy tongue. "I am trapped by this body. There is no place for me in the world, no refuge I can find. I cannot even depend on the kindness of others, because it will never be freely offered to me."

Mary worked her way across the glass-strewn floor to us. She took the first journal from Adam and stacked it with the second under her good arm. "Well. We have his research. We have his funds. We have his laboratory. It will be a while before he can set up again."

"I say we do not give him the opportunity." I looked around the home that had never been mine. The home I had always been desperate to be safe in. The home that, as a Frankenstein, I finally had claim to.

I knocked over the first vial I saw. Another, and another. I picked up a chair and swung it through the cabinet, destroying both Victor's chemicals and the Frankenstein family china. I did not realize I was screaming until at last my destructive energy had spent itself. The room reeked of his materials; refuse added to the disaster on the floor.

I walked to the door bearing the Frankenstein family crest. "Do you think you can tear this down, Adam? I need to start a fire."

He grunted in wordless assent. He easily tore the door off its hinges with his enormous hands, then threw it into the middle of the room. The second door followed. Adam went through the rest of the house, smashing furniture. Mary slowly dragged the trunk of money out with her one good arm while I retrieved the supplies I had hidden to use to kill Adam when I did not understand who the monster really was.

We threw it all together and formed a pyre in the middle of the dining hall. It was time to burn my history here, once and for all. We would rise from the ashes, reborn. Adam. Mary. And myself.

I took a match from the stove in the kitchen, then paused. "We should check the servants' quarters. I would hate to murder someone by accident."

"We only plan to do that on purpose," Mary added helpfully. "But if anyone were here, I think they would have responded to all the noise."

"The servants left when Victor returned," Adam said. "I have been watching."

"Good."

"Should we place the body on top?"

I looked at the ruined form of Judge Frankenstein. He had claimed me and held me captive, seeking to possess me for my money. He was not as bad as his son. But he was certainly part of the reason Victor was who he was.

"This is not for him. This is for me." I threw the match onto the pyre. We stayed until the fire drove us from the house. Then we stood, side by side, and watched as Frankenstein Manor was consumed.

"What do we do now?" Mary asked.

"Victor said he would chase me to the ends of the earth. I think I should make it a challenge for him."

Mary laughed. "I would love to make him suffer."

"You cannot mean to come with me! My road will be long and lonely and dangerous."

She stared ahead at the flames. "My uncle is dead. I loved the bookshop because I loved him. If I returned to it, I would spend the next years fighting to keep it and eventually losing it because I am a single woman and such is the nature of the law. Besides, Victor knows I know the truth about him. I cannot imagine he will forgive or forget my role."

"I think," Adam said, his deep voice like rocks scraping together, "I can give him a trail to follow. I am memorable."

What a strange company we were! But I was gladder than I could say that I would not do this alone. "Trying to follow us will keep him moving, prevent him from being able to set up another laboratory. We can save others in that way. But we need to lure him as far away from people as we can. In case things do not go as planned." After all, the three of us had failed once at killing him. "He hates the cold. So I say we move north as quickly as possible."

"Oh, we three fugitives will make this hell for dear Victor." Mary rubbed her hands together in delight.

I laughed, and Mary joined in, the noise brighter than the fire raging in front of us. Something in Adam seemed to release. He stood straighter, no longer turning his face from us. His black lips parted in a smile, and at last I saw the soul he carried. Victor had not made that. It was entirely Adam's.

We settled into silence, listening to the rain sizzle as it hit the flames, the heat so intense that our clothes dried as fast as they got wet.

This house had been a refuge, and it had been a prison. But even watching it burn, I was not free. Victor was out there. He would follow me. I knew his singular intensity and devotion to a goal better than anyone. He would find me.

I would let him.

TWENTY-SEVEN

THAT MUST BE OUR CURE:
TO BE NO MORE

I ALWAYS KNEW I would see the world because of Victor.

I had never imagined it would be because I was running away from him.

We stood on a plain outside Saint Petersburg. It had been a long, frigid journey. And we had yet more long and even colder journeys ahead of us. But as we looked on the onion domes of that glittering, frosted city, I finally felt something like peace.

"It is beautiful," I said.

"It is freezing," Mary said.

"It is both," Adam said.

I laughed, linking arms with Mary. And then, ever tentative, I reached out and linked my other arm through Adam's. He flinched at the touch—he always did—but then he softened. I did not look up to see whether he was smiling. I was trying to do things simply because I wanted to, or because they felt right, rather than because I was trying to elicit a certain reaction for my own purposes.

"You two should go into the city," Adam said. "Spend a few nights warm and cozy. I will wander the countryside and let people catch glimpses of me."

"What if someone tries to harm you?" I feared this constantly, that his monstrous visage would inspire violence. "That is not fair to you. We should all be warm or none of us."

He patted my hand. His dwarfed mine, at more than twice the size, but he was remarkably gentle. "I am faster and stronger than anyone who may wish me harm. I do not mind doing this task. The cold does not bother me. And I like the wide-open spaces. It is still exhilarating to run as fast as I can." He paused, then smiled shyly. It was such a tentative smile, like a new bud of a flower. So fragile and unformed. "And I like being reunited with you after."

I met his smile with my own, which helped his budding flower grow. "I like that, too. But I do not speak Russian. So we will be at a loss in the city and—"

"I do." Mary grinned, her breath fogging out in front of her face. "At least well enough to order dinner and get a room. My uncle loved Saint Petersburg. I want to see it for myself."

"That settles it." Adam patted my hand one more time and then gently pried it free. "I have already seen it."

"In another life," I countered.

"That is enough for me. I will meet you back here in three days." He loped away, within seconds too far away to argue with.

Mary climbed back into our open carriage and took the reins. "Come. I want to be warm for more than a few hours at a time."

I joined her, and we rode down toward the city. Our carriage was a sled, so she stopped on the outskirts and found a stable for the horses. We rode in a hired buggy to the center of the city. I wanted somewhere nondescript and anonymous. Mary chose the nicest hotel she could find.

That night at dinner, our bowls filled with soup and our glasses with wine, she glared at me. "We are in one of the most beautiful cities in the world. I want to go to an opera. I want to visit the cathedrals. I want to enjoy this expensive meal. And you are determined to be miserable. Adam is *fine*. He likes the solitude, and he likes coming back to us afterward."

"It is not that," I blurted out, and then I realized what it was. I looked down at my bowl and the silver spoon next to it. It blurred. "How can I enjoy myself when Victor is still out there? How can I enjoy myself when Justine is dead? William? Your uncle and Henry—not dead, but not alive, either. Not really. I bring their restless ghosts with me. They were killed because of me. Because of Victor's twisted need to possess me forever. How can I ever smile, how can I ever enjoy myself again, knowing what my life has cost?"

Mary reached across the table and took my hands in hers. I wore black now, all the time. She wore deep red tonight, complementing her beautiful complexion. She smiled at me, squeezing my hand. "Because I know my uncle. I see glimpses of him in Adam. In his kindness. In his wonder at nature. In his love for both of us. I am certain Henry is in those things, too. And your Justine is gone, but you carry her in your heart. Would she want that heart to be heavy and burdened for her sake?"

I shook my head. "She made me promise the opposite."

"I am not saying you should not feel remorse or sadness. But if nothing else, your past should teach you the value of life. The wild and precious joy of it. Do not let Victor steal that, too. He has already taken enough."

I nodded, freeing one of my hands to wipe my eyes. I held her other hand for a long time, until my chest felt light enough that I could breathe. And then I offered her a guileless smile for no reason other than that I loved her and I was glad to have her with me. She returned it.

That night, curled against her in the warmth of our bed in front of a gently crackling fire, I slept deeply. For the first time in months, no nightmares troubled me.

"I brought you a present," I said, smiling. Adam's blue eyes widened in surprise. Under the furs and supplies we had bought was a stack of books. Poetry, plays, philosophy—everything I knew Henry had loved, and that Mary knew her uncle had loved. And aside from those, we had brought books on a dozen other subjects, so that Adam could discover what *he* loved.

"Thank you," he said solemnly, running his misshapen fingers over the books. Mary and I both hugged him, and he wrapped his arms around us, to encompass us both. "Thank you," he whispered, and I knew the gift we had brought him was not a gift of words or knowledge, but of companionship. We would never leave him. He would never leave us.

The family that had nearly destroyed me had inadvertently given me a new family. I would keep my promises to Justine. I would embrace whatever strange life I had, for as long as I had it. And, with Mary resting her head on my shoulder and Adam driving the carriage, I allowed myself to smile for no one.

For *myself.*

Mary strapped on her furs, belting them in place until she looked more beast than girl. I laughed at her as I pushed aside the crate and checked the opening in the floor to make certain the hole we had carved in the ice for water and fish was still clear. I broke the ice forming around the edges, then pulled up the line. "Three fish!"

The wind howled around our tiny shack, searching desperately for a way inside between the mud and wood that sealed out the elements.

Snow had drifted so high it covered the single window, making even the daylight hazy and soft. We did not know who had built the shack or to whom it belonged, but we had been there for two weeks with no visitors. And if the owner did appear, we would happily pay for our time here. I could not imagine anyone idly venturing to us, though. The snow was a lashing, blinding constant. Adam frequently had to dig us out so we could go for supplies.

The shack was far emptier without his gentle, soft-spoken presence. I always felt better when he was home. But he did not mind the solitude during his trips to be glimpsed at villages within a few days' travel, and he felt uncomfortable with his massive bulk in our tiny space.

We did not mind, and we made certain he knew. He would be back the next day, and then we would discuss our next move. I would miss this howling shack. But it was time to make a decision about where to go next.

"He really is a genius, you know," Mary said.

"Who?" I put the fish on the stove, then shoved the crate back over the opening to the ice hole. I would cook the fish that evening for supper when Mary returned from her supply run. She would bring back food and any news she could find. So far we had heard nothing of Victor. No trace of someone inquiring about us. And, thankfully, no rumors of strings of murders in Geneva or anywhere nearby.

I wanted to imagine we could continue like this forever. Mary had begun to suggest that Victor had died from his wounds, or that our flight had been too successful. She wanted to go back to Saint Petersburg, find a secluded home to purchase for the three of us. To settle. Maybe Victor would find us in a month, or in a year, or never. I did not know what I hoped for. I only knew that, since Saint Petersburg, with Mary and Adam, I was . . . happy.

"Victor. Is a genius," Mary said, patting a stiff section of her furs.

She pulled them aside to reveal his journals. "Also insufferable. Did you know he was keeping a journal, too? He was writing an account of his life, but editing out the parts where he murdered people for their body parts. He made himself the hero. I think he fears his legacy, should anyone discover what he has done, and wants to control what they know. You are—if you were worried—an angel on earth, faultless, beautiful, and utterly and completely in love with him."

"I had no idea he had such a talent for fiction."

"Mm," she said. "You were also murdered by Adam on your wedding night! Such drama. Victor was committed to an asylum for some time after, so great was his mourning."

"That insufferable *ass,*" I hissed.

Mary laughed. "He certainly has a flair for talking about himself. And so many descriptions of mountains! He is quite enamored of their grandeur."

"You should burn his journals."

"That is *your* solution to everything, not mine. I have also been studying his work. He is insane, and a murderer, but his mind . . ." She trailed off, something like admiration on her face. Then she shook her head as though physically pushing the thought away. "If it makes you feel any better, I understand how you could have thought so highly of him and been blind to his true nature. His mind truly is remarkable."

I sighed. "It was not his mind I loved. It was his esteem for me. He valued me when no one else did. And I thought it made me special, that he loved only me. I should have realized that his inability to love anyone else just meant something was wrong with him."

"Oh, Elizabeth, you sweet, sad thing," Mary said brightly. "*I* think you are special. And I love a lot of people. Well. I love some people. . . ." She paused. "At least two people. I definitely love two people. As long as you count Adam as a person, which we do."

I laughed, hugging her awkwardly around her massive furs. "Hurry back."

She kissed my cheek, then attached her snowshoes. I braced myself as she opened the door. The wind flung it inward, blowing in snow and lowering the temperature dramatically. Mary was bent nearly horizontal as she pushed out and fought against the wind to walk on top of the snow. I wrestled the door shut, barring it with relief and feeding the stove.

That afternoon, with the soft, cold sunlight and the warm stove, waiting for my friends to return, I decided: We would not let Victor dictate our lives anymore. We had run. We had waited. We would settle and let him find us or remain forever a mystery. I did not mind where we ended up, so long as I had my little family of three.

Mary's desperate knock on the door sounded. I rushed up from the nap I had fallen into and unbarred the door. It flew open with even more force than normal, knocking me to the floor.

"Close it!" I shouted, lifting my arm to cover my eyes from the snow blowing in and the glare of the sun blinding me.

The door shut, and I lowered my arm to find Victor looming over me.

"Hello, my wife."

I kicked out at his shins, crawling back toward the table. Victor dodged, stepping around my legs and kicking my arms so I fell flat on the floor. We had pistols and rifles beneath the bed, but I could not get to them. I rolled over to face him.

He was holding a pistol of his own. He had come prepared. His dark hair was covered by a fur hat, which was caked with snow. How long had he lain in wait outside our shack to catch me?

All this time we thought we were setting a trap for him. And now I was trapped, alone.

"I have a sled outside with dogs. We will be miles away before that woman knows you are gone. And I know the monster is a full day away, even at his tremendous pace." He leaned down and smiled at me, the coldly possessive expression reminding me of his father. "Did you really think this would work?"

I scooted back. He watched me, ready to spring. I stopped when my back hit the crate. There was nowhere to run. I could not get the pistols before he could stop me. And if I struggled, doubtless he would drug me again, and I would lose any chance to fight.

"You will be happy to know I am finally ready," he said. "It has not been easy, but you would neither understand nor appreciate what struggles I have endured. Anticipating your gratitude after your change has sustained me. It has also allowed me to forgive you for your lack of faith in me."

"I will never be yours," I said, hollow and lacking conviction.

He crouched down so we were eye level. I no longer pretended for him, and he did the same. His true self was revealed. It was like looking at a portrait—flat, lifeless, no soul beneath the strokes. Had I really never seen it, or had I always chosen to look away, as he said?

"There was never another path for you. Consider how much worse it has all been for me. How much I have had to suffer. And how much of that suffering has been caused directly by you!" His face twitched and his fingers tightened on the pistol. Then he sighed. "It does not do to dwell on it. There is no point in fighting. This is your fate, Elizabeth Frankenstein. I will let no other claim you—not man, not death, not even God." He stood, holding out his hand.

"If I come, will you let Mary and Adam be?"

"Who the devil is Adam?"

"He is—" I would not say the monster.

Victor caught on. "Oh, Adam. A man's name for something so much less. But yes. They can do whatever they wish. I have no use for them."

He smiled. It was the smile I had taught him. And I knew he gave it to me now so I would not have to see the truth. Of course he would not let them live. Mary had tried to take what was his, and Adam was a reminder of failure. He would take me, and then he would destroy them. Or in Mary's case, use her body for something unspeakable.

What option did I have?

I smiled up at him, giving him the look that always soothed him so he could function. He let out a breath of relief, his eyes lighting. He still needed me. He would always need me. And some part of me still responded to that.

I had no means to kill him. But perhaps, after he had taken me, I could devise something. I smiled more sweetly still, and he leaned down to kiss me. I could not stop myself from jerking away from his hateful lips.

My movement dislodged the crate, my momentum carrying me backward into the hole in the ice.

The shock was immediate and overwhelming. Panic bubbled up like my breath as I struggled to orient myself and find the hole. I had to get out!

A hand grabbed for me, grasping blindly through the icy water. The hand that had reached out to me as a child, that had pulled me from my misery and into a life of a different kind of captivity. The hand that, guided by his brilliant mind, could accomplish delicate and sensitive operations that defied the fundamental laws of life and death.

The hand that would take my body and make it his own.

Victor would save me. And I wanted to live! Desperately. As I always had. For one moment I let myself consider it.

But if I lived, I would still die, and I would never have control of myself again.

I took his hand, and then I pulled with all my might. Victor, unused to meeting resistance from me, tumbled into the hole. He flailed, turning toward me in the blue depths. His eyebrows were drawn together in surprise and confusion.

I reached out and smoothed them, smiling. Victor would never hurt anyone again. I had saved them, and I had saved myself.

He struggled for the surface, searching for the hole. But he had not taken off all his furs. They were weights, dragging him down. I wrapped my arms around him, embracing him and sinking with him until he stopped moving. The water around me, deepest blue, turned from cold to burning heat and then peaceful nothingness.

I opened my arms to release Victor. His fingers, tangled in my hair, finally broke free. He spiraled down, staring up at me in surprise, until the black depths claimed him. I floated, weightless and finally, truly free.

And then, alone but not scared, I closed my eyes.

EPILOGUE

I SUNG OF CHAOS AND ETERNAL NIGHT

Taught by the heav'nly Muse to venture down
The dark descent, and up to reascend . . .

THERE WAS NOTHING.

And then a shock so great it yanked me free of the hold of eternity, pulsing pain to every sleeping nerve until I felt and saw the brilliant white that claimed me and forced me back.

I took a breath.

I opened my eyes. I did not know this room, this place. I did not know anything. I felt panic rising, until a cool hand rested on my cheek. Mary stared down at me, smiling through her tears. Adam loomed next to her, his tortured face alive with hope. "Welcome back, Elizabeth Frankenstein," she said.

I was free. And . . .

"I am alive," I whispered.

I am alive.

AUTHOR'S NOTE

Two hundred years ago, a teenage girl sat down and created science fiction.

She did it on a dare. The coolest thing I ever did on a dare was ask my now-husband out. Which, granted, changed my world. Mary Shelley? Changed the whole world.

Rarely does a story come along that reshapes the public imagination in such a startling and notable way. The fact that we are still talking about *Frankenstein,* studying it, remaking it, speaks volumes to the questions Mary Shelley asked. Because it isn't the answers in stories that are interesting—it's the questions.

When I sat down to write a retelling of a book that has meant so much to me, I wasn't sure where I wanted to start. I knew I wanted a female protagonist, but beyond that, I needed direction. I needed my questions.

I found them in Mary Shelley's own introduction to the book. In it, she deflects focus from herself, talking about her husband, the poet Percy Bysshe Shelley, instead. "My husband," she said, "was from the first, very anxious that I should prove myself worthy of my parentage, and enroll myself on the page of fame. . . . At this time he desired that I should write, not so much with the idea that I could produce any thing worthy of notice, but that he might himself judge how far I possessed the promise of better things hereafter." And then in the preface, the only part of the book written by him, Percy makes certain to note that if people knew Lord Byron was writing at the same time *Frankenstein* was drafted, they would certainly prefer his work.

Mary Shelley adored her husband. She kept his heart wrapped in a sheet of his poetry in her desk until she died. But that passage made me want to break something. *Frankenstein* wouldn't exist without Lord Byron and Percy Shelley's challenge—or Percy Shelley's encouragement to Mary Shelley to keep writing. But the genius was all Mary's.

Still, at publication, for decades after, even today, people gave all credit to the men around her. After all, how could a girl—a teenage girl—accomplish something so great?

So my questions began to take shape. How much of who we are is shaped by those around us? What happens when everything we are depends on someone else? And, as always: Where are the girls? Even Mary's wild and expansive imagination could not put a girl at the forefront of this story. They're relegated to the background, mere caricatures. And that was where I found my story. With a girl given to a boy as a gift. With a girl whose whole life revolves around the brilliant boy she loves. With a girl who inadvertently helps create a monster.

With a teenage girl, because, as Mary Shelley proved, nothing is more brilliant or terrifying than that.

ACKNOWLEDGMENTS

First and foremost, thanks go to Mary Wollstonecraft Shelley, whose stunning imagination continues to inspire countless stories, including this one. Thank you for being a badass goth genius and showing those poets what a real scary story is. You changed the shape of fiction forever.

Special thanks go to my own badass geniuses, Wendy Loggia and Beverly Horowitz, for asking if I would like to write a *Frankenstein* retelling. The answer, obviously, was yes. I'm so grateful you two prompted me to discover Elizabeth and her story.

Thank you as well to everyone at Delacorte Press and Random House, particularly Audrey Ingerson for her editorial help, Colleen Fellingham for gently reminding me how much I need a copy editor, and Aisha Cloud, my sublime publicist.

For Regina Flath and her design team, tremendous gratitude and awe. I am astonished by your creativity and ability to dream up a concept and make it into a gorgeous and unnerving cover.

Michelle Wolfson remains my ever-capable and steadfast agent, guiding my career and finding opportunities for me, even when the books are too scary for her. Sorry, Michelle. We both know I'm not getting any less creepy.

The drafting of this book would not have been possible without Natalie Whipple redirecting me, Jon Skovron being my resident

Frankenstein expert, and Stephanie Perkins reading each version and helping me craft my own lovely monster. I love you all.

To Lord Byron and Percy Shelley, thanks for being insufferable and thinking there was no way Mary could write something better than you two could. Joke's on you.

Thank you to Noah for being the foundation of my life, my sounding board, my support, my partner. And finally, to my beautiful children, thank you for sharing me these long months with all the monsters I had to bring to life. You're still my greatest creations.

Blue Lily

KIERSTEN WHITE is the *New York Times* bestselling author of the And I Darken and Paranormalcy series, *Slayer, The Dark Descent of Elizabeth Frankenstein,* and many more novels. She lives with her family near the ocean in San Diego, which, in spite of its perfection, spurs her to dream of faraway places and even further-away times.

kierstenwhite.com
@kierstenwhite